THE SPINSTER

Emerson Pass Historical, Volumn Two

TESS THOMPSON

Praise for Tess Thompson

The School Mistress of Emerson Pass:

"Sometimes we all need to step away from our lives and sink into a safe, happy place where family and love are the main ingredients for surviving. You'll find that and more in The School Mistress of Emerson Pass. I delighted in every turn of the story and when away from it found myself eager to return to Emerson Pass. I can't wait for the next book." - ***Kay Bratt, Bestselling author of Wish Me Home and True to Me.***

"I frequently found myself getting lost in the characters and forgetting that I was reading a book." - ***Camille Di Maio, Bestselling author of The Memory of Us.***

"Highly recommended." - ***Christine Nolfi, Award winning author of The Sweet Lake Series.***

"I loved this book!" - ***Karen McQuestion, Bestselling author of Hello Love and Good Man, Dalton.***

Traded: Brody and Kara:

"I loved the sweetness of Tess Thompson's writing - the camaraderie and long-lasting friendships make you want to move to Cliffside and become one of the gang! Rated Hallmark for romance!" - ***Stephanie Little BookPage***

"This story was well written. You felt what the characters were going through. It's one of those "I got to know what happens next" books. So intriguing you won't want to put it down." - ***Lena Loves Books***

"This story has so much going on, but it intertwines within itself. You get second chance, lost loves, and new love. I could not put this book down! I am excited to start this series and have love for this little Bayside town that I am now fond off!" - ***Crystal's Book World***

"This is a small town romance story at its best and I look forward to the next book in the series." - ***Gillek2, Vine Voice***

"This is one of those books that make you love to be a reader and fan of the author." -***Pamela Lunder, Vine Voice***

Blue Midnight:

"This is a beautiful book with an unexpected twist that takes the story from romance to mystery and back again. I've already started the 2nd book in the series!" - ***Mama O***

"This beautiful book captured my attention and never let it go. I did not want it to end and so very much look forward to reading the next book." - ***Pris Shartle***

"I enjoyed this new book cover to cover. I read it on my long flight home from Ireland and it helped the time fly by, I wish it had been longer so my whole flight could have been lost to this lovely novel about second chances and finding the truth. Written with wisdom and humor this novel shares the raw emotions a new divorce can leave behind." - ***J. Sorenson***

"Tess Thompson is definitely one of my auto-buy authors! I love her writing style. Her characters are so real to life that you just can't put the book down once you start! Blue Midnight makes you believe in second chances. It makes you believe that everyone deserves an HEA. I loved the twists and turns in this book, the mystery and suspense, the family dynamics and the restoration of trust and security." - ***Angela MacIntyre***

"Tess writes books with real characters in them, characters with flaws and baggage and gives them a second chance. (Real people, some remind me of myself and my girlfriends.) Then she cleverly and thoroughly develops those characters and makes you feel deeply for them. Characters are complex and multi-faceted, and the plot seems to unfold naturally, and never feels contrived." - ***K. Lescinsky***

Caramel and Magnolias:

"Nobody writes characters like Tess Thompson. It's like she looks into our lives and creates her characters based on our best friends, our lovers, and our neighbors. Caramel and Magnolias, and the authors debut novel Riversong, have some of the best characters I've ever had a chance to fall in love with. I don't like leaving spoilers in reviews so just trust me, Nicholas Sparks has nothing on Tess Thompson, her writing flows so smoothly you can't help but to want to read on!" - ***T. M. Frazier***

"I love Tess Thompson's books because I love good writing. Her prose is clean and tight, which are increasingly rare qualities, and manages to evoke a full range of emotions with both subtlety and power. Her fiction goes well beyond art imitating life. Thompson's characters are alive and fully-realized, the action is believable, and the story unfolds with the right balance of tension and exuberance. CARAMEL AND MAGNOLIAS is a pleasure to read." - ***Tsuruoka***

"The author has an incredible way of painting an image with her words. Her storytelling is beautiful, and leaves you wanting more! I love that the story is about friendship (2 best friends) and love. The characters are richly drawn and I found myself rooting for them from the very beginning. I think you will, too!" - ***Fogvision***

"I got swept off my feet, my heartstrings were pulled, I held my breath, and tightened my muscles in suspense. Tess paints stunning scenery with her words and draws you in to the lives of her characters."- ***T. Bean***

Duet For Three Hands:

"Tears trickled down the side of my face when I reached the end of this road. Not because the story left me feeling sad or disappointed, no. Rather, because I already missed them. My friends. Though it isn't goodbye, but see you later. And so I will sit impatiently waiting, with desperate eagerness to hear where life has taken you, what burdens have you downtrodden, and what triumphs warm your heart. And in the meantime, I will go out and live, keeping your lessons and friendship and love close, the light to guide me through any darkness. And to the author I say thank you. My heart, my soul -all of me - needed these words, these friends, this love. I am forever changed by the beauty of your talent." - ***Lisa M.Gott***

"I am a great fan of Tess Thompson's books and this new one definitely shows her branching out with an engaging enjoyable historical drama/love story. She is a true pro in the way she weaves her storyline, develops true to life characters that you love! The background and setting is so picturesque and visible just from her words. Each book shows her expanding, growing and excelling in her art. Yet another one not to miss. Buy it you won't be disappointed. The ONLY disappointment is when it ends!!!" - ***Sparky's Last***

"There are some definite villains in this book. Ohhhh, how I loved to hate them. But I have to give Thompson credit because they never came off as caricatures or one dimensional. They all felt authentic to me and (sadly) I could easily picture them. I loved to love some and loved to hate others." - ***The Baking Bookworm***

"I stayed up the entire night reading Duet For Three Hands and unbeknownst to myself, I fell asleep in the middle of reading the book. I literally woke up the next morning with Tyler the Kindle beside me (thankfully, still safe and intact) with no ounce of battery left. I shouldn't have worried about deadlines because, guess what? Duet For Three Hands was the epitome of unputdownable." - ***The Bookish Owl***

Miller's Secret

"From the very first page, I was captivated by this wonderful tale. The cast of characters amazing - very fleshed out and multi-dimensional. The descriptions were perfect - just enough to make you feel like you were transported back to the 20's and 40's.... This book was the perfect escape, filled with so many twists and turns I was on the edge of my seat for the entire read." - ***Hilary Grossman***

"The sad story of a freezing-cold orphan looking out the window at his rich benefactors on Christmas Eve started me off with Horatio-Alger expectations for this book. But I quickly got pulled into a completely different world--the complex five-character braid that the plot weaves. The three men and two women characters are so alive I felt I could walk up and start talking to any one of them, and I'd love to have lunch with Henry. Then the plot quickly turned sinister enough to keep me turning the pages.

Class is set against class, poor and rich struggle for happiness and security, yet it is love all but one of them are hungry for. ......Where does love come from? What do you do about it? The story kept me going, and gave me hope. For a little bonus, there are Thompson's delightful observations, like: "You'd never know we could make something this good out of the milk from an animal who eats hats." A really good read!" - ***Kay in Seattle***

"She paints vivid word pictures such that I could smell the ocean and hear the doves. Then there are the stories within a story that twist and turn until they all come together in the end. I really had a hard time putting it down. Five stars aren't enough!"

-***M.R. Williams***

Also by Tess Thompson

CLIFFSIDE BAY

Traded: Brody and Kara

Deleted: Jackson and Maggie

Jaded: Zane and Honor

Marred: Kyle and Violet

Tainted: Lance and Mary

Cliffside Bay Christmas, The Season of Cats and Babies (Cliffside Bay Novella to be read after Tainted)

Missed: Rafael and Lisa

Cliffside Bay Christmas Wedding (Cliffside Bay Novella to be read after Missed)

Healed: Stone and Pepper

Chateau Wedding (Cliffside Bay Novella to be read after Healed)

Scarred: Trey and Autumn

Jilted: Nico and Sophie

Kissed (Cliffside Bay Novella to be read after Jilted)

Departed: David and Sara

Cliffside Bay Bundle , Books 1,2,3

BLUE MOUNTAIN SERIES

Blue Mountain Bundle, Books 1,2,3

Blue Midnight

Blue Moon

Blue Ink

Blue String

EMERSON PASS

The School Mistress of Emerson Pass

The Sugar Queen of Emerson Pass

RIVER VALLEY

Riversong

Riverbend

Riverstar

Riversnow

Riverstorm

Tommy's Wish

River Valley Bundle, Books 1-4

LEGLEY BAY

Caramel and Magnolias

Tea and Primroses

STANDALONES

The Santa Trial

Duet for Three Hands

Miller's Secret

THE SPINSTER

Emerson Pass Historical, Volumn Two

TESS THOMPSON

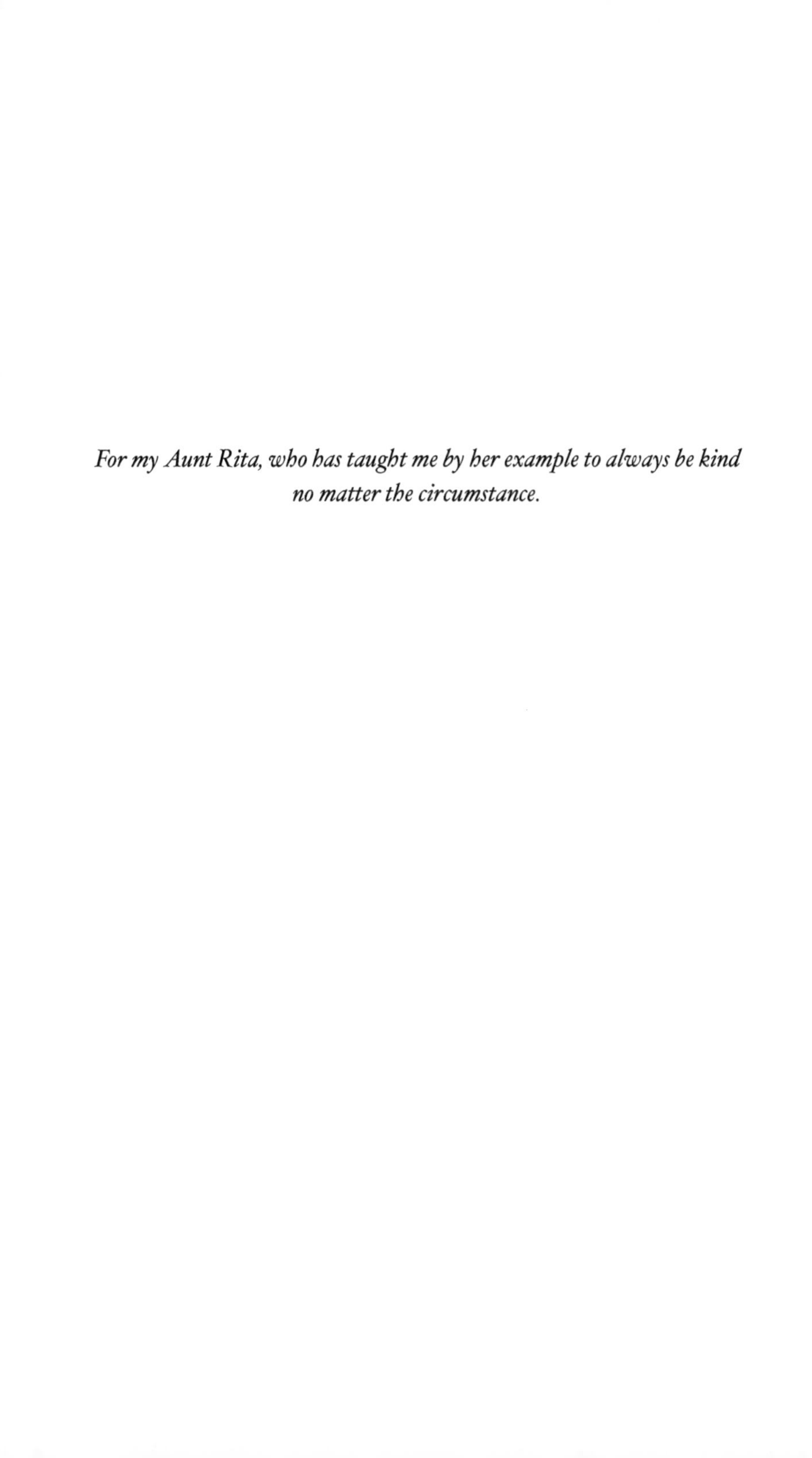

For my Aunt Rita, who has taught me by her example to always be kind no matter the circumstance.

THE SPINSTER

Josephine

The letter from Phillip Baker came on paper as thin as our pond's ice after a first autumn freeze. Perhaps that delicate paper should have been a clue as to what was to come. How my life would change. One could not skate on ice that thin. How right I was.

I read his correspondence twice, thinking through his offer. With a lightness in my steps that did not match my heavy heart, I walked to the window of my parents' sitting room. A first snowfall had blanketed the valley where my father's estate dwelt between two Colorado mountains. Our winter wonderland had come late this year. A brilliant, sunny, crisp fall had gone on for months. Given all that the last few years had bestowed upon us, we gratefully enjoyed every moment.

We'd survived the days and days of worry over my twin brothers fighting in France and the threat of the Spanish flu to the troops. Then, a second wave—the deadliest wave—of the Spanish flu had plundered the world. A third in the fall, threatening us once more. Emerson Pass had managed to remain isolated enough that we'd been spared.

Finally, though, it seemed as if the world would return to our lives before the war. Papa and Mama had seemed to be able to breathe again for the first time since the boys had enlisted, not yet seventeen, having lied about their age. Our dear friend Isak Olofsson had also survived. All three were home now. Not quite the same, but physically intact.

Not all of our boys returned to Emerson Pass. We'd lost Francis Lane. I hadn't known him well, but he was part of us. A soul lost. Buried in a cemetery across the seas. A young man who would never know what it was like to marry, have children, grow old.

And I'd lost Walter Green. He was not one of us. No one but I mourned him here. I had enough grief for a whole town.

The first letter from Phillip Baker had come in the fall of 1918. I could remember every word.

My name is Phillip Baker. I'm not sure if Walter ever mentioned me in his letters, but we knew each other for a brief time when we were children and then, by coincidence, were assigned to the same unit for basic training and sent to France together. I'm writing to tell you that Walter was killed in action last week. I was aware of your correspondence with him and that you would want to know. I'm sorry. He died bravely and without any suffering.

Just a month before the end, he'd been killed in action. The promise of our future together snuffed out before it began. I'd had only two weeks with him. Two weeks of bliss. Now I had only the memories. They would have to sustain me for the rest of my life. I would be a spinster. A librarian spinster and auntie to my six siblings' children.

I touched my fingertips to the cold glass. Snow fell steadily outside the windows. In Colorado, we had at least a dozen words to describe snowflakes. Today it was a dry, fat flake. Good for skiing, according to Flynn and Theo. A new sport they'd fallen in love with after their time in Europe. They'd come home determined to bring skiing here to Emerson Pass. The sport of the future, Flynn had declared. A way for our town to continue to grow and flourish. Shops would be built around the visitors. They'd seen it in the Alps. It would work here too, they'd told

Papa. He'd agreed to let them use part of their trust for the investment in their future. They were now happily planning away for the new version of our town. They'd cleared trees on the northern mountain for runs and built a lodge from the logs. In the spring, they would complete the rest of the needed details. By next winter, if all went well, skiing would have come to us for good.

I returned to the letter, reading the neat handwriting.

November 20, 1919

Dear Josephine,

I hope this letter will find you well. I'm also hopeful that you'll remember who I am. If not, I'll be mortified. Since returning from the war, I've been in New York City. Unfortunately, I became very ill last year with the Spanish flu. While convalescing, I remembered your descriptions of Emerson Pass from the letters you wrote to Walter. (He often read passages to me and the other men.)

Your descriptions of the wildflowers, sky, and trees have convinced me to travel west in pursuit of my own place of belonging. I've decided to take a leap of faith and come to Colorado, perhaps to settle for good. I'm writing to see if I might visit you and your family? I ended up with your letters and the books you sent. I feel guilty that I haven't sent them to you before now, as I'm sure you'd like to have them.

My request and trip may sound strange to you, but there's nothing or no one keeping me here. I grew up in an orphanage and have never truly had a home.

We all looked forward to your letters, as Walter shared many stories of you and your family with the rest of us lonely boys who, sadly, had no one writing to us. From your stories, I feel as if I know you all. I'd be honored to bring your letters, novels, and photograph and to meet you and your family.

I'm also hopeful that your father and brothers might have ideas for me in regard to work. Before the war, I apprenticed with a cabinetmaker. If they know of anything, I'd be pleased to hear of it.

If you're amenable to my visit, I thank you kindly and look forward to hearing from you.

Sincerely,
Phillip Baker

His request to visit wasn't the strange part. I found it odd that he made no mention of Walter, other than to say he'd shared my letters. An image of Walter laughing during one of our picnics flashed before my eyes. His sunny head of hair and light blue eyes had transfixed me from the start. He'd had an infectious smile that made me feel dizzy. I'd met him in Denver while I was attending a librarian conference. He'd been passing through on his way to report for duty. Our meeting had been pure chance. He happened to be out that warm evening while I walked in the park with colleagues. I'd thought at the time it was destiny. I now knew it was the day that led to my broken heart. Did I wish I'd never met him and be spared the pain of losing him? I couldn't answer that question.

I pressed my forehead against the glass. If only the coolness would numb the rest of me. Even for a few minutes. To feel like my old self instead of a worn-out, dried-up spinster. I would be twenty-three on my next birthday. Most women were married with a child by this age.

"What is it, Jo? Why did you sigh?" Papa asked from behind his newspaper.

I hadn't realized I'd sighed. Papa knew me too well. After everything we'd been through together, it was no wonder. I turned from the window and stepped nearer to the couch where he and Mama Quinn were having their tea. "It's a letter from Walter's friend. The one who wrote to tell me of Walter's death."

"Yes, we remember." Mama's eyes immediately softened with sympathy. "What does he want?"

"He wants to come out here for a visit and possibly to stay. My letters were a travel brochure, I guess."

Papa lowered the paper onto his lap. "How interesting." His English accent, according to my friends, remained as strong today as it had been when he came to America so many years ago. I, however, could not hear it. He sounded only like my beloved Papa.

"Does he have a wife and family?" Mama folded her hands together on her lap. I'd pulled her from reading. The novel, *My Ántonia*, was face-open on the couch next to her. Her fair hair was arranged in waves pulled back into a bun at the nape of her neck. Younger than my father by fifteen years, she was blessed with delicate, even features and a heart-shaped face.

Just over ten years had passed since she'd arrived to open the first school of Emerson Pass and my father's heart. Almost immediately she'd become the heart of our family. All five of us thought of her as our mother. Since their marriage, two little sisters had come, bringing our total to seven. Papa called us "The Lucky Seven."

"He has no family of any kind," I said. "In fact, he was raised in an orphanage. I have the feeling he's in need of a fresh start and work. He thought Papa might have ideas for him."

"How sad. We'll help him in any way we can." Mama set her teacup onto its saucer and fixed her kind brown eyes upon me. "Unless there's a reason you wouldn't want him to come here?" The anxious way she looked at me lately filled me with guilt. Papa, Mama, and my sisters had been worried about me. I hated knowing I caused them concern. My job was to be the responsible, steady eldest, not the sad, mopey mess I'd become.

"No, not at all," I said. "Should we invite him to stay with us? Just until he can figure out what to do next?"

"Yes, we've room for him if he doesn't mind bunking with the boys." Papa drained the last of his tea and set aside his cup. "I'm keen to help any man who fought in that terrible war."

"He says he trained as a cabinetmaker." I hugged my middle as I walked over to the fire that roared in the hearth, crackling and snapping. "He says Walter shared the contents of my letters with him and the rest of the boys. I find that...perplexing."

"Which part?" Mama asked.

"That he shared them. My letters were intimate, meant for

only one pair of eyes." I looked down at my hands to keep from crying.

"Darling, it doesn't really matter," Papa said softly. "If your letters brought them some relief, isn't it an honor?"

"I suppose." I sat in one of the armchairs and watched the fire. One end of a log looked like the nose of a fox.

Mama smoothed her hands over the top of her day dress made of crimson organza. "Phillip must stay for Christmas."

"Yes, I agree," Papa said. "He shouldn't be alone for the holidays. We'll take care of him until he can get on his feet. The boys can show him around town, do a little carousing."

"Alexander, carousing?" Mama raised her eyebrows and looked properly mortified. "Our boys do not *carouse*."

Papa didn't answer, but his eyes twinkled as he gazed at her. My chest ached with both gratitude and sorrow. Their love pleased me. Yet it also brought to light what I'd lost. I'd hoped Walter and I would share a life as they had.

Mama returned her gaze to me. "Jo, what's troubling you?"

"We don't know Phillip," I said. "What if he's awful?"

"I doubt he will be," Mama said. "He was so kind to write to you about Walter's death."

"That's true. If he's Walter's friend, he must be all right," I said.

"We didn't really know Walter," Papa said.

I sucked in my bottom lip to hold back a retort. Never in my life had there been any discord between my parents and me. However, they hadn't approved of my whirlwind courtship with Walter. Which was in no way his fault. He hadn't had time to come home with me and meet my family. "He was here such a short time. There wasn't an opportunity for him to court me properly. He planned to, when he returned from the war."

"Yes, of course, darling. We understand," Mama said in a soothing voice.

"Yes, yes, quite right." Papa followed up too hastily. No one wanted to upset me these days. I missed when my family treated me normally. Now it felt as if I were a fragile piece of china no one wanted to break.

"May I read the letter?" Mama asked.

I nodded and handed it over the tea set. She unfolded the letter and began to read.

"Sweetheart, have a biscuit," Papa said to me. "You're looking much too thin."

I obeyed, not having the energy to disagree, and put a cookie, which Papa called a biscuit, on a plate. He poured a cup of tea and set it on the table front of me. He believed most problems could be solved after a cup of tea. Given my troubled mother's death when I was nine, I'd known differently for a long time.

Mama folded the letter and put it back in the envelope. She had a strange look on her face, somewhere between puzzled and intrigued. "I think it might be good for you to have him here."

"You mean to tell me stories about Walter?"

"Not that exactly," Mama said. "He's someone of your own age group. Perhaps he will become a new friend?"

Mama and Papa exchanged a glance I couldn't decipher.

"I don't need friends. I have Poppy and my sisters." Poppy and I had grown up together. Their parents had died when Poppy was young and her older brother, Harley, had raised her while acting as groundskeeper and gardener. Poppy had been away for the better part of two years, working as an apprentice to a veterinarian in cattle country. I'd missed her more than I'd thought possible. She had just always been there and now she was off to her own adventures. "Poppy will be back in a few weeks. But I shall be a good hostess, don't worry."

"Regardless, we can't let a hero be alone during what's supposed to be the merriest time of the year." Mama had the biggest heart in the world, rivaled only by my sister Fiona, who seemed to think it was her job to look after every single person in the world.

"I'll write him this evening and ask if he'd like to stay with us," I said.

All four of my gaggle of sisters rushed into the room. Those who thought only boys were loud had never met my sisters. Harley had taken them into town in the sleigh to ice-skate for the afternoon. The pond in the center of town had frozen solid for the first time this season just last night.

"You won't believe what Delphia did," Cymbeline said, without concern over interrupting the adults.

Delphia, in preparation for the admonishment, tore a cap from her mushroom of blond curls and glared at her older sister. "I didn't do it."

At sixteen, Cymbeline lorded over the younger ones. Fiona, thirteen, was the protector. Adelaide, or Addie as we called her, was quiet and shy and obedient to bossy Cymbeline's wishes. Four-year-old Delphia, bless her, had the same fire as Cymbeline. From the time she could talk, she was having none of the dictatorship.

"She challenged a boy twice her age to a race," Cymbeline said. "And when she didn't win, she knocked him to the ground."

Delphia's bottom lip trembled. "I didn't."

"The whole thing was an accident." Fiona placed her hand on Delphia's head. "She slid into him because she was going so fast. Anyway, she learned it from you, Cym. You're always racing boys."

"That's different." Cymbeline's color heightened, making her even more beautiful than the moment before. God help us all, she was stunning and looked more like a woman than a girl. Mama always said we only had two types in this family. Fair and blond, like her, me, and the two youngest girls. Or dark hair and deep blue eyes, like Papa, the boys, Cymbeline and Fiona.

"Come here, little one," Papa said to Delphia.

She trudged over to him. He pulled her into his lap. "Tell me what happened."

She looked up at him with angelic eyes. "It's what Fiona said.

I was going fast, pretending that a monster was chasing me, and then I ran into him."

"Did you say you were sorry?" Mama asked.

"Yes, that's not the problem," Cymbeline said as she grabbed a cookie from the plate. "She said she was sorry and then she planted a kiss on him. On his cheek."

I had to cover my mouth with my hand to hide my smile.

"His cheeks looked like an apple," Delphia said. "I just had to kiss one."

I caught Mama's eye. She seemed to be trying not to laugh but kept it together enough to say, "Delphia, you mustn't ever kiss a boy."

"But why?" Delphia blinked her big blue eyes.

"Because it's not proper," Mama said.

I noticed Addie was shivering. "Come here, doll. I'll warm you up." I tucked her into the chair next to me and rubbed her cold hands between mine. Addie was quiet and serious like me. I adored her.

"Mama and Papa kiss all the time," Delphia said.

"They're married." Cymbeline plopped into an armchair next to me. "You don't understand anything about how the world works."

"Cym, don't say it like that. She's just a little girl." Fiona went to stand in front of the fire with her hands behind her back.

"I'm your baby," Delphia said as she gazed up at our father. "Right, Papa?"

"Yes, but that doesn't mean you're allowed to kiss boys." Papa put his chin on her head and looked over at me with eyes that danced with humor. Mama always says it was his dancing eyes that drew her to him. I knew exactly what she meant. "You're *my* baby, which means you can't love any boy but me."

"I won't do it again." Delphia let out a long-suffering sigh, as if all the fun in the world was taken from her.

"Besides the unfortunate incident with the apple cheek," Mama said, "what else happened?"

"That ridiculous Viktor Olofsson was skating with all the girls, one after another." Cymbeline shook her dark curls. "He had the nerve to ask me."

"What did you say?" I asked, knowing the answer, but teasing her anyway.

"Jo, don't be daft," Cymbeline said. "I would never let that big oaf touch my hand."

He was a large man but most certainly not an oaf. Although his shoulders were thick and wide like a Colorado mountain, he was a gentle, intelligent soul who I suspected had a deep and long-lasting crush on Cymbeline. "I think he's like a hero in a storybook. Brave and strong." I'd once seen him pick up a wagon off a man's leg when the horse had bucked and broken free, leaving his owner under a wheel. With almost white hair and light green eyes, he looked like the Vikings in one of the history books I had in the library.

Cymbeline's eyes flashed as she stuck out her plump bottom lip and scowled. Strangely, her sour expression did nothing to disguise her beauty. "He's such a show-off, doing tricks on the ice."

"You do tricks on the ice," Fiona said, not unkindly but more as a fact. "All the same ones Viktor does."

Her observation was correct. If Viktor learned a trick on the ice, Cymbeline practiced until she'd conquered it.

Mama had confided in me more than once that she was afraid Cymbeline would never be satisfied living in a man's world as we do. If she'd been old enough, I had no doubt she would have volunteered to be a nurse in the war effort overseas.

"Well, be that as it may," Mama said, "we have exciting news. Jo's acquaintance, Phillip Baker, is coming to stay with us for the holidays."

"The one who wrote to you about Walter?" Fiona asked.

"The same," I said. "How did you remember?"

Fiona shrugged. "I remember everything about my family.

Anyway, it wasn't like I could ever forget that day." Her eyes glistened. "I shouldn't like to ever see you that way again, Jo."

I held out my hand to her. "Come here, sweet sister." She sat on the arm of my chair and I patted her knee. "You don't have to worry. I'll never give my heart to anyone else. I'm the spinster of the family."

Phillip

The train chugged up a slope so steep I was certain we would not stay on the tracks. Across from me, a baby in her mother's arms cried. To distract myself from my fears of falling into the abyss below me, I pulled out the letter from Josephine. I breathed in the faint smell of her perfume that lingered on the paper. My imagination? Perhaps. Regardless, this one was to me, unlike the stack I'd read too many times to remember. Letters that were not written to me. By a girl who didn't belong to me.

It's a terrible thing to hate a dead man.

Yet I knew him for who he truly was. When I'd known him as a child in the orphanage, I'd recognized immediately how he used his charm to get what he wanted. Even the nuns fell for his act. When he ran away at age twelve, I genuinely think their hearts were broken. Women, even ones sworn to love Jesus, couldn't help but fall for Walter Green.

Hope lurked inside me, goading me into this fool's errand. After cheating death a second time by recovering from the Spanish flu, I would not rest easy until I came west and told Josephine the truth about the man to whom she'd pledged her eternal love. If not for me, I knew she would love a ghost, possibly forever. Josephine Barnes was a loyal woman. Nothing would deter her unless she understood what kind of man he really was under all that golden-haired, blue-eyed charm. I couldn't bear the thought of a woman like her spending the rest of her life remembering a man who never really existed. Walter Green was not the man she thought he was. I was the only one left alive to tell her the truth.

He hadn't loved her. There were other women who wrote to him. All who believed he would marry them when he returned from the war. All targeted for their wealth. Playing the odds, he'd said to me one time. The more he had waiting, the more likely he would marry into money. Those were to secure his future. Countless dalliances with nurses were just for fun.

Yes, I wanted her to know the truth. But it wasn't for purely altruistic reasons. I wanted her for myself. As I'd convalesced after the flu, I'd read the letters she'd sent to Walter hundreds of times. I'd stared at her photograph until I memorized every detail of her pretty face. The stories of her close family and the beautiful mountains where she lived had moved me more than they should have. In truth, I'd fallen in love with her. Was I lonely? Yes. I'd been lonely all my life. This was something else entirely. In addition to my yearning for a family and my romantic nature, I had this odd sensation of a deep connection between the two of us. The idea of fate, even soul mates, had crossed my mind. Was there a reason beyond mortal comprehension that I'd been the one who ended up with the box of her correspondence?

Could I pinpoint the exact moment I decided to write to her and ask if I might come to visit? Not really. It was more of a gradual thing, an expansion in my mind of what might be possible. Even though I knew her affection toward me was unlikely, I had to try. A man like me didn't win a rich, beautiful girl like her. I was poor and uneducated. My only skills were those of a cabinetmaker. Yet I had hope. I'd escaped the war and then the flu. I had to take a chance.

I glanced down at the letter, reading it one more time.

Dear Phillip,

My family and I would very much like you to come for a visit. Whether you decide to stay permanently in Emerson Pass or not, we'd be honored if you'd spend the holidays with us.

I hope you won't find my large and somewhat obnoxious family too overwhelming. I've asked them all to be on their best behavior, but that's not a guarantee. You'll bunk with my twin brothers. They also served in the war. I'm sure you'll all become fast friends.

Papa and my brothers will be happy to help you find employment if you decide to stay.

I shall look forward to meeting you soon.

Sincerely,

Josephine Barnes

I folded the letter and put it back in the envelope, then traced the letters of my name, written by her hand.

Walter, I thought, *you lucky, conniving bastard.* He'd held that hand in his own.

The train had made it to the top of the peak. I looked out the window to snow that sparkled under the sun. Josephine hadn't exaggerated about the piercing blue hue of the sky.

The baby stopped crying. Her mother, a pretty blonde woman wearing a gray traveling suit and matching hat, apologized to me for the noise. "The altitude hurts her ears."

"No need to apologize, ma'am. We were all babies once."

She peered back at me with obvious curiosity. "Do you know someone in Emerson Pass? Most people who head our way either live there or are visiting family or friends."

"I'm visiting the Barnes family."

Her face lit up with a bright smile. "The Barneses. They're very close friends of mine. I'm Martha Neal. I was the second schoolteacher in Emerson Pass, but now I'm married to the town doctor. He was an outsider who moved to town to take over the practice of our last doctor and somehow managed to make me his wife." She indicated the baby with a dip of her chin. "This one is named Quinn, after our first teacher in Emerson

Pass, who is now married to Alexander Barnes. But you know all that, I suppose?"

How much should I say? My natural tendency was to remain taciturn. When one's lived the kind of life I have, sharing too much led to either pity or fear, as if being an orphan or poor were contagious. "I served in the war with Josephine's beau, Walter Green. When he died he left a few items that I thought she might like to have. It's taken a while to get out here. My name's Phillip Baker."

Her eyes widened. "You're a friend of Walter's?"

Not exactly a friend. "That's correct. Did you know him?"

"No, no. I've only heard about him from Josephine. Those of us who attended school together are quite close. We meet for tea at least twice a month to discuss books and gossip. Oh dear me, where are my manners? I'm happy to meet you, Mr. Baker, and I'm terribly sorry about Walter. We lost one of our boys and the whole town cried for a week. What you must have seen, I can't imagine." Martha bounced Quinn on her lap. The baby babbled and chewed on her fist.

"Thank you. He wasn't a close friend. We served together, that's all." The car jerked, causing both Martha and me to sway slightly. I gripped my seat with both hands.

"Our poor Josephine. His death broke her heart. We all hoped she'd move on, but so far she hasn't."

"How so?" I couldn't help but ask. What luck to meet Martha. I'd gather as much information about Josephine as I could. The nuns often told us that the more we knew about a subject, the better we could make a decision or persuade others to our cause.

"She's sworn herself to spinsterhood and running the library. Which is disappointing to the eligible bachelors in town. Given half a chance, most of them would snatch her up if they could. She's remarkable. Did you know she brought the library to us with funding from Andrew Carnegie?"

I nodded. She'd written in detail about the building and

opening of her library. As if Walter had cared. I'm not sure he'd ever read a book. "Yes, Walter mentioned that to me."

"May I ask what you're bringing to her?" Martha adjusted Quinn to the other knee.

"The letters she wrote to him. There are stacks of them, and I thought she might like to have them. I wanted an excuse to come out here, too. I'm thinking of staying."

"I hope you will." She smiled at me. "We're friendly in Emerson Pass. I think you'll love it as much as the rest of us do. And how kind of you to bring the letters. Jo walked to the post office every Monday and Friday with a letter in her hand. Without fail, even though he almost never sent one in return. Do you know why he wrote back so seldom?"

He was too busy sleeping with nurses to reply to Josephine's heart-wrenchingly beautiful letters. "I've no idea, really. He wasn't the writing sort, I guess."

"Have you brought the books she sent, too?" Martha asked.

She knew about the books? "Yes, I wanted to return them to her for the library. They gave me such pleasure during difficult times. I wanted to make sure others could enjoy them."

"You like books?" Martha watched me with a more serious expression on her face.

"More than anything."

"And Walter?"

"Excuse me?"

"Did he like books? Martha asked.

"I can't say that he did, no." He'd always tossed them over to me the moment he took them from the box Josephine had sent. The candy he'd kept for himself. He'd had a terrible sweet tooth.

Her glaze flickered to the window. "How odd."

"Ma'am?"

"Josephine told me he'd written to her two times about how much he enjoyed the books, even mentioning specific plots and characters. She was thrilled, of course."

I flushed. I'd told him what to write in those letters so that she continued to think of him as a scholar. Both times he'd tricked me into describing the plots. I couldn't help myself but to discuss books with enthusiasm.

Martha peered at me through narrowed eyes. "May I be frank about something?"

"Of course." Where was she going with this?

"I've suspected there might have been others. Women, I mean."

I bit back a bark of surprise. Martha was no fool. I almost smiled with triumph. "What makes you think this?"

"When my husband was courting me, he was already a busy country doctor, yet he wrote me love letters at least once a week, and we lived in the same town. All he had to do to say hello was walk over to my parents' store. All of which leads me to believe that Walter's feelings weren't what he'd professed them to be. What's the old saying? Actions speak louder than words."

"I'm sorry, but it's not for me to say."

"You shouldn't play poker."

"Poker?"

The baby began to fuss. Martha reached into a bag by her side and came out with a hard-looking biscuit and handed it to Quinn. "I can see by the look on your face that there was more to this Walter than Josephine knew."

I moved my gaze away from her, flustered by this interrogation, and looked out the window. We were now on actual ground, passing through a dense forest of fir and pine trees. If Martha was an example of what I was to face in Emerson Pass, then I better get my story straight.

Given that I was only four when they died of yellow fever, I had only a few memories of my parents. One of them was of my mother scolding me for lying about taking a cookie without asking. *Tell the truth, Phillip, even when you know you could get away with a fib.*

However, Martha was a stranger to me. I didn't want

Josephine needlessly hurt. If she were to learn Walter's true character, it should come from me.

"Mr. Baker?"

I returned my gaze to Martha. "Men don't speak often of matters of the heart."

"But what about men who face death daily? Don't they confess their fears? Their loves?"

I was starting to feel rather sorry for Martha's husband. "I'm not sure what you're asking."

"You are sure."

I didn't say anything.

"I'll be clearer," she said. "Was he in love with Josephine? Was he planning on marrying her as she thought?"

"Respectfully, Mrs. Neal, I'm not sure I know, even if it were for me to say."

One eyebrow rose. "I see."

I was afraid she did.

"May I ask," I said, drawing the words out long, "if his intentions were not completely pure, what would you advise me to tell Josephine?"

She stared at me for a few seconds. Even the baby had stopped chewing on her cookie to focus on me. "I suppose that depends on your intentions. Have you come to hurt her?"

"Of course not. The opposite."

She gave me a satisfied smile. "May I take a guess, Mr. Baker, about your actual intentions?"

"Of course." Despite the chill of the train's car, my shirt clung to my back.

"You've fallen in love with her photograph. And perhaps you've read her letters, which made you aware of her intelligence and good heart. You most certainly are the one who told Walter what to write about the books."

I coughed and returned to the view of the landscape.

"You've come to get to know her," Martha said. "To see if your instincts about her are correct."

"What if I have? Will you rat on me?" I turned back to my interrogator.

She gave me another satisfied smile. "How fortunate that we were to meet today."

I swallowed and waited for the blow. Was there any other way for her to interpret my actions? Traipsing across the country because I thought I was in love with a girl I'd never met would not be greeted with approval.

"Josephine is my dear friend whom I love very much. However, I also have excellent instincts about people, and I've thought from the beginning that something wasn't quite right with this Walter character. Josephine has been practical and steady her entire life, but in this particular instance, I think she was taken away by the idea of love."

"Don't underestimate his charm," I said drily. "He'd perfected it over time."

"How long had you known him?"

I drew in a deep breath. I was in too far now. "I knew him for a brief time when we were children. We were at the same orphanage for a year or so. Until he ran away."

Both eyebrows raised this time. "Ran away? To where, I wonder?"

"In all truthfulness, I don't know." He'd run away at twelve, unable to abide by the nuns' rules. Even during all the hours we'd spent together during the war, he'd not filled me in on exactly where he went or how he survived during the time before he joined the army. I had a distinct feeling that he'd been involved in criminal activity.

"Were there other women? Is he a charlatan? Did he want her money?" Martha asked. "Please, Mr. Baker, tell me the truth."

"I believe all those things to be true."

"Believe or know?"

"Know."

"And the others?"

"All from wealthy families. He was ensuring his future upon his return."

She was quiet for a moment. Her cheeks had flushed red and she repeatedly tapped her foot as if she wanted to bore a hole through the floor. Finally, she turned to look at me.

"This is what you're going to do, Mr. Baker. Give it a few days before you tell her of Walter's true intentions. I'm afraid it'll drive her away. Kill the messenger, if you will."

"Yes."

"Spend time with her. Maybe use a little charm of your own to thaw her out, perhaps show her how much life there is to live."

"Being charming's not really my strength. I've nothing to offer, really."

"But you've come anyway?"

"Ever hopeful."

"You're handsome. That will help."

I almost laughed. "I am?"

"Yes. Have you not seen yourself in the mirror? Strong jawline. High cheekbones. Sapphire-colored eyes. Enough hair for three men. My husband will be jealous of that, I can assure you."

"Walter looked like the god of the sun or the like," I said. "All golden."

"Yes, I can imagine the type." She wiped drool from Quinn's chin with a handkerchief before looking back at me. "One piece of advice. If you win over her family, that's half the battle. They're as tight a clan as they come."

I nodded. "That much was clear from the letters."

She made a noise somewhere between a yelp and yap. "You did read them. I knew it."

"I'm ashamed to admit it, but yes. He'd stored them all in a box. I took them with me after he was killed."

"Did you not have letters of your own?"

"No. There's no one. Never has been."

"There should be."

It was my turn to study Martha. "What makes you think I'm any different from Walter?"

"My parents own the dry goods store in town. I've spent my whole life watching people from behind the counter. I can tell an honest man when I see one."

I had no idea what I'd done to make her think I was honest, but I didn't ask. She'd figured out everything else rather quickly.

"Her family invited me to stay for the holidays," I said. "Which astounded me."

"Get ready, Mr. Baker. That's just the beginning. In Emerson Pass no one's allowed to be a stranger for long. Before you know it, you'll feel like you've been here forever."

As if the train agreed, it slowed as we approached the station.

"Welcome to Emerson Pass," Martha said. "Where you can belong if you only ask."

Josephine

The house was quiet the afternoon we expected Phillip Baker to arrive. After lunch, I wandered down to the sitting room, where I found Theo at one of the windows.

Papa was at the office. My sisters, other than Delphia, were all at school. Mama and Jasper were downstairs working with Lizzie on the plans for the holiday festival in town. On hiatus during the war, we'd happily brought back the tradition last season. This was to be our most exciting one yet. We would have lights for the first time. At considerable expense, Papa had ordered lights to hang over our frozen pond and to decorate the tall fir that stood next to the gazebo. There would be food, music, ice-skating, and Santa for the children.

"Theo?" I asked from the doorway.

He flinched as if I'd startled him, then turned my way.

I walked over and took his hands. "How are you? Do you need anything?"

He brought my hands to his chest. "I'm fine. Simply enjoying the quiet."

I looked into his eyes, large in his narrow face. He seemed young and old at the same time. There was a weariness to him that hadn't been there before the war. But I remembered it from when he was a child. He'd been the one to find our mother. She'd been mentally ill and had gone outside on one of the coldest nights of the year and had frozen to death. For years after that, Theo had been quiet and haunted. I could still remember the smudges under his eyes. They'd gone away when Mama Quinn had come to us. Now, though? I wasn't sure anything could bring back the old Theo. I'd woken in the night to hear him crying out in his sleep, followed by the soothing tones of Flynn.

"When I was away, it became impossible to imagine that any place could be this tranquil." Theo let go of my hands and walked over to the fire. "I wasn't sure we'd ever get back here."

"Do you regret enlisting?" He and Flynn had told the recruiter they were eighteen when they'd not yet turned seventeen.

"I couldn't let Flynn go without me. It would have been worse for me to worry about him than be there too."

"It's over now. You're home where you belong."

"It's not completely over." He tapped his temple. "Not here, anyway."

"Oh, Theo, don't say that. You'll forget, won't you? Over time?" I regretted it as soon as it was out of my mouth. He shouldn't have to pretend for my sake.

"Yes, of course." Theo grabbed a log from the stack and tossed it into the fire. His tone betrayed his words. He didn't believe for one moment that he would ever forget. I'd seen him pretending to be fine for Mama's and our sisters' sake many times since he'd come home. I knew him almost as well as I knew myself. Something had broken in him over there.

Flynn rushed in, flushed from the outdoors and yanking off his coat. He rarely slowed down these days. In addition to working long hours on the ski area, he spent a lot of time in the barn with the horses, taking the sleigh out for long drives, teasing the girls, playing chase with Delphia. Sometimes I wondered if the demons would catch up to Flynn when he slowed down long enough to think. Would he have the same haunted look in his eyes as Theo? Or would he always outrun the ghosts of that horrible war?

Last summer and fall, the twins had begun work on their ski lodge and clearing part of the northern mountain for ski runs. Although they were partners, it was more Flynn's dream and passion. Like the war, Theo would not let him go it alone.

"Just the two people I wanted to see," Flynn said.

"Here, give me your coat," I said. "I'll hang it in the closet for you."

"Thank you, dear sister." He kissed my cheek.

My heels clicked on the hardwood floor as I crossed into the hallway. By the time I'd returned, my brothers had poured themselves tea and helped themselves to one of Lizzie's scones.

"Jo, sit down with us," Flynn said. "Let's talk."

I did as he asked. "I have nowhere to be today." I'd recently hired someone to staff the library a few days a week, freeing me up to concentrate on procurement. In the years since I'd first secured funding from Carnegie, I'd been busy, but now I didn't have as much to do. No man to write to. The library was up and running. Mama didn't really need help with the little girls. Fiona and Cymbeline were nearly grown and fully ensconced in their studies and their friends. There were days I felt somewhat useless.

I poured myself a cup of tea and settled back into a corner of the couch. "What are you two doing today?" They were dressed in wool jackets and knickers.

"We're taking Papa up to the mountain to show him the ski runs," Flynn said. "Now that the snow has finally come, we want to show him how the pulley system works." When they'd skied in Europe, they'd studied systems for pulling people up the mountain. Theo, always clever with engineering, had repurposed abandoned mining equipment into the rope pull that would take the skiers to the top. All they had to do was hold on to the rope and let the machine do the rest. "He wants to try out the slopes himself." I smiled at the pride in his voice. Flynn, of all of us, craved Papa's praise. Not elusive to any of us, of course. If anything, Papa admired us a little too much. According to him, there wasn't anything his Lucky Seven couldn't do.

"I can't imagine why anyone would want to put sticks on their feet and slide down a mountain," I said.

"Jo, you won't believe how much fun it is," Flynn said. "We can't wait for you all to learn."

"What about you, Theo?" I asked. "Did you fall in love with it as much as Flynn?"

"I did. Not that I was challenging Frenchmen to races like my brother."

"Cymbeline will be doing so the moment she masters the skis," I said.

"That's my sister," Flynn said. "I'm so proud of her."

"Delphia's going to be just as bad," I said. "Yesterday at the pond, she ran into a boy and kissed him."

"That child scares me a little," Theo said.

"She's a rascal," I said. "Wild. Like you and Cymbeline."

"I have no idea what you're talking about." Flynn grinned before taking a large bite of scone.

Theo set down his teacup. "Are you going to the festival with anyone, Jo?"

"You mean with a man?"

"Is that such a strange idea?" Flynn asked.

"I'm not interested in any of that," I said. "There's no one who could hold up to Walter."

"You knew him such a short time," Theo said softly. "Don't you think it's time to move on?"

"I've moved on." I prickled with defensiveness. "I have my work."

"You don't appear to have moved on." Flynn spoke in his gentlest tone, which softened me somewhat.

"What am I supposed to act like? Running after every eligible man in town? Acting silly and ridiculous? I had true love, and now I'm going to devote myself to my work."

Theo cocked his head to the side, obviously trying to soften what came next. "Two weeks doesn't seem like enough time to know if you love someone or not."

"They were the best two weeks of my life." I stopped talking, afraid I would start to cry. "He was just everything I ever wanted. Smart and funny. He made me laugh, and you know how I barely have a sense of humor."

"Not true," Flynn said. "You've been laughing at me my whole life."

"*At* you, brother, is different from *with* you," Theo said.

"We would be married now if he hadn't died," I said, ignoring their obvious effort to make me smile.

"But Jo, he didn't formally propose," Flynn said. "Or ask Papa."

"We didn't like that," Theo said.

"Not one bit," Flynn said.

"He would have, but he had to report for duty." A gnawing shadow of doubt niggled at me. Not just at the moment, but in the middle of the night when I lay awake staring at the ceiling. I would never admit it to anyone that his lack of steady correspondence hurt. One time I'd snapped at poor Martha when she asked me about how unequal it seemed to be. I knew she was only expressing concern, but it bothered me. Still, who knew what it was like over there, gunshots and tunnels? I couldn't expect him to have sat around writing to me all day. Perhaps he hadn't wanted to scare me. Which, as it turned out, I should have been more afraid. I'd been so certain he would return.

"Papa didn't want you to marry him," Flynn said.

"Why would you say that?" I stared at him, shocked.

"He said in his letters to us that he thought you were worried about becoming an old maid, which made you susceptible to his charms. All the girls in your circle were getting married and you weren't."

I huffed as I crossed my arms over my chest. "That's ridiculous. I wasn't worried about getting married. Not at all." This was a blatant lie. When Martha had married Dr. Neal and then Elsa had married the dentist she'd met in Denver, I was terribly jealous. The weddings had been such fun. They'd been beautiful brides, and I'd looked around the garden and wondered when it would be my turn. "Anyway, it doesn't matter now. I'm going to be a spinster, whether I was afraid of it or not."

Flynn laughed. "Jo, there's no way you're going to be a spinster. You're too pretty."

"And clever," Theo said.

I looked over at them, both smiling at me. I'd always been able to tell them apart, and not just because of Flynn's scar. Their personalities were direct opposites. In a moment of anger, I'd once called outgoing, competitively ruthless Flynn a scoundrel. Whereas Theo was the scholarly type, bookish and shy. "I'm dedicating my life to the library. I'll never let myself be hurt like that ever again."

"Give it some time," Theo said. "Someone new will come along."

"I told you. I'm not interested." I tightened the grip of my hands on my elbows. "What about you two? Do you have your eyes on anyone?" I asked, desperate to change the subject.

"Nah, I'm too young," Flynn said.

"Not too young for war but too young for a wife?" I asked.

"I think I'll be a bachelor," Flynn said.

"You must have thought of someone while you were away? Did you write to anyone? Theo?"

"I didn't write to anyone but I would've liked to." The tips of Theo's ears turned pink. "But I know she wouldn't have wanted a letter from me. Flynn, probably, but not me."

Flynn groaned. "Not this again. He thinks he's in love with Louisa and that she's in love with me."

"Louisa?" Louisa Kellam Lind had a bit of a history with our family. When Quinn had first opened the school, Louisa came without her father's permission. Later, we found out he'd been hurting her. After Mr. Kellam was killed, Pastor Lind and his wife, Pamela, had taken Louisa in as their own. Since then, she'd thrived, changing from a skinny, shabby little girl to a beautiful young woman. I'd no idea Theo liked her. Did she have eyes for Flynn? I hoped not, for Theo's sake. "When did this happen?"

"Never mind," Theo said. "It's not anything to talk about."

"Does she know you like her?" I asked Theo.

"I told her after we enlisted," Theo said. "She wasn't interested."

"She's been away at finishing school," I said. "But Mrs. Lind says she's coming home for the holidays and not returning. It's because they adopted Louisa when she was already nine. They want more time with her."

"Isn't that what we all want?" Theo asked. "More time?"

Footsteps in the foyer drew our attention. Harley appeared in the doorway, carrying his hat. "Sorry to interrupt, but I wanted to let you know I'm headed out to the train station to pick up Mr. Baker."

"Thank you, Harley," I said. "I'll be here."

"What do you know about this Baker character?" Flynn asked after Harley left.

"Not much," I said. "Other than he was kind enough to write me when Walter died."

"I hope he's as handsome as the devil," Flynn said. "And brings you back to the land of the living."

"Don't be ridiculous," I said. "This isn't a romantic novel where a stranger arrives in town to capture the maiden in distress's heart."

Phillip

The moment I walked into the Barnes home I smelled the aroma of cookies. I didn't have too much time to think about that, however, because Josephine appeared. Her photograph had lied. She was prettier in person. I hadn't thought that possible. She wore a green wool dress that flattered her slender figure. However, she was smaller than I'd imagined—medium height with narrow shoulders and a small bust. Her eyes were the color of an emerald and slightly upturned, as if they were smiling. Golden hair piled on top of her head shone under the overhead light.

My stomach churned from nerves as she stepped forward to offer her hand. I brushed my lips against her gloved knuckles. I dared not hold on to her for long.

"Phillip, welcome to Emerson Pass," Josephine said.

"Thank you." As so often happened, my words were stuck in the back of my throat. Walter would have known what to say. Words had dripped from his tongue like warm honey over a biscuit. No one could resist the way he made you feel when you were with him. That had been his secret weapon in the war of love. "You're lovely...I mean, your home. Is lovely. I'm sorry. I don't mean to be forward."

She smiled, dazzling me. "Thank you for the compliment. Both of them. How was your trip?"

"Harrowing. I met a friend of yours, though. Mrs. Neal. She and baby Quinn sat across from me."

"Oh, how serendipitous. Did she entertain you with stories of our little town?"

I swallowed a nervous laugh. "Yes, I guess you could say that."

From behind her, a young man entered the foyer from a room off to the right.

"This is my brother Theo," she said.

We shook hands. As I looked into his dark eyes, I sensed a kindred spirit. There was a seriousness in his countenance as well as shyness and sensitivity. I wondered how he'd fared in the war. Had it broken a part of him as it had me?

"Pleased to meet you," Theo said. "Flynn and I are excited to show you around."

"I'd be grateful," I said.

A man dressed in a formal black suit appeared. "Dear me, I apologize, Mr. Baker, I didn't realize you'd arrived." An English accent. I knew from the letters that Josephine's father was British and that this was their faithful butler, Jasper.

"Not to worry, Jasper," Josephine said. "He's only just gotten here."

"May I show you to your room?" Jasper asked.

"Yes, and then we'll have tea," Josephine said to me. "Lizzie's made sandwiches and cakes for us."

I nodded but didn't trust myself to speak further. Jasper took hold of my suitcase and headed toward a stairwell made of dark wood. I followed him up the stairs and down a hallway to a bedroom with two sets of bunk beds. "You'll be here with the twins. The bathroom is just through that door." I spotted a white claw-foot tub and floor made of white tiles. "Will you mind sharing the room?"

"Not at all."

"Would you like me to put away your things?" He gestured toward my suitcase.

"No, I prefer to take care of it myself. But thank you." I didn't want anyone to see my meager belongings.

"As Miss Josephine indicated, the Barnes family has tea every day around four. Whoever is around takes part. This household is loud, Mr. Baker, and can be overwhelming, so please take respite here in your room if need be. No one will hold it against you. I hope you'll let me know if you need anything at all. If you require a trip into town, I'll have someone take you there in the sleigh. After the first snowfall, we put the motorcars away and use the horses. Safer that way. You've met Harley. His wife's called Merry and she assists me in the running of the household. My wife's called Lizzie and she mostly rules the kitchen, along with Mrs. Wu. We all have children now, and they're in and out of the downstairs, but please let me know if they bother you at all."

"I grew up in an orphanage. It'll be like home."

Jasper's formal expression twitched into a smile. "I often joke with Lord Barnes that we're like an orphanage. All told, including the grown Barnes children, we have a dozen young ones here. Although I don't suppose I can consider the twins or Josephine children any longer. But when you've been with a family as long as I, it's hard to think of them as anything but children.

"May I ask about attire for tea and dinner?"

"You're expected to dress for dinner but for tea, what you have on will do nicely." Jasper cleared his throat. "One thing I'd like to say—we're all grateful for what you chaps did over there. I say that as an Englishman and American. It's an honor to have you here."

"Yes, sir. Thank you."

Jasper frowned. "It's a frightfully long train ride from back east. If you'd like a bath before tea, take all the time you need. The Barnes family are not sticklers for formalities. They tend to meander in and out on their own timetables, so you may do the same without offense."

"Much obliged." I'd done nothing but say thank you since I'd arrived. "Also, would you mind giving this to Josephine for me?" I opened up my bag and pulled out the box of her letters to Walter. I'd kept her photograph in the pocket of my suit. I'd have to give that to her later. I wasn't quite ready to part with the image that had anchored me to hope for so many months.

"Consider it done. Again, welcome to Emerson Pass." Jasper walked away, the tapping of his heels as precise as his speech.

I went first to look at the bathroom. Electricity and running water? Luxury living. I didn't belong here. I had no chance with a woman like Josephine. For the hundredth time that day, I questioned my sanity. What had made me think this was a good idea to come here?

Believe in yourself. No one else does. Men like us have to be scrappy to get what we want.

That had been advice from Walter.

A twinge of guilt rattled me further. Sure, Walter had been deceitful and conniving, but he'd been my friend. He'd seen us as the same. The type of men who weren't invited to the club and had to worm our way in by nefarious means. However, I wasn't that way. Despite my circumstances, or perhaps because of them, I held integrity and honesty above all else. Without them, who was I? A poor man who was also a liar? I had to claim something to be proud of. My character was all I had.

I tried to put my trepidations aside to enjoy a bath with the hot water and nice-smelling soap. Afterward, I shaved at the mirror. I didn't look too bad considering the long train ride. My dark hair looked nice after a good wash. Dark smudges under my eyes had been there since I joined the army, so there was nothing to do about them. Nightmares plagued me and disturbed my sleep. Perhaps here in the quiet, I would sleep better.

Although I'd seen the same dark circles on Theo. Maybe the quiet didn't help.

When I was done, I put on a fresh shirt and my light gray suit. At a few minutes to four, I headed back downstairs.

I can do this, I told myself as I walked into the sitting room. Dark paneling and brightly colored furniture gave the room a cheery feel, as did a roaring fire and the scent of cinnamon.

A tall, rather intimidating man stood by the fire. Sitting on the couch, a petite blonde woman had a book open on her lap. Two little girls played with dolls under a large desk.

"Hello there, you must be Phillip. I'm Lord Barnes, Josephine's father." He bounded across the room and pumped my hand, then slapped me on the shoulder. "We're awfully glad you came." His British accent made him seem even more posh to me.

The pretty woman on the couch had risen by this point and came forward, introducing herself as Quinn Barnes, Josephine's mother. "Please call me Quinn. We're not formal here." She giggled. "Other than Jasper, that is."

She didn't look much older than Josephine. I knew from the letters that Quinn Barnes was her stepmother and quite a few years younger than Lord Barnes. However, I hadn't been prepared for radiant beauty. The kind that came from the inside. "Thank you, Quinn."

"Come sit," Quinn said. "Are you famished? We have all this." She gestured toward an impressive spread on the coffee table. "Sandwiches and little cakes. Lizzie was excited to welcome a new guest and made way too much."

I sat in one of the chairs, eyeing the food as my stomach growled. Quinn handed me a small plate. She had this way about her that made me instantly at ease. "Help yourself to whatever you want. I can remember the first time I came here, having traveled such a long distance, all I could think of was food. I was practically starved back then."

"She rationed out her food to one meal a day," Lord Barnes said. "I've been fattening her up ever since."

"Darling, you're making me sound as if I'm a cow you're preparing for market," Quinn said, laughing.

"The attempt to fatten you clearly hasn't worked," I said. "You're positively beautiful." Why had I just said that? What an idiot I was.

"Why, thank you, Phillip. What a nice thing to say."

"I agree," Lord Barnes said as he knelt to kiss his wife's cheek. He straightened to his full height. "The ladies are having tea, but I was thinking of a whiskey. Care to join me?"

"No, sir. I don't drink whiskey." This wasn't entirely true, but I wanted to make a good impression.

"I'll pour you a cup of tea," Quinn said. "In this house, we have a lot of tea. I'm outnumbered with all the British folks."

"A hot cup of tea is most welcome." I filled a plate high with six small sandwiches cut into neat squares. From what I could tell, they were ham and cheese.

"Please, eat," Quinn said. "Jo and the others will be down any minute, but let's not wait for them. The early bird gets the worm."

I did as I was asked, only too gladly. The bread was soft and instead of cheese, I discovered they were spread thick with butter. "This is...delicious."

Quinn smiled and nodded her head approvingly. "Lizzie is the greatest cook the world has ever seen."

"Oh, dearie me, not true." A voice came from behind me. I turned to see a redheaded woman making her way into the room with another tray of sandwiches.

"This is Lizzie," Quinn said.

"Welcome, welcome," Lizzie said. "You must let me know all of your favorite foods and I'll make them all for you while you're here."

"That won't be necessary," I said. "I don't want to cause any extra work for anyone."

"Nonsense. This is what I live for." Lizzie's face and figure were round. Pink cheeks glowed with health and good humor.

"This is the best sandwich I've ever eaten," I said.

"I'm going to like you. Now I must get back to the kitchen. I wanted to get a good look at you first, Phillip Baker." Lizzie looked over at Quinn. "He'll do just fine, don't you think?"

"Lizzie, mum's the word," Quinn said.

"Yes, yes, quite right." Lizzie curtsied and then scampered from the room. I wondered if she'd left fairy dust in her wake.

While I ate, Lord Barnes joined his wife on the couch. The little girls approached, shooting shy glances as me.

"Ah yes, come meet our guest," Lord Barnes said.

Quinn gestured for them to come closer. "This is Delphia, our youngest, and Adelaide, who is seven. Girls, this is Philip Baker, Jo's friend."

"Nice to meet you," I said.

Delphia peered at me. She was an exceptionally pretty child, with large blue eyes and hair the color of dried grass. "Did you come from far away?"

"Yes, New York City."

"Papa and Mama went there once," Adelaide said, then flushed, as if embarrassed that she'd spoken. She was also fair of skin but didn't have the robustness of her sister. A little too thin, and very serious eyes made her seem older than seven. She had the same shade of blue eyes as her sister, but her hair was so blond it was almost white.

"Papa hates it there," Delphia said. "Too many people."

"Delphia," Lord Barnes said, laughing. "When did you hear me say that?"

Delphia shrugged as she turned her gaze toward the cakes. "I don't know. You say a lot of things. Can I have cake?"

"You two will have a sandwich first and then you may have a cake," Mrs. Barnes said.

They climbed onto a wide easy chair and sat together. Delphia's legs were too short to dangle over the seat and stuck out straight in front of her. Adelaide sat with her hands folded on her lap as Mrs. Barnes gave them each a square of sandwich. While they nibbled, they watched me.

"Girls, it's not polite to stare," Quinn said.

"Why?" Delphia asked.

"Because it might make a person self-conscious," Mrs. Barnes said.

"What's self-commerce?" Delphia asked.

"I'll explain later," Adelaide said to her sister. "For now, you should be quiet."

Delphia's eyes flashed with annoyance but she kept whatever retort she had to herself.

"How was your trip out here?" Mrs. Barnes asked me. "The train scared me to death the first time I took it from Denver to here. I thought I was going to die by falling off one of those steep tracks."

"I thought the same."

We were interrupted by Josephine's arrival. She rushed in looking flushed and sat in the chair next to me. I caught a whiff of perfume that reminded me of jasmine. It was the smell from her letter to me. I'd been right. "I'm sorry I'm late. I lost myself in a book and didn't realize the time."

Delphia, having finished her sandwich, asked for a cake.

"I'm going to give you each one, and then you'll go off to play and let the adults talk," Quinn said.

"As long as we get cake, I don't care," Delphia said.

"Delphia, please mind your manners," Quinn said.

"Sorry, Mama."

The next few minutes we talked further of my trip out here. I mentioned that I'd met Martha Neal.

"This is a small town," Lord Barnes said. "Not surprising. Tell us, Phillip, what can we do to help your transition into our little town? What kind of work are you interested in finding?"

"I trained as a cabinetmaker before the war. Other than that, I don't have many skills."

"Would you want to set up a shop?" Lord Barnes asked.

"Eventually, yes. But I'd need capital for that. Until then, I'll take anything. If you have anything around here that needs fixing, I could help."

"But you're our guest," Josephine said. "We can't put you to work right away."

"No, I'd prefer to work," I said, hastily. "I like to earn my keep. It would help me feel less of a burden. Your offer to stay here at the house is the kindest thing anyone's ever done for me." A tickle of guilt bothered me.

"Good man," Lord Barnes said. "Everyone in this family works one way or the other. There's a place for everyone in Emerson Pass. When you get settled, perhaps we can talk further about your shop."

"Thank you, sir." I could have teared up right then and there. Would this be the place I finally found a sense of belonging?

The rest of the hour passed pleasantly. At five, Josephine asked if I'd like to get bundled up and take a walk out to the barn. "I could show you the animals."

"Can I come?" Delphia asked from the corner. She'd put her doll facing the wall, as if she'd been naughty. I had a feeling Delphia herself had faced the corner quite a few times.

"No, sweetheart," Lord Barnes said as he patted his knee. "You and I are going to read a book so that Jo can show Philip around."

"All right, Papa." Delphia climbed into his lap and snuggled close.

Josephine stood. "Phillip, would you care for a tour or would you rather rest?"

I jumped up, both excited and terrified at the prospect of spending time alone with the lovely Josephine. "No, I'd love a tour. Show me the way."

"We'll see you at dinner," Mrs. Barnes said.

I thanked them for tea and followed Josephine to the foyer. The idea of Josephine alone had me reeling. Part of me wanted to run and hide. However, the bold part of me that lay dormant most of the time urged me forward. I'd come this far. No turning back now.

"Do you have a coat?" she asked.

"No, just my suit jacket."

She tugged open the closet door and pulled out a green-and-black-checkered hunter's jacket. "There's an old one of Theo's or Flynn's in here. Would you like it? The snow stopped, but it'll be cold."

"Yes, please." My first instinct had been to say no, but that would have been foolish. The weather was frigid here. I would have been completely chilled on the way from the train station had Harley not had wool blankets in the sleigh.

I helped her into her coat first. She put a fur-lined cap over her head while I put on the jacket. "A good fit," I said.

"Yes, you're almost exactly the height of my brothers. Check the pocket. There's probably a hat and gloves in there."

I reached into both pockets. Sure enough, there was a knit hat and a pair of gloves inside. After I'd donned both, I asked if she was ready.

"Yes, we should go before it gets completely dark."

We walked out to the covered entrance. If she didn't think this was dark, how dark did it get here? She pointed toward the lit barn, then turned a switch on near the door. The lanterns that lined the drive came on, dazzling me with their bright lights. "So pretty," I said under my breath.

"Aren't they? Papa had them put in just last year. They're especially festive this time of year."

We headed out to a shoveled walkway that led to the barn. I let her take the lead.

"Our family loves animals," Josephine said. "Don't be surprised if they ask at dinner about what you thought of our horses."

"What should I say?" I concentrated on not slipping on the icy path.

"Something about how they're the most beautiful horses you've ever seen. That's what they think, anyway."

"Then I shall say it for certain."

She laughed, and her breath made a cloud in the cold air as she yanked open a side door and motioned for me to go in first.

The space was large and tall with stalls for a cow, a pig, and several horses. Chickens lay on nests. A rooster eyed us suspiciously.

"That's Doodle," Josephine said. "He's mean, so keep an eye out for him."

She pointed to a hayloft. "I used to go up there to be by myself when I was younger. I love my brothers and sisters, but sometimes I needed a little peace and a place to read."

"That sounds nice. I'd have liked a place like that at the orphanage." I'd never had any time alone there. We'd slept in small beds all lined up in a row and ate all meals together. "The only place I could escape to was the pages of a book."

We locked eyes for a split second.

"I understand perfectly." She took two apples from a bucket near the door. "Would you like to feed one of the horses an apple?"

"Sure." I'd have liked to say no. Horses scared me a little with their large teeth.

We walked over to the stalls. The horses both whinnied at the sight of Josephine. "These two girls are Lucy and Pearl. They're a little older than the other two, so we use them for the small sleigh." She pointed to the other pair. "These two are only three years old." She held the apple up to one of the horses. "This one is Willie. And that's Oz."

I held out the apple in front of Oz. "Will he just take it?"

"Bring it closer."

I did so and flinched as Oz sucked it from my hand.

"You haven't been around horses much, have you?"

"No, not really," I said.

"These two are gentle. They won't hurt you."

She took my hand and put it on Oz's nose. "Stroke him with your thumb. He loves that."

I would have preferred to stroke Josephine's nose, but I did as she asked. Oz flicked his tail.

"He likes you," Josephine said.

"How can you tell?"

"He's smiling. See." She pointed at his mouth, which looked exactly as it had when we first walked up to him.

"Did Walter really read you all parts of my letters?" Josephine asked.

"We loved the stories of your family's antics. Everything is exactly how I pictured it from your descriptions."

"Perhaps my family is more entertaining on paper than the real thing."

"I found them entertaining just now."

"Wait until you meet Cymbeline. Was it really my letters that made you want to come here?" Josephine asked.

"Yes. I wanted to get out of the city. As your father said—there are too many people. When I was so sick, I told myself if I survived, I'd come out here to see it all for myself." *And you.* I kept that to myself.

"I hope you won't find the town too quiet." Josephine leaned against the stall.

"I don't think I will," I said. "I've a confession to make."

"Yes?"

"I read through all your letters when I was well enough. They helped me get better. I know that probably sounds ridiculous."

"No, not ridiculous." She watched me, carefully, as if I were an oddity she wanted to figure out but couldn't quite. "Sweet, actually. Reading letters from a girl you didn't know seems a romantic thing to do."

"They gave me joy when I needed it most. Like a good book."

"I can imagine doing the same in your situation. You were lonely and scared and needed a distraction." Josephine took in a deep breath and looked up at the rafters. "There were parts meant just for Walter. I'm slightly mortified to think what I put in there. I must have sounded like a lovesick girl."

"You made me long for someone to feel that way about me."

"Don't be ridiculous," she said. "I'm not that good a writer."

"I beg to differ."

She was quiet for a moment. "I was taken aback when you said he'd read parts of the letters to the other men. I imagined him reading them as I did his. Savoring every bit. Reading them over and over and keeping them to myself. Holding them close. Like a secret love."

"We needed your stories of family doing ordinary things. You can't imagine how much. There were days...when things were really bad and I felt certain none of us would ever make it home." I paused, thinking about how much I wanted to tell her. How truthful did I want to be? "They hinted at the possibilities of life. If I could just make it out alive, there might be a girl who would love me as you had Walter. Then later, when I was sick, they held the idea of promise. Of better things to come."

"I'm glad they gave you something to hold on to. After your letter that Walter had died, I was lost in that way, too. Looking for anything that would lead me into the future. That they gave you all something to look forward to and enjoy during such a hard time gives my life meaning." Her voice wavered. "I struggle to understand why certain things have happened and what my place is supposed to be now. Is it just my work at the library? Should that be enough?"

"You could love again, couldn't you?" I asked. "Someone worthy?"

"My father did. After Mother died, he was able to fall in love. But me? I don't know. There's never been anyone else I felt that way for."

Bitter jealousy churned my stomach. If she only knew how undeserving my friend had been.

"What about you, Phillip Baker? You must not have a girl back in New York or you would've brought her with you."

"Right, there's no one."

"Do you want someone?" Josephine asked.

"I want a wife and family more than anything in the world."

Her eyes softened. "Oh, that's nice. You'll get it. A wonderful, very lucky girl will come to you soon."

"I don't have much to offer a woman. Not yet."

"You're enough just as you are." She smiled and brushed the collar of my coat with her fingertips. "I have a feeling the young ladies of Emerson Pass will be tripping over one another to meet our new handsome bachelor. I'll be sure to tell you who to stay away from and who is good."

I knew the girl I wanted. She was standing right in front of me. Now I just had to win her heart.

Josephine

The night of Phillip's arrival, we dined with my parents. The little girls had already eaten and been tucked into bed, but Fiona and Cymbeline were allowed to join the adults. My brothers had stayed in town to eat at the café before working from Papa's office.

The chandelier shed soft light over the dining room table. Mama and Papa always sat on either end with my siblings and me on either side. Tonight, Cymbeline and Fiona sat across from each other on the end nearest Papa. Phillip and I were opposite, near Mama.

Phillip had dressed for dinner in a dark suit and white shirt with a bow tie. I hadn't expected him to be quite so nice-looking. I'm not sure why, but it had never crossed my mind what he looked like one way or the other, only that he'd been Walter's friend. He'd been through a lot, and I have must seemed like a spoiled rich girl. What did he think of me? I was surprised to realize I hoped I'd lived up to my letters and that I wanted very much for him to like me.

Before the first course of squash soup, Papa raised his glass. "To Phillip. Welcome to our home."

"Thank you, sir. I'm pleased to be here."

We all lifted our glasses to toast. My sisters looked fetching in their dinner dresses. Fiona was in a soft blue and Cymbeline in gold with small beads sewn into a lovely pattern. This was her first formal dress as a young woman of sixteen. She'd been the same height for several years and most likely wouldn't grow taller. She was curvier than Fiona and me and strong as an ox. One day a few years ago, I'd caught her standing in front of the mirror, crying over the fact that her breasts had seemed to arrive out of nowhere. "I don't want them," she'd said. "They're pulling me forward when I skate or run." I'd had to bite the inside of my lip to keep from laughing. Only Cymbeline would be dismayed by her chest, whereas I wished I had much of anything at all in that area. My sister was not your ordinary girl.

"Papa, please tell us about the slope," Cymbeline said. "I can hardly wait to try skiing."

Papa's eyes lit up as he set down his glass and answered my sister. "The rope pulled me up the mountain with limited effort. Theo's system is genius."

"Did you go fast on the way down? Were you afraid?" Fiona asked, her eyes wide.

"I was not afraid, but remember, I skied in Switzerland on holiday as a child," Papa said. "I'd forgotten how exhilarating it is."

"Dear me, I do hope you won't make me do it," Mama said. "I'm not keen on heights or speed."

Papa flashed an indulgent smile her way. "You, my love, will stay in the lodge sipping a hot toddy and watching your husband conquer the mountain."

"That sounds lovely," Mama said, smiling back at him, looking pretty in a beaded cream dress with her golden hair piled on top of her head. Long white gloves ran the length of her arms.

"What's the lodge like?" Fiona asked. "Will it be fancy?"

"I was imagining it more rustic," Phillip said. "With large beams and high ceilings."

We all turned to look at him.

He flushed at the attention. I had the feeling he hadn't meant to speak.

"Are you familiar with ski lodges?" Mama asked.

"Not really," Phillip said. "I imagine them that way, for some reason."

"Do you fancy architecture?" Papa asked.

"Nothing so complex as that," Phillip said. "Cabinets and furniture suit me fine."

"We don't have a furniture shop in town," Cymbeline said, her eyes sparkling. She'd inherited Papa's excitement around business. If she'd been born a man, I could easily see her opening a business of her own. Now, if all went well, her best hope was to work for my brothers. She was a born leader but needed something to focus on or she got herself in trouble.

"True enough," Papa said. "I'd like to have one so we are as independent from the city as possible. As it stands now, people make their own or have them shipped at great expense on the train. Perhaps you could make something for us in the barn to show me an example of what you can make. A business loan could be arranged if I like what I see."

I stole a glance at Phillip. He was leaning forward slightly with his spoon hovering above his bowl. "I'm not a braggart, Lord Barnes, but I'm skilled. Where would I get wood?"

"We have a forest of it right here." Papa pointed toward the windows. "Cedars, firs, quaking aspens. If you can cut it down on my land, you can have it."

"I've not cut down a tree before," Phillip said.

"I have," Cymbeline said. "With an ax. There's nothing to it."

"You could take him out, Cym, and show him how we do it in Colorado," Papa said.

"I'd love to," Cymbeline said. "You have to be patient, chipping away at it one swing at a time."

"Patience is something I'm good at," Phillip said.

"Don't forget the triangle part," Fiona said.

"Right. You make a forty-five-degree angled notch in the trunk," Cymbeline said. "We'll show you."

"Girls chop down trees in Colorado?" Phillip asked, looking from Cymbeline to me, then to Papa.

"We do whatever a boy can do here," Cymbeline said with a flash of rebellion in her eyes. "If we want to, anyway. Jo doesn't care for rough jobs, but I do."

"The noise it makes when the tree falls scares me," Fiona said. "But I try to be brave so Cymbeline doesn't get impatient with me."

"I worry about their safety, of course," Mama said. "But these girls know the woods as well as their papa. However, might I suggest that a trip to the local sawmill, where they have cut wood, might be more efficient?"

Lord Barnes laughed. "As usual, my dear, you're correct."

"The Barnes ladies open libraries, chop down trees, and roam the woods, and what else?" Phillip's blue eyes twinkled as he gazed across the table at me.

A little buzz started in my chest. He was absolutely too handsome and personable. He already had my sisters twisted around his finger. If I weren't careful, I might like him. No, my heart belonged to my poor dead soldier. I'd promised him.

"My wife was our first schoolteacher," Papa said.

"What about you, Miss Fiona?" Phillip asked. "What will you do?"

"I sing and play the piano," Fiona said. "I might be a teacher like Mama was before I get married and have lots and lots of babies."

"Fiona's a very good singer," Cymbeline said, sounding proud. "She's going to sing in church this coming Sunday."

"Would you like to come and hear me?" Fiona asked Phillip.

"I'd love nothing more." Phillip returned his attention to his soup.

Mama smiled over at me before taking a bite of her soup.

"Speaking of businesses in town, I spoke with the boys who run the saloon," Papa said. "They're worried about January."

Prohibition took effect in January. The café, as it was now called, would most likely still serve drinks but in secret. Fortunately for them, our local law enforcement were frequent patrons of the saloon. Papa felt certain they would look the other way. He purposely stayed quiet about how he felt about the Eighteenth Amendment for fear of alienating either side of the political argument. He was a businessman and the self-appointed father of Emerson Pass. He saw his job as one of support and inspiration, not rules.

"What's your opinion of Prohibition?" Mama asked Phillip. "The twins are adamantly opposed. I suppose coming from their time in Europe, the idea seems provincial."

"I can't say I have an opinion one way or the other," Phillip said.

Papa chuckled. "Very diplomatic of you."

"I'm quite for it," Mama said. "Nothing good ever happened between the walls of a saloon."

"How do you know?" Cymbeline asked.

"Have you been to one?" Fiona asked.

"I've never set foot in a place like that, no. However, some things a woman just knows," Mama said. "Are you a drinking man, Phillip?"

"I've had a drink before," Phillip said.

"Quinn, stop quizzing our new friend," Papa said, laughing. "If he'd like a whiskey with me after dinner, then he shall have one."

"I shouldn't like to upset the mistress of the house," Phillip said, smiling. "So whatever she advises is what I'll do."

"That's wise," Fiona said in her innocent way. "Mama only wants what's best for us."

"You're very lucky to have a mama such as this one," Phillip said.

"We know," Cymbeline said. "Our other mother died."

"And God sent Mama to us," Fiona said.

"We don't remember her," Cymbeline said. "But we've seen a painting. Jo looks just like her."

My stomach churned. I didn't like it when the girls talked about how much I looked like our mother, even though it was true. She'd left us when we needed her. I couldn't forgive her for that. We were better off with our Mama Quinn anyway. But still, thinking of the way Mother had died angered me. How could she leave us that way? She'd purposely walked into a frozen world where she knew she would die. Leaving Papa to raise five children on his own. Leaving me, at nine years old, to take her place, robbing me of my childhood. I knew the answer. She'd been unwell. Her sense of reality damaged. Yet there it remained. The anger like a red-hot knot in my stomach.

I looked up from my soup to find Papa watching me. I smiled at him to assure him all was well. He knew my thoughts, though, and where I went sometimes in my mind. We'd lived through all of it together. Only once in a long while would I see him drift away to that dark time. Theo, too. The others had escaped without the permanent damage we'd endured.

"You're absolutely right, dear husband," Mama was saying. "I'm only teasing you, Phillip. You may do as you please. Consider our home your home."

Phillip's brow wrinkled. "Speaking of which, do you think there's a place in town I could rent? A room somewhere?"

"There's the boardinghouse," Papa said. "But there's no reason you shouldn't stay here. We have more than enough rooms."

"We'd really like it if you'd stay here," Mama said. "I promise not to ask too many questions at dinner."

"I don't mind," Phillip said. "I'm only too happy to answer anything. The nuns used to tease me that I was incapable of lying, even when I'd done something wrong and fibbing would've saved a knuckle rapping."

"What's that?" Fiona asked.

"It's when they took a ruler and smacked our knuckles," Phillip said. "No one liked it, I can assure you."

"Were you often in trouble?" I asked.

"Not often," Phillip said. "I wanted nothing more than to please the kind women who gave their life to take care of children no one wanted. The only times I got in trouble were because of Walter. He was forever coming up with ideas about how to escape or steal food."

"Walter? Really?" I couldn't imagine him to be an unruly boy. During our time together, he'd been the perfect gentleman. Well-mannered and polite, deferring to my wishes. "In my experience, he was a rule-follower."

"Was he?" Phillip asked me. "Perhaps you brought that out in him."

"Boys can be rascals and grow up to be fine young men," Mama said. "Flynn was always in scrapes when he was little."

I glanced at Papa. His gaze was fixed on Phillip with obvious interest. I knew that expression. He was attempting to suss out what Phillip had meant when he said Walter had led him into trouble. A twinge of irritation pushed its way in. As much as I adored my father, his attitude toward Walter annoyed me. He hadn't known him. Who was he to judge? He and Mama had fallen in love quickly. How was my experience different?

"How long were you and Walter together at the orphanage?" Papa asked.

"Only a few years," Phillip said. "When we were twelve, one of his attempts to run away was successful. The next time I saw him was in the army."

"Why did he want to run away?" Mama asked.

"I don't know," Phillip said. "The nuns were good to us. It wasn't as if we had anywhere to go."

"Isn't it strange how you ended up together in the army?" Mama asked.

"Yes ma'am, it is. I could hardly believe my eyes." Phillip set aside his spoon as our maid, Lila, brought up the main course—

roast beef with carrots and potatoes. She took the platter to Mama first and then to me. The aroma of rosemary and onion wafted up from the platter as she scooped a small portion onto my plate.

"Thank you, Lila, this smells delicious," Mama said.

Phillip's face lit up when it was his turn to be served. "I've never eaten as good as I have today, and I've only been here six hours." When everyone had their portion, it amused me to see the way Phillip dug into his food. I liked his humility and easy way with my sisters and his politeness to my parents. This was a good man. Coming here would be good for him. Everyone needed community and a sense of belonging.

He needed some good luck after everything he'd been through. My letters had brought him here. Something good had come from my writing. This brought me a sense of relief. Walter could not come back to me. But at least I'd made a difference in a man's life that truly needed some luck.

Four days had passed since Phillip's arrival. I hadn't seen him as much as expected. He'd spent most of his days with Harley in the barn and shed, learning how he could be of service. I was busy at the library and had only seen him during dinners, but already it felt as if he'd always been with us. He spoke enthusiastically about the animals and all that he'd learned from Harley. On the way upstairs one night, he confessed to being physically exhausted at night and falling fast asleep.

On that fourth afternoon, I returned early from work and instead of going inside the house, I went out to the barn to look for Phillip. We hadn't had much opportunity to talk, and I wanted to ask him questions about Walter's death. I found him tossing hay into the horses' stalls. Oz and Willie were already eating. Pearl and Lucy were patiently waiting.

"Hello," I said.

He turned quickly and smiled. "Jo, hey."

I hustled over to him. "How are you holding up? Have they worked you too hard?"

"Not a bit. I love it. I'm even getting used to these beauties." He patted Oz on the nose.

"Is it all right sleeping with the boys?"

"Sure thing. It's fun, actually. Reminds me a little of being with the other boys at the orphanage, except we don't get in trouble for talking past nine."

"I'm glad. I wanted to make sure you knew you were invited to the festival with the family."

"Your mother already told me I was to come," he said. "I'm looking forward to it."

Before I could ask him anything else, Theo and Flynn burst through the barn doors, their voices loud and excited. They both stopped when they saw us.

"Just the man we wanted to see," Flynn said.

"Phillip, we wondered if you could come to town with us in the morning," Theo said. "We're helping to set up for the festival and could use another strong man."

"Sure, I'd be happy to help," Phillip said.

"Do you skate?" Theo asked Phillip.

"No. Never," Philip said. "I don't have skates, so I'll watch."

"We'll get you a pair tonight," Flynn said. "Everyone in Emerson Pass skates."

"Do skates cost a lot?" Phillip asked, his gaze on his feet.

He would be worried about the money for something that wasn't a necessity. Shame on us for being insensitive. We should have thought of that before announcing that he would be obligated to skate like the rest of the young people in town.

"Our treat," Flynn said, obviously thinking fast. "In exchange for helping us set up tomorrow."

"Right," Theo said. "Consider it a gift for helping out around here. Papa says you're doing a great job. Flynn and I are busy with our skiing enterprise and don't have time to pitch in like we should."

"Yes, all right." One corner of Phillip's mouth twitched into a half smile. "I'll feel foolish, but if I'm going to fit in around here, I need to skate."

"That's the spirit," Flynn said. "Let's head to town now. Mrs. Johnson will have your size."

"I'll see you later, then?" Phillip asked me.

"You can count on it." I waved them off and turned to the chickens. Lizzie might need extra eggs for the desserts she was making for the festival. She loved how everyone fought to have her cake over all the others.

There were three eggs, all warm from the hens' nesting. I placed them carefully in the bucket we kept for this purpose.

Doodle came strutting toward me as I crossed over to the door. For a split second, I thought of Walter. What was it about Doodle that had made me think of him? I put the thought aside and locked the barn door.

I was thoroughly chilled by the time I went back inside the house. Jasper, as if he'd been waiting for me, stood by the foyer closet.

"Are you all right, Miss Josephine?" Jasper asked. "Your eyes look tired this afternoon. You're not coming down with a cold, I hope?"

"I didn't sleep well, but I'm fine. Thank you for asking." I'd tossed and turned all night for no reason at all.

"Your mother would like to see you in the sitting room," Jasper said.

I thanked him and went to the sitting room, where Mama was at the desk writing. She looked up as I approached. Her gentle smile welcomed me. "Hello, darling. You're home early."

"We were slow, so I left Dolly in charge."

"Are you hungry? You look tired. Have you eaten today?"

"Yes, I'm fine. Did you need me for something?"

"Nothing in particular. I haven't seen you much this week."

She stood from the desk and asked if I'd join her near the fire. It wasn't yet teatime. The fire crackled as I sat in one of the armchairs. A yawn escaped before I could swallow it. I ignored Mama's concerned glance.

"I was just out in the barn," I said. "Phillip seems to be adjusting to country life."

"I'm delighted by the young man. He's such a hard worker. Nothing seems to deter him, either. He just cheerfully goes about his work."

"He seems to like it here," I said.

"He's handsome, isn't he?" Mama asked.

"Is he? I hadn't noticed."

"Lying doesn't look good on you, Jo."

"Mama, I'm not lying. Why would you say such a thing?"

"I've seen the way you look at him."

"I *do not* look at him any way at all, other than as Walter's friend."

"Do you think it's odd that Walter ran away from the orphanage? Why would he have done that?"

"Maybe it was awful there." Where was she headed with this? I tried not to bristle, but it was already too late.

"Phillip said the nuns were good to them," Mama said.

"As you said, Phillip tends to see things very positively."

"Isn't that a wonderful quality?"

"Mama, what are you trying to say?" I asked with an edge of impatience in my voice.

"Nothing, darling. Just that you two have a lot in common. You'd have to be blind not to notice those eyes of his."

"Well, I haven't. Walter was the love of my life. There's no need for a Phillip."

"*A* Phillip?"

"Don't sound like that. I'm merely saying that he's nothing to me, other than a friend of the man I loved and lost."

"Many people have fallen in love through letter writing without once meeting in person."

Fall in love? Had she lost her mind? "The difference is that those letters weren't to him. He read them as a *distraction* while he was convalescing. Not because of anything genuine between us, since I wasn't even aware of him. He said he read them as if they were a good book."

"I think he came here for more than the fresh air," Mama said.

"I'm sorry to be impertinent, but that's ridiculous."

"Aren't you at all curious about why you're so insistent on remaining loyal to Walter?"

"I don't need to be curious. I already know why."

"A fear of losing someone again isn't a good enough reason. Your whole life will pass you by, Jo, holding on to a ghost. Your sisters and all your friends will marry and have families and what will you be doing? Escaping forever into a book instead of living your own life?"

I'd like to have pretended that Mama's words didn't bother me. However, they did. She was right. I would have to stand by and watch from the corner of the room like a wallflower as my sisters and even Poppy fell in love and married. "I made a promise. Shouldn't that mean something?"

"It should. But promising the rest of your life to a dead man makes no sense at all, and you know it. I've never known you to be afraid of anything, Josephine Barnes. Until now."

I rose wearily to my feet. "I'm not sure what you're doing, Mama, but goading me into forgetting about Walter isn't going to work. I loved him with all my heart. What would you say to me if it were you who'd been left a widow because Papa died? Would you just *move on* as everyone seems to want me to do?"

"Walter wasn't your husband."

I stared at her with my mouth partially hanging open for a second or two. "He would have been."

"Are you sure about that? Because he certainly never made that clear to your papa. He didn't write to you but once a month." She put up a hand. "Don't make excuses for him. He was simply too lazy or didn't care enough to write to you after every letter he received. Is that what you would have accepted as a wife? A man who only filled you up halfway? Don't you dare sit there and tell me his lack of correspondence didn't hurt."

"It's no good speculating at this venture, Mama. I'll never know what it's like to be married to him. As you've so aptly said, he's dead."

"We didn't raise you to accept second best, Josephine."

"Walter was the best. Writing letters isn't the totality of a man's character." With that, I strode to the door and fled up the stairs. The moment I was in the bedroom, I threw myself on my bed and burst into tears.

Josephine

The evening of the festival, my sisters and I were all bundled up in our warmest outerwear and tucked under blankets in the large sleigh. Papa and Mama were in the front, sitting together as closely as two people could. Overhead, the stars blessed us with their beauty. A sliver of the moon hung over the northern mountain. In the quiet of the evening, even the horses seemed hushed, their hooves making a pleasant pitter-patter through the soft snow. All morning and into the late afternoon, powdery flakes had tumbled from the heavens. Around three, the clouds had parted and drifted away, replaced by a sky more purple than blue until the short day transitioned into darkness.

I had the little girls on either side of me. One thick blanket was tucked over all three of us, creating a pocket of warmth from our bodies. The sweet scent of their freshly washed hair tucked under their matching blue caps mingled with the smells of the piney forest.

Delphia's excitement was palpable. She leaned forward, the muscles in her neck straining to see around Mama. "I can't see town yet, Jo."

"You will. Be patient," Mama said.

"Look at the stars instead," I said to Delphia.

Delphia jerked her head upward, moving the blanket, which let in a burst of cold air.

"The stars," Addie said with a sigh as she tilted her face toward the sky. She shivered, either from the chill or the poignant beauty of the night. I put my arm around her narrow shoulders and pulled her closer to my side. There were times with all my sisters that I could hear their thoughts despite the lack of words, but no one more than with my dear Addie. Like me, she could not fathom the beauty of the night. There were things that could not be explained, both good and bad in this world. I wished Addie would only know nights such as this one but I feared that would not be true. Still, I knew this one undeniable truth. One must keep on despite disappointments and losses, because good times would come again. Sweet was stronger than sour, courage stronger than fear.

"Fiona, sing to us," Papa called out from the driver's seat.

"'Silent Night,' please," Mama said.

Fiona's rich voice rang out from behind us where she and Cymbeline sat together. "Silent night, holy night."

I turned around to take a peek at them. Fiona sat straight as a board, her neck long as she sang. Cymbeline stared upward, unusually still, as if mesmerized by her sister's musicality. They were as bright as the stars just then.

The lights of town appeared as Fiona sang the last verse. As we approached the center of town, Delphia squealed at the sight of all the people.

"I thought we'd never have a night like this again," Mama said. "All this seemed far, far away during the war."

"We're all safe and well. Tonight we celebrate our good fortune." Papa stopped near the gazebo to let us out. "You girls go ahead. I'll take care of the horses and meet you there."

"Do hurry, Papa," Cymbeline said. "Everyone's waiting for you."

"Not to worry," Papa said. "I'll be as quick as I can."

Cymbeline and Fiona each took the hand of one of the little girls and ran ahead. Mama and I had been polite to each other since our spat the day before but hadn't spoken of it.

"Jo, I'm sorry about yesterday."

I threw my arms around her. "I'm sorry too."

"It's only that I want you to be happy. You've always been such a good girl, putting everyone before yourself. I don't want you to do it for Walter. Whether or not he would have been what you wanted, he's no longer here. Can't you see that?"

"I do. But regardless, I'm simply not interested in Phillip Baker. Please, don't get your hopes up just because the rest of you seem to have fallen in love with him overnight."

"Fine. I won't say another word."

"All right, then." We shared a smile and then linked arms and walked toward the crowd. I scanned the people, looking for Phillip, and found him with Theo over by the ice. They had their heads together, talking closely. "There's Phillip," I said, under my breath. "There with Theo."

"Were you looking for him?" Mama asked.

"What? No. I mean, yes. He's our guest and I wanted to make sure he was all right. The boys may have worked him too hard."

"He seems to be fine," Mama said. "You'll have to stay close to him, though. Show him around. Introduce him. Maybe to some young ladies? I mean, since you're not interested."

I didn't like the idea. Why was that? *Oh, never mind*, I told myself. *You're being silly.* I didn't want him. I shouldn't keep others from him. "Good idea, Mama. He's a very sweet man. Any woman here would be lucky to have him."

Fortunately, we were engulfed in the crowd at that moment or the conversation might have become more heated. I'd never had words with Mama or been chastised. I didn't like it. I also thought she might just be right. My loyalty might be disguising a deep lack of courage.

I put it aside to take a good look around. Mama's mother

and sister, Annabelle, were helping Annabelle's husband, Clive Higgins, who owned the meat shop, serve sausages to a long line of hungry patrons. They'd set up a temporary booth and were handing out raw sausages wrapped in paper. People had brought their own sticks for roasting the sausages over a large firepit.

A long table was lined with every treat imaginable: cookies, cakes, and pies. Papa had paid the local baker, Mr. Cartwell, to make enough rolls for a whole town. Cartwell looked as jolly as old Saint Nick tonight with his round belly and full pink cheeks. The Johnsons had sponsored pork roasts, which had been cooking over an outdoor fire since dawn. I didn't like to think of the poor pigs having sacrificed their lives. The wonderful smell, however, could not be denied.

Over the years, the Johnsons had expanded their store to meet the growing needs of our town. They'd become wealthy because of fair business practices and good customer service. However, while some might have become greedy for more, they were grateful and generous. Tonight, they'd donated candy for the children that later would be handed out by Pastor Lind playing Santa. I could hardly wait to see my sisters' faces.

A vat of spiced apple cider hung over a smaller firepit. Isak Olofsson was manning the cider, using a ladle and filling cups people had brought from home.

Flynn and a group of men had huddled together around the gazebo to pass a flask around, adding whiskey to their cups of cider.

"Oh, dear, I hope everyone behaves themselves tonight," Mama said.

"Don't fret, Mama. Just enjoy yourself."

"Yes, yes. You're right. I just don't like the men drinking with all the children here."

"The little rascals aren't paying any attention to what the adults are doing."

The Cole family, who owned the café in town, had made pots

of chili. The line for the spicy scented beans was as long as the one for sausage.

Delphia, Addie, and Fiona circled back to stand with us. "May we have a sausage, Mama?" Fiona asked.

"Oh, dear. I forgot the roasting sticks in the sleigh," Mama said.

Just then Papa appeared with the twigs the girls had carefully carved yesterday. "Go on, off with you," he said after he handed them out to each of the girls. "Where's Cymbeline?"

I spotted Harley and Merry with their little ones standing in line for a sausage. Jasper and Lizzie were sitting together on a bench, watching their daughter play with some of her school friends. Even Mrs. Wu had agreed to take the night off and come into the town. Li was away at music school in Chicago. Fai, her granddaughter, was surely here somewhere, but I didn't see her at the moment.

I finally found Cymbeline. She was standing with a group of girls from her class, gesticulating wildly with her hands. "There she is," I said to Mama.

"She's bound to cause trouble tonight," Mama said. "I can see it from here."

"She'll be all right," Papa said.

"I'm worried for others, not her," Mama said. "She's growing wilder by the day."

"Don't worry," I said. "The world is big enough for Cymbeline's spirit. Anyway, we're here to have fun and celebrate our second Christmas of peace."

"That's right," Papa said. "All troubles are forgotten tonight, my darling wife."

"You're both right. I don't know what's gotten into me lately. Worrying over everything."

"It's all part of being a mother to seven," Papa said. "There's always one to worry over."

Theo, with Phillip by his side, approached. I found myself smiling shyly at Phillip. His eyes were beautiful. Even in the dim light thrown from the lanterns around the gazebo, they beckoned to me.

Phillip greeted us with a bob of the head. "Nice to see you."

"You as well," Papa said. "Thanks for helping the boys this afternoon."

"We had a great time," Theo said.

"We did, sir," Phillip said.

"Phillip and I are becoming great chums," Theo said. "We couldn't have done it without him."

Phillip beamed.

"Papa, we have everything set up." Theo motioned toward Flynn to come join us.

"Jolly good," Papa said.

Flynn came running over, grinning like he used to when we were children. "All right, let's get on with it. If all goes well, the lights will come on one after the other."

"Pond lights first," Theo said. "Then the tree."

We followed the boys over to the gazebo, which was located between the tree and the frozen pond. A band would play there after the lighting ceremony.

Phillip leaned close to my ear. "You're looking beautiful tonight."

"Thank you. How was your afternoon?"

"More fun than I can say. I almost felt like I've lived here all my life."

"I'm glad." Indeed, he seemed so happy that I couldn't help but feel the same. This man was a good reminder to appreciate many aspects of family and community I often took for granted. He was so easily pleased. His almost childlike joy humbled me.

The crowd hushed as Papa took the stage.

"Good evening, Emerson Pass," Papa said in his booming voice. "What a turnout. I won't bore you with a long speech, but I do wish you all a merry Christmas. I'd be remiss if I didn't say how grateful I am that we are now in a time of peace and good health. May the new year bring good fortune our way. Without further ado, let us have light." Within a second, the lights strung over the frozen pond lit up, followed by the tree. The crowd cheered.

For some reason, unshed tears stung my eyes. Seeing the whole town out enjoying themselves touched me deeply. Papa's dream of a community had come true.

I glanced up at Phillip. He stared at my father with a mixture of respect and admiration.

Next, I thought about what Mama had said to me earlier. Was she right? Had he come for more than the fresh air?

"Eat, drink, and be merry," Papa shouted out to the crowd.

People dispersed to various areas of the festival. The pork had been taken down from the spits and cut into pieces, drawing a crowd of men. Many of the young people put on their skates and began to make their rounds. Cymbeline had already made at least a half dozen circles before I had my skates attached.

Mama had taken Phillip over to a bench and was helping him with his skates. I did a lap before pulling up beside them, breathing hard. "Are you ready? Mama, will you take him out with me?"

"Yes, of course. Now don't worry if you can't get it right away," Mama said to Phillip. "It took me two whole seasons before I stopped falling."

Papa, holding the hand of each of my little sisters, flew by.

"Hello, Jo. Hi, Mama," Addie called out to us.

"Look at me. Look at me," Delphia said.

"You look great," I said.

We each supported one side of the large man as he got unsteadily to his feet. I could feel the strength in his arms and torso as he gingerly moved forward.

"That's right, just tiny steps at first," Mama said.

The three of us managed to make it halfway around the pond before his feet slid out from under him, bringing us all down onto the ice. To my mortification, my legs entangled with his. My skirt rose up above my knees. I scooted away from him as quickly as I could while simultaneously pulling my skirt over my stockings.

"Ladies, I'm sorry." Phillip's legs were spread out into a V shape as he supported himself with the palms of his hands. "Are you hurt?"

Mama scoffed. "No, it takes more than some ice to hurt us. We're women of Emerson Pass."

Papa skated up to us. The girls were with Fiona now, skating in a pack on the other side of the pond. Papa held out his hand to help Mama up, then did the same for me. Poor Phillip remained on the ice, looking up at me with shining eyes. Dark tufts of hair poked out from under his knit cap, and his cheeks glowed from the cold. My heart might have skipped a beat.

"I'd like to skate with my wife now," Papa said. "I'll leave my daughter to help you, Phillip. She'll teach you everything she knows."

My parents exchanged an amused look before skating hand in hand. What they found so funny, I couldn't say, but I had a feeling the joke was on me.

I took pity on Phillip despite my embarrassment over my earlier entanglement with his legs and held out both hands to him. "Let me help you."

He raised one eyebrow as if skeptical but placed his gloved hands in mine. I tightened my grip and attempted to raise him up to no avail. His feet once again slipped out from under him, and this time I landed squarely on top of his chest. For a second I was as frozen as the pond under us, staring into his eyes. A girl could get lost in them and be stuck forever.

A deep rumble of a laugh came from inside his chest. I could feel it even through our layers of clothes.

I rolled off him and onto my knees. "How will we ever get you off the ice?"

"What's it called if one scoots there on his or her backside?"

I giggled. "There's no name for it, but it might be our only way out of here."

He raised his knees and using his hands for support began to inch toward the side of the pond where an empty bench waited. When he finally reached his destination, I was already there waiting.

I planted my feet securely in the inches of snow. With one hand firmly gripping the back of the bench I offered the other one to him. Somehow, I managed to pull him up and onto the bench.

"Good God, that was awful." His breathing was labored but his eyes twinkled at me. "Why would one ever do such a thing on purpose?" He ripped his cap from his head. "I'm hot, if you can believe it." His wavy hair was mussed, like a little boy just out of bed. I shocked myself by wondering what it would feel like to put my fingers in that mass of curls.

I forced myself to look away. "You'll get accustomed to it after a time." I sat next to him, making sure to keep a distance between us. The feel of his powerful chest and thighs against mine was not something I would soon forget. In fact, I was more alive than I'd been since the news of Walter's death. *No, no*, I told myself. *This is Walter's friend.* Shame flooded me. How could I betray Walter this way? I'd only just met Phillip, and I was thinking about his hair. What kind of woman was I?

"I'm never going out there again." The corners of his eyes crinkled as he laughed.

Martha Neal appeared with two cups of steaming cider. "Hello there. I thought you might need a hot drink."

"Martha, nice to see you again," Phillip said.

"You as well," Martha said. "Did Phillip tell you we met on the train?"

"He did," I said as I took the cup from her.

"And how are you faring so far?" Martha asked Phillip.

"Hard to say," Phillip said. "Other than I cannot skate."

"Not yet," Martha said. "Give it time."

I could have imagined it, but they seemed to have exchanged a collusive glance. Over what, I couldn't be sure. Surely Martha wasn't playing matchmaker? She knew I'd sworn myself to Walter. Perhaps I was being paranoid, but my parents and Martha both seemed to be up to no good.

"I hope your husband knows how to set broken bones," Phillip said. "I'm not sure I'll get out of here tonight without a broken arm or leg."

Martha laughed as if that was the funniest thing she'd ever heard. "My husband does indeed know how to fix broken bones. But don't worry. Josephine will make sure you're all right. She's a most loyal friend."

Martha gave me a sweet smile, which I returned with one of my own, even though she was acting strange.

"Have fun," Martha said. "I've got to get back to my mother. We're monitoring the sweets table to make sure none of the children make themselves sick with too much sugar. You can return the cups to me when you're done." She wriggled her fingers and then made her way down the trodden path of snow toward the dessert table.

I took a sip of cider and nearly choked. There was whiskey in it. "This is spiked," I said. What was wrong with Martha? I'd never seen her have a drink in my life. At our monthly book club meetings, she always declined sherry even though some of the other women had one. So far it seemed the impending Eighteenth Amendment had only made our citizens take more interest in imbibing than ever before, including the young men tonight who were passing around flasks and filling their cups of cider with whiskey. But Martha? I would have never guessed.

He looked down at his cup, then back at me. "I might like to drink mine if you don't mind?"

"Don't hold back on my account."

"Do you think it will make me skate better?"

I laughed. "I don't think so, no."

He sipped from his cup and made an appreciative grunt. "This is good."

We sat in silence for a few minutes, watching couples and

groups of children skate by.

The drink seemed to have relaxed Phillip. His shoulders had softened. He gave me a lazy smile and took another drink from his cup. There was something endearing about the man, despite his obvious masculinity.

"What was it like growing up at the orphanage?" I asked. "Were you always there?"

"I was sent there when I was four or so. After my parents died from yellow fever within days of each other. There was no other family, so off I went. The sisters were good to us." The wistful quality in his voice caused goose bumps to spring up on my arms. "I always think of them this time of year. They somehow managed to give each of us a Christmas present. There were thirty or so of us at any one time. Occasionally, a baby or toddler was adopted, but the older children were there for life."

"Do you remember your parents?"

"A little. Mostly they're images in my head—certain moments in time forever etched in my consciousness." He reached into his pocket and pulled out a piece of paper the size of a postcard. Faces of a man and woman were drawn in pen and ink. "I drew this of them one night during the war. I'd suddenly worried that the horror of that time would erase them from my memory. Isn't that strange? What happened over there—what we saw—it changes a man."

"My brothers aren't the same since they got back. Nothing overt, but I can see it in their eyes sometimes when they think no one's watching." I took the paper from him to get a better look, holding it up to capture the light from the bulbs overhead. The depictions were detailed and well drawn. I could see he favored his father just from the drawing. His mother had a delicate chin and wide-set eyes. "This is quite good."

"Not really, but drawing relaxes me. Takes my mind off my troubles."

"Everyone needs that from time to time."

"What's your way?"

"Reading," I said. "That's why building a library here was so important to me. I wanted anyone to be able to have what I had when escaping into a book, no matter if they're rich or poor."

"It's quite something—what you did."

"I had a lot of help from Mama and Papa." I gave him back the drawing. "Nothing compared to what you boys went through in the war."

"Honestly, I didn't think I'd make it home. I've never had much luck in life. When we lost so many of the boys that night... I didn't think it would be me that survived." He tucked the drawing away inside the inner pocket of his jacket.

"The night Walter died?"

"That's right. One day you look around and think, how am I still here when the others are gone? I vowed not to be so satisfied with simple survival. Instead, to live life with boldness. Like your father."

"How so?"

"In your letters, it was apparent he's not a man satisfied with complacency simply because he could be. He didn't do what was expected of him, but what he wanted. Coming here and building this town. Making a community. What could be more important than that?"

I nodded. It was true what he said. Papa had given up his title as the eldest son of English aristocracy to come to America and make his own way. "He always says the first time he stepped off the train in what was then an abandoned mining town he knew this was the exact spot he wanted to live for the rest of his life."

"It's extraordinary. Reading about him in your letters made me want to be a better man. I've spent too long in the background, letting others take what I wanted."

"What is it that you want?" I asked.

He shifted on the bench as his gaze looked away from me toward the Christmas tree. "In one of your letters, you described when Delphia was born. Do you remember what you wrote?"

I nodded. "I think so."

"Your described how the doctor said your mother might not make it because of an infection. You wrote how your father wouldn't leave her side for days, alternating between praying on his knees and wiping her brow with a cool cloth. That image stayed with me as if I'd seen it with my own eyes. I want a love like that."

My throat ached. I wanted that too. I'd thought I had it with Walter. "Mrs. Wu's tea did its magic."

"Mrs. Wu's tea?"

"She makes this concoction with herbs and other plants—we don't know what exactly, and she won't give the recipe to anyone but her grandchildren. We all believed it cured her of the infection."

"You never mentioned that in your letters."

I turned my gaze back to the skaters, wishing I could think of a better explanation than the truth. "Oh, well, I didn't think Walter would understand about the tea."

"Why do you say that?"

"An instinct I had about him. He said a few things when we were together in Denver that made me think he didn't like that people who weren't of European heritage came to America. My family doesn't think that way. We think what makes our community special are all the different cultures who've come here." I waved my hand toward the pond. "Everyone here came from somewhere else."

"Was that the kind of man you wanted?"

"It was a small thing. Compromises have to happen."

He set aside his now-empty cup. "How am I going to get my boots back on?"

I laughed, the tension between us broken. "Are you sure you don't want to try skating again?"

"If you're willing to fall with me, then yes."

Fall with him? Or was it fall for him?

I stood and held out my hand. He took it.

Phillip

I went home in the smaller of the sleighs. The twins were in the front and Josephine and I tucked in the back under a heavy blanket. Lanterns hung from the front of the sleigh helped to find our way in the dark. Above us, the stars twinkled brightly. I stared up at the sky, marveling at the beauty. The plodding noise of the horses tromping through the soft snow was steady as we made our way home. Tomorrow we would return to clean up and take down the tables. For now, however, the sparkle of the night was still upon us.

"You all right back there?" Flynn asked.

"Fine," Josephine called out to him. "Are you fine?" she asked me softly.

"Better than I've been in a long time. I had such fun. Thank you for inviting me."

"Hopefully you won't wake in the morning with any bruises." Josephine yawned. "Is it midnight?"

"A little after." I'd checked my watch before we loaded into the sleigh.

"I never stay up this late." She yawned again, then rested her head against my shoulder. "Are you glad you came here?"

"So far, yes."

"Even after the skating?"

"Yes, even after the skating."

As we turned a corner, a light in the distance appeared.

"Almost home," she said.

We didn't speak for the rest of the way. Flynn stopped the horses very near the house. "Go on in," Flynn said. "I'll take care of Lucy and Bell."

"I'll help you," I said.

"As will I," Theo said.

I threw the blanket off our laps and dismounted from the sleigh and helped Josephine to climb down as well. Our eyes locked for a split second before she looked down at her hands. "Good night, Phillip. Good night, boys."

I watched her walk away and slip inside the house as I headed to the barn. Each twin led a horse into the barn and got them into their stalls.

Flynn reached into his coat pocket and took out a flask. "Anyone care for a drag before we go inside?"

"Sure thing," Theo said.

"Me as well," I said, not wanting to sound unmanly.

We stood just outside the horses' stalls. Theo handed me the flask. "How was your night?"

"Good, thanks," I said before taking a swig. "I've fallen for Emerson Pass. I knew I would."

"That's not all that's caught your eye," Flynn said, grinning at me. "You and Josephine seemed chummy tonight."

"Flynn," Theo said. "We agreed to stay out of this."

"You trying to woo her?" Flynn asked.

"What if I was?" I asked.

"Might be rough going." Flynn took another drink from the flask. "She's under the impression that Walter Green was her one and only."

"I gathered that," I said.

"Declared herself a spinster," Theo said. "Which we think is ridiculous."

"You do?" I peered from one twin to the other.

"We weren't keen on the idea of Walter, if you want to know the truth," Flynn said.

"May I ask why?" I asked.

"The family—our family—didn't think she knew him well enough," Theo said.

"And he promised to marry her but there was no ring, no formal proposal," Flynn said.

"Which we found suspicious," Theo said. "Our father wasn't consulted, either. No letter of introduction or to ask for her hand."

"We didn't care for that," Flynn said. "A lack of respect."

The way they finished each other's sentences was like they were one person.

"Our sister has never once done something that didn't make sense or was impractical or overly romantic," Flynn said.

"Until Walter Green," Theo said.

"An outsider. A stranger. Someone she met in the city." Flynn said *city* as if it were a bad word.

"We have a theory about why she says her heart's closed forever," Theo said. "She doesn't want to risk losing anyone again."

"And she believes Walter to have been the only one for her," Flynn said.

"As well as the finest man in the world," Theo said.

"The likes of which does not exist." Flynn rolled his eyes.

"He wasn't a fine man." I hadn't meant to say this out loud, but there it was.

The twins watched me with their pairs of identical eyes.

"Go on," Flynn said.

"Yes, please tell us what you know," Theo said.

"Why do you think I know something about Walter?" I asked.

"Instinct," Theo said.

"I hate to speak ill of the dead."

"Go on," Flynn said.

"Walter Green had more women than Josephine writing to him. All five of them with expectations that when he returned, he would marry them. Like your sister, the other ladies were from wealthy families."

By the time I finished my diatribe, both men's complexions had reddened.

"You were witness to this?" Theo asked.

I nodded. "We were together every day. Not much escaped notice."

"You must tell her," Flynn said.

"I don't know," I said. "Causing her further hurt is the last thing I want. She has an idea of him. One that gives her comfort. Shouldn't I let well enough alone?"

The twins looked at each other, then back to me.

"This would be the unselfish thing to do," Flynn said. "But self-sacrifice doesn't get the girl."

"I'm sorry to say, I agree," Theo said. "As her brothers, we'd rather have her know the truth about someone she's foolishly closed her heart over so that she might be happy with someone else."

"A man worthy of her love," Flynn said.

"A man like you, for example," Theo said.

"You don't know me," I said. "What if I'm the same as Walter? Here for the money."

"Are you?" Theo asked.

"No. I came to see if the girl I fell in love with from her letters was real. Or if my feelings were only a romantic ideal."

"And?" Flynn asked.

"I'm prepared to do whatever it takes to win her heart. Also, to convince your father and the two of you that I'm worthy of her."

"Well, all right then," Flynn said. "Let's get on with it."

We were quiet as the twins and I entered the house. No sooner had we taken off our outer jackets than I saw a movement out of the corner of my eye. Josephine stood in the entryway of the sitting room.

"Jo, you're still up?" Theo asked.

"Yes, I wanted to have a word with Phillip," she said.

"I'm tired and headed to bed," Theo said.

"You two behave yourselves," Flynn said.

Flynn shot me a look before heading toward the stairs with Theo at his heels.

I followed her into the sitting room. The fire had died down to embers. A lantern shed a yellow light.

She stood in front of the fire with her arms crossed over her middle. "I've something to ask you, and it can't wait a moment longer. I want to know how Walter died."

I inwardly cringed. Knowing few details of his death would certainly frustrate her, as it had me. "What do you want to know?"

"Were you with him when he died?"

"No. That day we fought hard, pushing the Germans farther north. By the time darkness fell, we'd successfully taken back some of the French territory previously lost." The day had been rife with casualties on both sides. Good men—soldiers who had become brothers-in-arms—had fallen before my eyes. "I lost track of Walter sometime during the battle. When the fighting was done, he wasn't one of the survivors."

Josephine's eyes glistened with unshed tears. "So you don't know if he suffered or exactly what happened to him?" She moved to the chair, sitting on the edge of the seat.

"No, but I doubt he suffered. The bullets flew fast. Most men never knew what hit them." This wasn't exactly true. I'd held too many men in my arms and watched the life drain out of them. Almost always their last words were of their mama or wife. The last thoughts not of enemies or wars but of the women they loved. "The battle was brutal and confusing. We weren't sure who we'd lost until it was over. There weren't many who survived that day. I knew only that he was somewhere in the piles...of dead men." My voice grew raspy with the effort it took not to break down in front of her. I didn't want to describe the horrors of that day or so many others. In fact, I didn't want to remember them. I did what I could to forget. That was my idea of survival.

Some of the men had been taken away by ambulance in the hopes they would live. Most were buried where they fell.

"There were men who came after the battles to bury the soldiers where they were killed. We weren't expected to do that." As those who fought, we weren't asked to bury our fallen friends. An unfortunate group came after each battle to do so.

"I expected him to be there at the end," I said. "He was tough. Strong and scrappy. Tougher than most, other than me."

"Why? What do you mean?" The way she asked in a small but desperate voice, wanting to know more, broke my heart.

"I guess because of the ways we grew up. For me, being raised in the orphanage and Walter living as he did. On his own so young." How much did she know about Walter's past? I knew there had been lies or omissions by the questions she asked in her letters.

"I have something for you." I reached into the breast pocket of my jacket and pulled out her photograph. I leaned forward to place it on the arm of her chair.

"Why was it in your pocket?" Her tone sharpened.

I flooded with heat. How did I explain that? I hadn't thought that through, anxious to change the subject from the battle. "For safekeeping?" It came out as a question. "I'll sound creepy but I wanted to make sure nothing happened to it until I could give it back to you."

"How kind of you." She brought the picture onto her lap and stared at the photo with such intensity I half expected it to catch on fire. "It wasn't on him when he died?" Her chest expanded as she drew in a deep breath.

"No." I hadn't thought she'd ask that particular question.

She looked up at me. "Where was it?"

"It was in the box with the letters. I was the one who took it out of there. I'm sorry. I know it didn't belong to me."

She was quiet for a moment as she drew a handkerchief from the sleeve of her dress and pressed it against her mouth. "He said he kept my photograph in his pocket. The one next to his heart." Her words were wooden and strangely calm.

I hesitated, unsure what to say. "He sometimes stretched the truth."

Her head snapped up. "Why would you say that? What do you mean?"

"He used his charm to his advantage." *Leave it at that*, I told myself. *She doesn't need to know about his deceit. Not yet.* Not until she trusted me more.

"Do you mean he lied to me?" She set the photograph on the table next to her chair. "He *did* lie to me. This was not where he said it would be. If it had been, you would not have found it with the letters because it would have been with him when he died."

"Maybe he was worried that it would be harmed."

"No, he said specifically that it would be near his heart for protection. But why would he lie about such a thing? Numerous times."

"I don't know."

"I think you do. There's more you're not telling me. Your eyes are evasive."

Feeling trapped, I muddled through, babbling like a brook after a storm. "He was captivating and smart and he used that to his advantage. His charm was intoxicating. To me, too, in the beginning. But his intentions were not always pure."

"Say what you mean," she said.

"You were not the only one who wrote to him. Or that he wrote back to."

She stared at me. Her bottom lip trembled. "How many?"

"I'm not sure. Four, I think," I said. "Actually, I know. There were five. All with the same expectations as you."

"Why would he do such a thing?"

"He was interested in moving up in the world. In fact, that was his main goal. He targeted women he thought could bring him social standing and wealth."

Her bottom lip trembled as if she might cry, but instead she seemed to gather herself. A tone eerily calm but with unmistakable anger delivered the next words. "Why should I believe you?"

My answer came quickly and surprisingly articulately. "Why did you believe him? You knew him for two weeks before declaring yourself in love with him. Did you truly know him, or was he merely someone you wanted him to be?"

"I'm not that kind of person. I'm not a romantic fool."

"You can choose what you believe or not, but I'm incapable of lying. Even small fibs." I bowed my head in deference to her. "Anyway, I've no motive for lying to you."

"You carried my photograph in your pocket." She said it matter-of-factly while staring right at me with eyes that bored into me.

I swallowed as a wave of heat flooded through me. What defense did I have? She'd understood my reasons only too well. "Yes, I did."

"Perhaps your reason for telling me these astonishing things are to make him look bad so that you might...might try to make an argument for yourself."

"Yes, my intentions were selfishly motivated, but I ask only that you examine what you thought you knew about him carefully. Go back over the conversations and his letters as if you're a detective. You'll see gaps and lack of details in his stories. Read him like you would a book. After tonight, I'll leave you be, but I'm pleading with you not to ruin the rest of your life over a false promise. He didn't have the photograph in his pocket like he said he did."

"Your reasons for coming here and telling me this were purely selfish," she said.

"Regardless of my feelings that are not completely benevolent, I'm telling you the truth about Walter. Yes, I fell a little in love with you in the pages of your letters." I raised my arms over my head and let out a deep breath. No more dalliances in the vague shade of gray. I would tell her the exact truth. "Actually, I fell deeply in love with you. So much so that I risked your wrath by coming here and telling you what I know to be true. A truth which will surely get me cast away. Don't you see? I had to take the risk. To find you here pining away for a man who was no better than a charlatan—that's reason enough for me to tell you. You've given up the possibility of happiness with a man deserving of your love for the memory of a man who lied to you. I can't leave here thinking you'll choose spinsterhood for that man."

All color had drained from her face. Her eyes were wide and glittery, almost as if she had a fever. "Is that why you came here? To win me? Is it some sick game to beat Walter?"

"God, no. It's about you, not him. I fell in love with you." I hung my head. "But I've done nothing but hurt you. I'm sorry I've caused you pain."

"You didn't do this." A tremor in her voice made my chest ache with guilt. Why hadn't I left well enough alone? I was an awful, grasping man who deserved to be alone and isolated. "It was Walter who lied, not you."

"Still, I hate to see you hurt. It's the last thing I would ever want."

She jerked to her feet and went to the fireplace. With her back to me, she used a poker to spread out the embers, then with a quick movement grabbed a skinny piece of wood and hurled it into the fire. "How did you know how many women there were?" She whipped back round. The color had returned to her cheeks. "How did you know about them? Did he brag? Did he laugh at me?"

"No. A man like that—the way he'd had to scrape his way along to keep himself from starvation—this was a means of survival. He thought of it more like an investment in his future. The outcome he wanted was more likely to happen if he had more than one woman in love with him."

She bit out the words. "By tricking women into thinking he was in love and wanted to marry them? Marry us? Yes, I suppose it's an us. Five of us. There are other ways to get what you want out of life. Opportunities that come along for honest, hard-working men."

"Which he wasn't."

"I believed every word out of his mouth. Every word in his letters."

"It wasn't your fault," I said as gently as I could. "He was good at the art of seduction."

"I've prided myself in being practical. Not like some of my girlfriends, so quick to declare themselves in love when really it's just an idea they're attracted to. What a fool I was. I did exactly as they had. Papa was right."

I watched her helplessly. What did I do now? She believed me, yet I'd hurt her. Secondarily, she now understood my reasons for coming here.

She stumbled back to the chair and sank down into the cushion. "Do you think I could have a small glass of whiskey? Pour one for yourself, too."

I sprang to my feet to retrieve her request. My hands shook as I poured us each a tumbler. "Here," I said. "Sip, though, so you don't choke."

She mumbled a thanks as she stared into the glass.

"I've hurt you. That was never my intention. I can't tell you how sorry I am."

The anger seemed to drain out of her along with a sigh. "Don't be sorry. Despite my reaction, you're right. The truth is better. Pining away for a mendacious ghost is not the way to live one's life."

"I'll go if you want me to," I said.

She looked up from her glass. "Did you truly think you were in love with me? From letters?"

"I did. I do."

I held my breath as I waited to hear what she said next.

"You couldn't have. I'm not that good a writer."

"I beg to differ."

Josephine

I stared into the fire as the pungent scent of whiskey tickled my nose. The log had caught, giving the dim room additional light and warmth, but I shook as if I were outside without a coat.

I hadn't expected any of what had transpired. Now, faced with this earnest man's eyes staring back at me, I didn't know what to do or think. I hadn't wanted to believe what he'd said was true about Walter, but the evidence was right here in front of me. The photograph told the story of a man who'd sworn he kept my image close to his heart, day and night. Only a fool would deny what was obvious.

Everything I'd thought I'd known was now in question, especially about myself. Was it true that I'd made Walter into the person I'd wanted him to be? If so, what did that say about me? Had I been so desperate for love that I'd concocted a story around a man who was essentially a charlatan?

Instead of taking Phillip's advice, I downed my glass of whiskey. The alcohol caused my eyes to tear up, and I coughed. He got to his feet. "Are you all right?"

I waved him back to his chair. "Yes, yes. I'm fine." I turned away, trying to gather myself. In love with me? How perfectly ridiculous.

Who was I to judge him? My heart had been given to someone with complete abandon. I'd mourned a man for years who didn't exist. A sudden urge to explain myself to Phillip surged through me. "I'd never been in love before. I had no experience with men. Nothing that would tell me if he were lying or not."

"You couldn't have known."

His kind blue eyes stared back at me with so much sympathy I had to turn away. "I've wasted years of my life."

"No, don't think that way," he said.

I observed him for a moment, trying to see what was beneath his angular features. "If you had been there and seen what those two weeks were like—how utterly charming and clever he was—you would see how it happened."

"I know, because I was charmed by him once, too. When we were kids, I thought we'd be great friends forever. He had this way of making you seem like you were better than you really were, which, for a boy like me all alone in the world, made him seem very shiny."

I barked out a bitter laugh. "Shiny. That's a good word for it." The other women. Had they sent their pictures, too? What were they like? How had they been fooled?

Did they know the truth now?

I returned my gaze to Phillip Baker. "Did you tell the others the truth about Walter?"

He shook his head. "I wasn't sure I was even going to tell you."

"I wonder if you should. Perhaps they're wasting their youth away as I was."

"I could, I suppose. Maybe they've all married someone else by now? And, as you said, my reasons for telling you were selfish."

I blushed. Don't think of it, I told myself. This is just a nice man who thinks he's in love with me. He's come all this way under that assumption, but it can't possibly be real. He's a romantic. That's all.

"What made you wait so long to come see me?" I asked.

"When I got back to the States, I didn't feel well. Not like some of the boys with the shell shock, mind you. Not that bad. Just uncertain about everything. And the noise. Every horn or crash caused my heart to beat faster. Then I became ill with the Spanish flu. I nearly died. Recovery took longer than I'd wanted."

"But you're all right now?" I very much wanted him to be all right.

"I'm fine. When I started feeling strong again, I thought about my life. What I wanted. The thing first on my list was to finally meet you. It took me this long to have the courage to write you."

"I'm glad you did."

"Even though I've brought unwelcome news?"

"My parents always say the truth is what matters most. I've made decisions based on what I thought to be true. It will take some time to recover from that and to examine exactly what it is in me that allowed that to happen."

"You're not angry with me?"

"I was for a second, but it makes no sense to kill the messenger. You didn't do anything wrong. Other than read letters not written to you." I smiled to let him know I was teasing. "But seriously, you must stop all this nonsense about being in love with me. People can't fall in love over words."

"I disagree." He gave me a slight smile. "You're not inside my mind."

"Is it all sunshine and roses inside there?"

"It's actually a bit cloudy. I'm roaming around half-blind, unsure where I'm going or what I'm doing. But there's one thing I know for sure, and that is how I feel about you."

I turned away from his gaze, shy. Could it be possible? Was there a chance I could feel the same way?

"No one's loved me for a very long time," Phillip said. "But I remember what it was like to bask in the glow of my mother's love. I know it's the only thing worth fighting for. It's true that I don't have much in the way of worldly goods, but my heart's pure. I'm going to work like the dickens to make a life I could offer to you."

"I don't care two figs about money," I said. "My father's set it up for me to have a comfortable life whether I marry or not."

"The success would not be for you but for myself. A man has to feel worthy of the extraordinary woman who chooses him."

"I see."

"If you'll allow me to spend time with you over the winter and perhaps into the spring, you'll know by then if there's the slightest chance of falling in love with me. My intention is to win your heart."

"You must believe there is or you wouldn't have come here." I chuckled to myself. The whiskey had warmed me and loosened my inhibitions. "Which shows an arrogance and boldness that reminds me of my father."

"All my life I've only had myself to rely on. Not many things have gone my way, which makes it easier to come for what I want. Nothing good ever came from timidity."

"Well, I shall sleep on all of this and we can talk tomorrow. In the meantime, I need to go to bed or I'll turn into a pumpkin by morning." I needed out of there. To think through all that he'd told me tonight. And to keep myself from giving him too much hope. I didn't know him. I wasn't going to make the same mistake I'd made in the past. *Be guarded and wary*, I told myself. *Even though he seems like the most sincere man in the world.*

He rose to his feet and offered his hand. I allowed him to help me up out of the chair even though I was perfectly capable of doing so myself. A tingle ran up my arm. We stood there, staring into each other's eyes for at least three seconds before I removed my hand from his. "Good night, Phillip."

"Good night, Josephine."

I walked out of the room knowing that his gaze traveled with me. When I got to the doorway, I didn't look back for fear that if I did, I might run straight into his arms.

THE NEXT MORNING, it was only Papa, Mama, and my younger sisters at breakfast. Flynn had taken Phillip and Cymbeline into town to help clean up after the festival. There was no sign of Theo, but he must have decided to sleep in after our late night. All of which gave me the perfect opportunity to tell Mama and Papa about Walter.

Surprisingly, I'd slept well. After I'd parted from Phillip the night before, I'd been so weary from the emotions of the day that I'd fallen immediately asleep. I was refreshed in the morning. Strangely, lighter too, as if a burden had been lifted. This was not the reaction I thought I'd have upon learning my love was not my love after all.

I waited for Fiona to take the little girls upstairs for some playtime before addressing Mama and Papa. He was reading the paper and sipping another cup of coffee. Mama was nibbling on one of Lizzie's biscuits while taking surreptitious glances in my direction.

"You're awfully quiet, Jo," Mama said. "Is everything all right?"

Papa put down his paper and fixed his gaze upon me as well.

"I'm fine." My voice wobbled, which did nothing to convince them. "It's just that I've learned some things from Phillip. About Walter."

"About how he died?" Mama asked. "Did you get the answers you were seeking?"

"Not exactly." Again with the shaking voice. I swallowed and took in a deep breath. "He wasn't who I thought he was. There were other women. Five, to be exact, from whom he received letters. They all thought he would come home to marry them."

"I don't understand," Papa said. "How could you *all* think he was to marry you?"

"Because he told us all the same thing," I said. "We're all from wealthy families. Phillip said he was interested in marrying someone with money to secure his future. I guess because he grew up all alone, his main goal in life was to have wealth and lead a life of leisure."

Mama's eyes had turned a deeper shade of brown. "He lied to you?"

"Why so many women?" Papa asked. "Why not just one wealthy one if that was his goal?"

I almost laughed at Papa's obvious naivete. "Phillip said he was hedging his bets, so to speak. Hoping one of us would come through after the war. The more he had lined up, the more likely it was to lead to marriage."

Papa was shaking his head. "If he weren't already dead, I'd kill him."

"Alexander, no," Mama said. "But thank God he didn't come back. You would have married him."

"How do you know Phillip's telling the truth?" Papa asked.

"Because he brought my photograph back to me," I said. "Walter had promised to keep it close to his heart for good luck. But it wasn't on him when he died. Phillip said it was in the box with the rest of his things. Just tossed in there with the others." I paused for a moment to gain my composure. Saying all this out loud was harder than I'd thought it would be. "He told me in every letter that he kept it in his inside jacket pocket. He lied to me about that over and over again. He ended every letter with the same sentence. 'I keep your image in my pocket next to my heart.' If he lied about that, it means he lied to me about other things too. I've no idea if any of his feelings were genuine."

"And you shouldn't care," Papa said. "Not after learning this."

"I feel like a fool." I hung my head. "You were right. I didn't know him well enough. I should have known better. I was too blinded by love—infatuation—to see it clearly."

"Thank the good Lord for Phillip Baker," Mama said. "Or you might have pined for Walter the rest of your life."

"He was very brave to tell you," Papa said.

"He had a motivation of his own. He thinks he's fallen in love with me through all those letters I wrote to Walter."

"He read them?" Papa asked.

"Again and again. He said that's why he's here. To win my heart. His words."

"How romantic," Mama said.

Papa's mouth was twitching as if he were trying not to laugh.

"It's all quite ridiculous," I said. "I'm not the type men fall in love with. It was only my writing that gave him a false sense of me. Now that he's here, he'll see that I'm the spinster type. Perhaps I should stick to writing and come up with a novel."

"Why would you say such a thing?" Mama asked.

"I'm boring and bookish and no fun at all. I think that's why I fell so hard for Walter. He seemed to see me differently than I did myself. But I was right all along. He was only interested in my money."

"Is that really what you think of yourself?" Papa asked.

I didn't answer, merely looked down at my plate of food I'd hardly touched.

"I don't know who you're talking about because it's not my clever, beautiful, kind, and funny Josephine," Papa said.

"He's right, darling," Mama said. "No one sees you that way. Everyone in this town adores you, and I'm quite right in saying you could have your pick of eligible men. The only reason why no one's approached you is that you made it quite clear you had no interest in anyone but Walter. Before and after his death."

"I don't want to hear you ever talk that way about yourself," Papa said, gruffly. "I won't have it."

"I'm sorry, Papa."

"Is there any part of you that thinks you could fall in love with Phillip?" Mama asked.

I smiled, remembering our argument. "As you say, there is the way I look at him."

"Well, yes, there's that," Mama said. "But it would be unkind to point that out again."

"And, as you said, we have a lot in common," I said. "He's easy to talk to, and I like how he is with the little girls. He's a hard worker. Honest and kind. I didn't want to admit any of those things to myself because I didn't want to be disloyal to Walter." I choked up. "Aren't I pathetic?"

"Darling, no. You're not the only one who has believed someone's lies," Mama said. "The only thing that matters is what you do now that you've learned the truth."

"There's a fine man right in front of you," Papa said.

I laughed as I wiped away tears. "Not you, too?"

"Have you seen his eyes?" Papa asked.

"Like sapphires," Mama said.

I looked at him and then to Mama. Their love wrapped me in a warm cloak.

"He *is* handsome," I said. "And has very nice manners. Best of all, he likes books." I was too shy to say anything more. I wouldn't have been able to explain how he touched a place deep inside me with his earnest heart.

Again, my parents exchanged a glance. This time they kept their thoughts to themselves.

Phillip

We'd just finished sweeping up the last of the debris left from the party and returned the bales of hay to the livery when Mrs. Johnson brought out a jug of hot apple cider for the helpers. The morning was cold but sunny, taking an edge off the frigidity in the air. Someone had added logs to the embers of last night's firepit. Some of the young people were gathered around warming their hands over the flames while laughing and talking.

I noticed Cymbeline was sitting alone on the bottom step of the gazebo. I grabbed a steaming cup of cider for myself and one for Cymbeline.

"I brought you some cider," I said as I handed her the cider.

"Thanks, Phillip."

"May I sit with you?" I asked.

"Please do." She peeked up at me from under a red cap.

"You don't want to join the group by the fire?" I plopped down next to her.

Cymbeline had dressed in boys' overalls for the occasion, but that hadn't seemed to distract the young men and boys from staring at her. Never having been an older brother, this feeling of wanting to throttle all of them was new to me.

"I would, but my nemesis is there." She pointed to a tall and broad-shouldered boy, with a face out of a Viking picture book. Blond hair peeked out from under his cap. "That's him. Viktor."

"Why is he your nemesis?"

She shrugged. "Isn't it obvious?"

I stifled a laugh. "Not to me, no. Isn't he older than you by a few years?"

"Yes, and he never lets me forget. Around here, I'm the best skater. The fastest skater. Except for Viktor."

"Well, he *is* a young man," I said. "He's bound to be faster."

"Don't say it," Cymbeline said, sounding disgusted. "I'm as strong and fast as any boy. Except for Viktor."

I'd observed Viktor stealing glances her way several times that morning. I suspected he didn't think of her as his nemesis.

"Is that the only reason you don't like him?" I asked.

"I have other ones. But I don't know how to describe them. There's something about him that makes me want to punch him."

I almost spit out a mouthful of cider. "He seems perfectly nice."

"Nice? Who cares about nice? That's all anyone can ever talk about in my family. Being kind and nice and of service to others. All of which makes me feel quite mean."

"Nice and kind are good qualities, aren't they?"

She didn't answer, other than to kick her boot into a drift of snow.

"He's a good worker. That you can admire, can't you?" I'd seen the young man tossing bales of hay as if they were matchsticks. "Being a good one yourself, that is."

"I haven't noticed."

We sipped our cider, quiet for a moment. I glanced over at the firepit. Viktor was watching us with an expression on his face that I recognized immediately. Jealousy. I might need to hang a sign around her neck with the number sixteen written on it. Translation: too young for all of you.

"Don't look, but he's been glancing over here. I think he might be jealous that you're talking to me."

She growled like a disgruntled puppy. "I don't think so. He sees me as a kid."

I doubted that, but I'd keep it to myself for now.

"I had to sneak out of the house this morning," Cymbeline said, abruptly changing the subject. "Before Papa saw what I was wearing. He's very old-fashioned."

"I've never seen a girl wear overalls before," I said.

She squinted at me as if I'd said something so outlandish that she thought she'd heard me wrong. "Dresses get in the way of real work. Men have liked to have us wear them as a way to keep us down. And corsets? How ridiculous that we be squeezed into something made of bones, which are supposed to be on the inside of your body, not outside. They were made to make sure we couldn't breathe, lest we think too much."

I smiled to myself.

She continued her diatribe. "Did you know women in Colorado have the right to vote? We have since 1893. The second state in the Union to do so. After Wyoming. Are you against women voting?"

"Absolutely not. There were a lot of women overseas, helping the war effort. Nurses. Ambulance drivers. They were very brave. It seems to me women can do pretty much whatever a man can do."

She gave me a nod of approval. "I couldn't agree more. If I'd been old enough, I would have gone to the front lines in a second. I'd like to drive an ambulance." Her eyes flashed with ambition as she flattened her empty hand and pushed it through the air in a mimic of an ambulance. "I would have driven right into the fighting to rescue injured soldiers."

"Let's hope we never have another war, so you won't have to."

She sighed. "I suppose you're right. But if I have to marry some man and keep house instead of doing something exciting, I'd rather die young."

"Don't say such things. No one should ever have to die young."

She flushed. "I'm sorry. That probably sounds awful of me. Did you lose a lot of friends in the war?"

"Yes, sadly." I'd leave it at that. Let her keep her romantic ideals of war. Her brothers had come home. She hadn't had to suffer the grief so many families experienced.

"Did you know Walter well?" she asked.

"Pretty well."

"Was he a heel?"

"Why do you ask?"

She shrugged as she pulled her legs up and wrapped her arms around her knees. "I didn't like him."

"Did you meet him?" I asked, surprised.

"No, but I read some of his letters. The few that he wrote."

"And?"

"I'm Josephine's sister. I understand things about her that others don't." She straightened her legs and pushed the toes of both her boots into the snow. "He wasn't right for her. Fiona and I both thought so. And now we find out he didn't even read the books she sent."

I nodded. "Read by me and some of the other fellas," I said. "Not a wasted effort."

"Fine, but that's not the point. How could Josephine marry a man who doesn't love reading? She's a librarian. That's heresy."

"Heresy? A strong word."

"I like that word. A lot. It has the proper seriousness. Anyway, he hardly ever wrote to her." She shifted to face me. "Jo wouldn't admit to it, but his lack of attention hurt her. She made excuses for him. The front lines and all that. But I knew something wasn't right. It's because she doesn't see herself properly."

"How so?" This girl was like finding a textbook on Josephine.

"First, she doesn't think she's pretty. Second, she thinks men find her boring because all she does is read and take care of people. She actually told me one time that she didn't expect to ever have a man fall in love with her."

"Ridiculous," I said, under my breath.

She lifted her chin slightly as she peered at me through narrowed eyes. "I agree. But you see, that's what it was with Walter. He paid attention to her, and she took that as love. It's sad because he preyed on that vulnerability. Which is why a girl should never let her guard down. Always distrust people until you know more." She bent her legs and leaned over her knees. "Jo's the only one who remembers our mother. That's why she's the way she is. She witnessed our mother's madness. She had to see things no child should."

"Like what?"

"She saw her standing over Fiona's crib with a knife in her hand."

I swallowed back an exclamation. How horrid. She'd not shared that story in her letters.

"She doesn't talk about it much," Cymbeline said. "But occasionally, when it's just the three of us older girls, she talks about our mother. And other things, like how hard it was after she died. Papa was devastated, and she had to take care of him and us. Fiona was a tiny baby then, and I was a toddler, plus the twins. We had Jasper and Lizzie, of course, but it was still hard for Jo. It wasn't until Mama came that she was allowed to be a child again. As Mama says, though, the damage had already been done. Jo was already like an old woman. Too worried. Too willing to accept scraps. Too devoted to a life of service."

"Is that a bad thing?"

"No, unless it's at a personal cost, which, in her case, it is. She doesn't think she's worth anything unless she's taking care of others. That's why she liked that rotten Walter in the first place. He needed her, and she sensed it."

"That's insightful of you," I said.

She raised both eyebrows. "The others don't think I'm as smart as them because I don't care much for school. It's just so stuffy inside, and there are so many things to do and learn that have nothing to do with academics. However, I know things about people, especially my family. I know things about you, too."

"You do?"

"You look at Josephine all soft in the eyes. Like this." She widened her eyes and made them appear glassy and blank. "Lovesick eyes."

"And if that were true? What would you think? Would you approve, since I like books?"

"Liking books is to your favor, yes. However, I'm not sure about the rest of you. I like that you think women can do what men can do. Still, I'm the wait-and-see type. My sister Fiona loves everyone without any discernment whatsoever. It's maddening. The others are almost as bad." She pointed to her eyes. "I'm watching you. Don't forget that."

I laughed. "When I was a kid, I was like you. When a new boy or girl came to the orphanage, I observed for weeks before making a judgment one way or the other."

"Is that why you came to us? To find a family?"

"That's appealing, yes. But I came for Josephine. To see if she was as remarkable as I thought. She is, but you know that."

"I do. I'm not sure you'll have any luck with her. She might not like you."

"Why?" My stomach clenched. Cymbeline's insightfulness unnerved me.

"Because you don't need her. You're strong all on your own. She won't have to take care of you. I'm not sure she'd know what to do with a man like that."

I nodded and turned toward the crowd surrounding the firepit. "Maybe I'm exactly what she needs then. I could take care of her."

"I'd like that for her." She reached her arms overhead and stretched. "For my other sisters, too. Just not for me. I won't be tied down by a man and made to obey. I'll have my own work and money and adventures."

"I've no doubt you'll make the kind of life you want."

She grinned as she rose to her feet. "You can count on that. But Phillip, in all seriousness, you've got to figure out how to skate, or you'll never fit in around here. Jo cannot marry a man who can't take her for a twirl around the pond. That's just not done."

"I'll do my best, but I'm an old man."

"Nah, you need more practice, that's all. I can help you." She motioned for me to get up. "Come on, old man. Let's get Flynn and head home."

Home. What a lovely word. If only Cymbeline knew how much she would miss home when she left. As determined as she was, this girl loved her family. It wouldn't be as easy as she thought to leave them.

Josephine

For most of the morning, I paced around the house, going over every detail I could remember of my two weeks with Walter, examining them as Phillip had suggested. Sadly, I couldn't find the holes in his stories. Like it was only yesterday, I could recall with perfect clarity the sincerity in his eyes and the sound of his laughter.

I went upstairs and opened the box of letters for the first time. I'd stored them under my bed next to the much smaller cluster of those Walter had sent to me. I pulled them both out and sat on the floor between my bed and Cymbeline's. We shared a room with three single beds as we always had, all lined up in a row according to age.

I read through several of Walter's first. There was nothing of note in them, other than flowery speech about his love for me. They were short, no more than a few paragraphs, with no details of what his days had been like. At the time, I'd excused the lack of length and detail on the war. Strategic battle secrets shouldn't be passed through letters. Now, however, it was obvious. He hadn't cared for me as I had him. Did we truly only see what we wanted?

I burned with shame. Having such an error in judgment over

something so important was not like me. Or was it? Did I have a completely false impression of myself?

Did Phillip really think he was in love with me? Was he as deluded as I had been about love? Were his fantasies about me and my life here only wishes, born from loneliness? They had to be. Yet at the same time, his passionate statements thrilled me.

Which led to further shame. What kind of woman was I? Declaring my eternal love to a cunning ghost one day and thinking of a man I'd just met the next.

Was my thrill only an illusion? I'd convinced myself before of a relationship that hadn't existed. Would this prove more of the same?

I set his letters aside and opened the box with mine. Neatly stacked, they'd been put into chronological order. By Phillip, I suspected, not Walter. Damn him. How could he have lied to me this way? Tears leaked from my eyes. I put the lid back on and slouched over the box and silently sobbed. A creak in the floorboards drew my attention. I looked up, drying my eyes with the backs of my hands. Fiona stood just inside the room.

"What're you doing, Jo?" The way she asked the question, gently with a tinge of sadness, I knew she knew exactly. She came to sit across from me on the floor.

"Stirring up ghosts, I guess."

She held out her hands. "No good will come from this. Give them to me."

I gave her the box. "Mama told you?"

"Yes. I'm sorry." She shoved the box under the bed, then put the Walter letters back into the stack. She set those aside, as if she wanted them for later.

"I feel foolish and embarrassed," I said.

She leaned close to brush away strands of hair that had stuck to my cheeks. "You've been sad for too long. It's time."

"Time for what?"

"Dancing."

"Dancing?" I giggled and shifted so that my back was against the bed. Fiona joined me and rested her head on my shoulder.

"I was wondering about something," Fiona said. "Did it ever occur to you that you couldn't love Mama Quinn because you'd loved our real mother first?"

"No. It was clear to me that Quinn was what we all needed."

She nodded and made a humming sound. "Hmm..."

We were silent for a moment. My sister wasn't exactly subtle.

"Our real mother was disturbed," Fiona said. "But you loved her anyway."

"True."

"Perhaps the way to look at this is that Walter was disturbed. You loved him anyway. We can't always control who we love. Sometimes those people don't deserve our affection, but that doesn't mean it isn't there. Loving someone, no matter how it ends, isn't something you should ever feel sorry or ashamed about. You didn't know."

"I've wasted too much time on him."

"Then don't waste another minute," Fiona said.

"Is it really that simple? I just will away all the memories and regrets?"

"It's not that simple," Fiona said. "But all that might be easier when a new chance at happiness shows up at your door."

"Fiona, how did you get so smart?"

"I'm not really. I just know a good person when I see one."

After my talk with Fiona, I decided to go outside for fresh air. If she was right and I should forgive myself for mistakes, perhaps a walk through the powdery snow would help me sort out exactly how to do so. We'd been blessed with another sunny cold day. Icicles hung from the roof of the house like long, pointed teeth. Several winter sparrows twittered from bare aspen branches.

I wore tall boots and had hiked up my skirt to keep it from brushing along the snow, allowing me to walk briskly. My restless and tormented thoughts eased the farther I walked. I took in the smell of the firs as I passed over the meadow and into the forest. The more steps, the better I felt. Perhaps my wise little sister was correct. I'd made a mistake, but not one that I couldn't forgive myself for. Mama always said there were no mistakes we couldn't learn from. What a large mistake I'd made. Would my growth equal the mistake?

I turned back and traipsed out of the forest and back over the meadow. A movement caught my eye as I approached the house. For a moment, I thought it was a deer behind a group of aspens. As I drew nearer, I realized the object was Theo. Wearing nothing but his long underwear, he sat under an aspen with his knees pulled up to his chest. He stared with blank eyes into nothing. My heart pounded hard and fast. My mother had been alone in the snow when he'd found her. Seeing him here was eerily similar. Wearing so little, he would be nearly frozen. How long had he been there?

"Theo?" I called out to him as I ran toward him as quickly as I could.

He didn't respond. I fell to my knees in front of him. "Theo, what are you doing out here?"

This time, his eyelids flickered. He raised his gaze to me, then blinked. "Jo?"

"Yes, it's me. What's happened? Why are you here?"

"I don't know. I'm not sure how I got here."

I rose to my feet. There was no time to waste. I needed to get him inside as soon as possible. "Come on. Let's go back to the house." I took off my coat and put it over his shoulders.

Surprisingly docile, he allowed me to take his hand and assist him in standing. He was heavy, but I managed to get him upright. I gasped when I saw his feet, which had been buried beneath the snow until now. He wore wool socks, wet from the snow. Depending on how long he'd been out here, he could have frostbite. I was beside myself by now, shaking from cold and fear.

I took hold of his arm and pushed him forward. "Go, quickly."

We began the trudge through the snow to the house. "Do your feet hurt?" I asked.

"No. Numb, that's all."

Walking out here had seemed quick. The trip back seemed to take forever. I wanted to lift him in my arms and run, but that was impossible.

I shouted for help when we reached earshot of the house. Seconds later, Jasper and Papa came running. "My God, what's happened?" Papa asked when they got to us. The terror in his voice brought tears to my eyes.

"I found him in the snow," I said. "Just sitting there."

"Theo?" Papa shook him slightly. "Are you all right?"

"Yes sir."

"Take one side of him and I'll take the other," Papa said to Jasper. "Theo, lift your feet. Get them out of the snow."

Theo, like me, had started to cry. "I'm sorry, Papa." He repeated the same statement three times as the men lifted him up and out of the snow and carried him into the house.

Once inside, they set him on the bench by the door. Papa knelt and stripped Theo of his socks. "Rub one and I'll do the other," he said to Jasper.

I sat next to Theo and took both his cold red hands and rubbed them as vigorously as I could. A moment later, Mama came rushing down the stairwell with Fiona on her heels.

"What happened?" Mama had both hands over her mouth and stared at Theo as if she couldn't believe her eyes.

"I found him like this in the snow over by the aspens." My voice sounded wooden even to myself. Perhaps it was my turn to be in shock?

"Oh, my poor boy," Mama said as she broke away from Fiona and hustled toward my brother. She sat next to him and took one of his hands in hers and began to rub it as I continued to do the other. "What were you doing out there?"

Theo had stopped sobbing by then and was staring at the top of Papa's head as if he once more wasn't sure where he was. "I don't know." His voice sounded bewildered and small. I had a sudden memory of him as a little boy the morning he'd come back from finding Mother. His little face had been red from the cold and exertion of running into the house to find Papa. "She's in the snow, Papa. No clothes. She won't move." He'd cried as the words came out. I'd been at the bottom of the stairs, just having come down with the infant Fiona in my arms. Since I'd witnessed my mother over the baby's crib, I didn't let her out of my sight. I'd begged Papa to put Fiona's crib in the room where Cymbeline and I slept. If Mother came to her again in the middle of the night, I would be there. Papa had installed a lock on the inside of the door. Every night I'd locked it before going to sleep. When the baby cried in the middle of the night for food, I'd taken her out of her crib to Mother. Papa would watch her feed the baby from her breast and then bring her back to our room and change her.

When Fiona was only three months old, Mother had walked into the snowstorm and perished.

I blinked to rid myself of the image of Theo that morning, but it was to no avail. Only six years old then, he'd curled up into a ball in front of the fire and stared blankly into the flames for hours. He'd been fragile for years afterward. And now, after what he'd experienced in the war, he seemed as fragile as our fine crystal. Why had they joined the army? Why had Flynn insisted they go? He should have known that his twin was not strong enough. Madness ran through our blood. What if we never got our Theo back?

Where was Flynn, anyway? He should be here. How could he have not heard him wake and wander out of the room in his pajamas? Flynn was supposed to look after him.

"There's no frostbite," Jasper said. "He must not have been out there too long."

His hands had returned to a normal temperature. Papa and Jasper rose to their feet. "Let's get him upstairs and into a hot bath."

Jasper nodded and they took a nearly comatose Theo up the stairs. The moment they'd disappeared, Mama burst into tears. "Jo, I don't understand. What was he doing?"

Fiona came to kneel on the floor next to us, seeming not to notice the melted snow that dampened her skirt. She placed her hands on Mama's knees. "Don't cry, Mama. Jo found him in time."

Mama wiped under her eyes with her handkerchief. "Thank God. But what were you doing out there?"

"I was taking a walk. To think."

The door opened and Flynn came through, followed by my sister and Phillip. "What's wrong?" Flynn's gaze went from Mama to me.

"Is it Theo?" Cymbeline asked.

"Yes, it's Theo." I jumped up from the bench, ready to strike as if I were a venomous snake. "I found him in his pajamas in the snow. He had no shoes on." Shaking with anger, I pointed a finger at Flynn. "Why didn't you know he got out of bed?"

"He was still there when I left this morning," Flynn said, uncharacteristically subdued. "I would have known if I was home."

"Has he done this before?" I asked.

"He sleepwalks sometimes," Flynn said. "It's not that unusual."

"Not unusual?" I asked. "Of course it is. What in God's name are you talking about?"

"Jo, don't shout," Fiona said. "Please."

"Josephine, we fought in a war. Give him time. He'll be fine eventually."

"I may not have been there, but I can certainly see how it's haunting him," I said through gritted teeth. "Anyone can see that. He's not fine now."

"Darling, please, this isn't helping," Mama said.

"I'm sorry, Mama, but I won't be quiet." I turned to face Flynn. "You were the one who insisted on enlisting. You were the reason he was over there in the first place instead of at university where he belonged. If it wasn't for your fighting spirit—your ridiculous need to compete—he wouldn't have been there at all."

"I didn't ask him to join me," Flynn said.

I ignored the hurt in his eyes. He didn't get to be forgiven. Not this time. I pointed my finger at him. "You didn't have to. He would never have let you go without him. That's not how he works and you know it. Instead, you thought only of yourself and what you wanted. He's not like you. He's sensitive and peaceful, and the war has destroyed him."

"Josephine, stop." Fiona had risen to her feet. Tears dampened her dark lashes. "Don't say anything more."

The tearful tone of her voice jerked me out of my anger. Everyone stared at me in various expressions of shock and discomfort. Cymbeline, eyes wide, pressed against the closed door, as if to keep the enemy from entrance. Phillip stood by the closet with one arm out of his coat. Mama sat on the bench with her hands clasped together on her lap, all color drained from her face. Her lips looked almost blue. Flynn's arms were crossed over his chest as he glared at me now with defiant eyes. Only Fiona seemed pliable, still of the living world and able to move about. She came close to me and took my hands. "Jo, the war wasn't anyone in this house's fault. You know that as well as I."

"But why did our brothers have to go?" I asked. "Why did my sweet Theo have to go and come back a shell of himself? Fiona, you were only a baby when Mother died. You don't know what she was like. How her mind slipped into madness."

"Triggered by us," Flynn said. "Isn't that what you think, Josephine? That she was fine until she gave birth to twins. Isn't that what you've secretly thought all along?"

I turned on him, spitting with rage. "How dare you say that to me? That couldn't be further from the truth. I've spent my life trying to protect you two. And the girls, too. It all fell on me after Mother died. It was my job to protect you, but I couldn't do it this time. Not when you lied about your age to go fight in a war that had nothing to do with us."

"We're English," Flynn said, "as much as we are Americans. The Allies needed us. Do you really think we could stay in isolation when our brothers and sisters were in danger of losing their freedom to the Germans?"

"They didn't need two underaged boys," I said. "Boys who should have been home finishing school and preparing for university."

"I'm sorry, but I disagree," Flynn said. "What we did over there is the most important thing we'll ever do with our lives."

"Yet one of you may be ruined for the rest of his." I'd had enough. Still shaking from rage and grief, I nudged Cymbeline away from the door and yanked it open and ran outside. Too angry to feel the cold, I staggered out to the path that led to the barn, crying. Already I regretted my outburst. I'd not known how deeply resentful I was of Flynn's insistence that they join the fight until I saw Theo utterly helpless and confused. He could have died out there like Mother. That thought made my stomach churn with fear. I couldn't lose him. I couldn't watch him sink into insanity. He had to get better.

I entered the barn. Chickens scattered as I tromped across their path to the hayloft. My grip on the rungs was slippery in my gloves. I didn't care. When I reached the top, I crawled into the dwelling on my hands and knees before getting to my feet. The room was tall enough that I could walk around without slouching. Bales of hay were stacked to the ceiling. We used the ones from the outside first, creating layers. I sat on the bottom row. Breathing hard from my anger and exertion, I wrapped my arms around my waist. Never in my life had I shouted at anyone. Had my siblings irritated me at times? Yes, but not in any way serious. This was unprecedented territory for me. I didn't like it. Not at all. In fact, I felt sick to my stomach.

The sound of the barn door opening and shutting startled me. *Please, do not be Flynn. Not yet.* I needed time to think through what to do next.

I got up to peek over the railing. To my surprise, it was Phillip. Also surprising? I was glad to see him. Better him than my parents or one of my siblings.

"Josephine? Are you in here?"

"Up here," I called down to him.

He lifted his gaze upward. "Ah, yes, there you are. May I join you?"

"I'm not particularly good company right now."

"I don't care. I've just come to see if you're all right." He crossed over to the ladder and peered up at me. Doodle strutted behind him. *The rooster looks like Walter.* How had I not seen that before now?

"Come up if you want," I said. "Be careful. The ladder's rungs are slippery."

I needn't have advised him. He came up the ladder with apparent ease. When he reached the top, he dropped to his knees on the floor before straightening. Too tall, he had to bow his head, as my brothers and Papa did.

I retreated to my bale of hay.

"May I sit with you?"

I nodded, scooting over to give him more room. When he sat, I smelled the spicy scent of his shaving soap.

"I'm sorry you had to see me like that," I said. "We don't often fight."

"I understand."

"My mother was very sick before she died."

"I can see why it would worry you to see Theo that way. After what you all went through."

"One time I saw her standing over Fiona's crib with a knife."

"Cymbeline told me about that this morning. I'm very sorry you had to see that."

"Cymbeline told you about that?"

"Yes. As a way to explain certain things about you."

"Oh." I sat with that for a moment. What else had Cymbeline told him about me?

"She thinks your mother's illness and death had a great effect on you. And that you rarely talk about any of those times. That you've taken the brunt of your mother's death and it's made you too willing to make compromises or accept less than what you deserve."

"She's right."

"Any time you want to talk to me about that or anything else, I'm here to listen." Phillip plucked a piece of hay from my shoulder. "There's nothing you could say that would turn me away."

I lifted my gaze to him. There was such understanding and gentleness in his eyes that a lump formed at the back of my throat. "If anything happened to Theo, I don't know what I'd do. He and I always had a special bond, both bookish and without an ounce of competition in us. We always just wanted peace and a good book. Cymbeline and Flynn are so driven. So relentless about everything, as if the world isn't large enough for them."

"Theo had to go with him?"

"As different as they are, he would never have been able to let him go alone."

"To have a bond like that must be something," he said.

"Both a blessing and a curse." I looked at my hands. "It's not true that I blame the twins for our mother's illness. I've never ever thought that."

"Flynn must believe that to be true and has assumed others do, too."

I hadn't thought of that. Had Flynn been carrying around that guilt all these years? I touched the cuff of his jacket with the tips of my fingers. "Thank you for coming to find me."

"Do you mean just now or in general?" He smiled as he placed his hand briefly over mine.

"Both, I guess? Yes, both."

WHEN WE ARRIVED BACK in the house, a hushed silence greeted us. After taking off our coats, Phillip spoke softly to me. "I'm going to skip tea today so that you can talk to your family alone."

"Thank you. For the talk. Everything."

"My pleasure." He brushed his fingers against my arm but then seemed to think better of it and withdrew.

"You're part of our circle now," I said lightly. "I hope you won't live to regret it."

"I can't imagine how that would ever happen."

I watched him head toward the stairs before I went into the sitting room. Only Papa was there, staring pensively into the fire. He looked up when I approached. His face was pale and drawn.

"Papa?"

"Come here, darling." He held out his hand. I gripped it in mine for a moment before sitting in the chair next to him.

"How is he?"

"Theo or Flynn?" The corners of Papa's eyes crinkled from a half smile. "I hear you gave Flynn quite the tongue-lashing."

I stared down at my hands. "I was angry. I shouldn't have said the things I did. I'm sorry for it."

"He knows. You'll apologize, and all will be well."

"I was hateful, Papa. I'm ashamed of myself."

"If anything, it was good to get it out in the open that way. He admitted to me that he's racked with guilt over what the war has done to his brother."

"I'm scared, Papa. He looked like Mother out there."

Papa turned back to the fire. "I'm scared, too. He's always been sensitive. No young man should have to fight, but he's particularly vulnerable to the horrors. What he had to do over there has broken him."

I hadn't thought until that moment that it was not only what he saw, but what he had to do. Theo, my peace-loving, bookish brother, had had to kill.

"What do we do?" I asked.

"We love him. And we pray." He tilted his head, peering at me. "We're the Barnes family. We get through whatever comes our way, together."

I STOPPED IN MY BROTHERS' room before heading to mine to dress for dinner. Flynn was sitting in one of the chairs by the window watching Theo sleep. He greeted me with a smile that didn't reach his puffy eyes.

Phillip was by the window, reading. When he saw it was me, he excused himself. "I need something from downstairs."

"Thanks, Phillip," Flynn said.

"Not a problem." Phillip gave me a smile as he passed by.

"I'm sorry," I said as I sat next to Flynn.

"No, I'm sorry. Everything you said is true. I should never have enlisted, knowing what it would do to him. I've been selfish and thoughtless." His voice broke. "And now, Theo is sick."

"The war did this, not you."

"He'd never have been there if it weren't for me."

From the bed, Theo shifted in his sleep. His eyes flew open, then he sat up. "Why are you two staring at me?"

Flynn and I both darted over to Theo's bed, standing on each side. I had a sudden memory of the twins snuggled up in one bed when they were about three years old. Often Papa would put them to sleep in their own beds only to find them curled up together in one.

"What is wrong with you two?" Theo asked. "Why are you in

here, Jo?" He glanced at the clock on the table between the two beds. "Is it morning or night?"

"Just before dinner," I said. "You slept all day."

"Jo found you in the snow," Flynn said quietly. "This morning. Still in your pajamas."

His eyes widened for a moment before he fell back onto his pillow.

"Do you remember when I brought you inside?" I asked.

"No, nothing since last night when I went to bed," Theo said.

"We think you were sleepwalking," Flynn said. "But Jo found you in time. No damage to your feet."

"I'm sorry, Jo," Theo said. "I must've scared you."

"You did." My eyes filled with tears. "We were worried about your feet. Papa and Jasper got you up here and into a hot bath. You don't remember any of that?"

"I can't say I do," he said.

Tears streamed from my eyes. I knelt by the bed and stroked my brother's arm. "I just want you to be safe. And happy again."

"Ah now, don't cry," Theo said. "Flynn can lock me in here at night from now on."

"How often has this been happening?" I asked.

"Flynn says about once a week," Theo said. "But usually I just wander the hall and come right back to bed. I'm not sure what I was doing outside."

A cold dread filled me. How would we keep him safe? Flynn couldn't watch him constantly. What if there were a fire and they were locked in here?

"Jo, whatever you're worrying about, don't," Theo said. "No harm can come to me with this one watching me like a hawk."

I wiped the tears from my eyes. Causing Theo more stress from my angst was not what he needed at the moment.

"How do you get him back into the room?" I asked Flynn.

"The couple times I woke and realized he wasn't here, I went out to the hallway and he was walking back to the room. Eyes open but clearly asleep."

"I think we should talk to Dr. Neal," I said.

"No doctors," Theo said. "This will fade." He placed his hand on top of my head. "Let's talk about something else. Tell us about Phillip."

"What do you mean?"

"I mean, do you like him?" Theo asked.

Flynn laughed, and for a moment we were back in time before the war, young and carefree.

"Stop teasing me," I said. "Anyway, it's none of your concern."

"She does like him," Theo said, sounding triumphant. "What a lucky man he is."

Phillip

❧

The next day, Josephine asked if I'd like to help her take books out to some of the folks who lived outside of town and weren't able to make it into the library. I happily agreed. On our way, Josephine explained how she'd applied for the grant and given enough for the building itself as well as hundreds of books. "Carnegie's putting them all over America. It's truly wonderful."

Now, as she pulled a book from a shelf, she turned to me. "The patrons tell me what they like to read, and I choose something for them. Each person gets one book a week. I take back the one I delivered the previous visit after I drop off the new one."

"Many of these books came from Papa's own library," she said. "He had loads to donate. If you look inside them, you'll see his name and date he purchased them."

"That was generous of him," I said.

"He wanted every citizen to have the opportunity for an education and a book whenever they wanted. When Mama first came here, she taught adult classes at night. Anyone who wanted to learn to read in English could."

"Do the night classes continue?" I asked.

"Yes, Mama still teaches whomever wants to learn, but there aren't as many these days. She'll often invite them out to the house instead and teach them in our sitting room. Our population hasn't grown terribly much over the last few years, so the need lessened."

"How come?"

"I don't know. Living in the Rockies isn't for everyone. There's more opportunity in Denver or other cities."

"Do you ever think of leaving Emerson Pass?"

"Not if I can help it," she said. "Emerson Pass is my home. Everyone I love is here." She put one last book on the stack. "All right, we've got them all. Are you ready?"

I held up a copy of *Howards End*. "I've always wanted to read this one."

"Superior choice." She picked up half the stack of books on the desk and put them into a crude wooden box. *I'll make her a nicer one*, I thought. Maybe one out of cedar, so the scent seeped into the pages of the books.

I put the other half of the stack in the box and insisted on carrying it out to the sleigh. The horses and sleigh were parked under a wooden awning at the back of the building. We'd covered the horses with heavy blankets. Even so, she'd said it was imperative we move quickly before the horses got too cold.

Oz and Willie looked up as we approached. I set the box in the back and joined Josephine. Seconds later, we were gliding over the snow. If I'd been a lesser man, I might have felt cowed under the competence of the woman by my side. Instead, I swelled with pride at the independence of her, the sheer capabilities she possessed. Running a library. Taking books out to the people of the farms. What a woman she was.

She looked fetching in her fur cap and wool coat. Leather gloves covered her hands. Although she drove straight-backed, she still appeared tiny. Too small to handle these horses. But the gentle creatures obeyed her commands without any troubles.

She looked over at me. "Do I have something on my face? You're staring."

Flustered, I turned my gaze to the horses' chestnut-brown hindquarters. "I'm sorry. I can't help but admire you."

Her lips twitched into a smile, but she didn't say anything. The bells around the horses' necks rang out merrily as we picked up speed. Sparkles from the sun on the snow danced before my eyes.

"We'll go out to the Cassidys' first."

Soon, we came upon a white farmhouse and red barn. From a brick chimney, a sliver of smoke rose up into the blue sky. "The Cassidys raise cattle and have fallen on hard times since Mr. Cassidy died last year. Mrs. Cassidy suffers from terrible headaches. I went to school back in the early days with Nora, Shannon, and Alma. They're all younger than me, closer to the twins' and Cymbeline's age. Alma's away at college, studying to become a nurse. She'll have a job with Dr. Neal when she returns. Shannon and Nora both quit school so as to look after their mother and help on the farm. It's a pity—stuck out here and missing so much of the fun in town.

"It's strange to remember how young and carefree we all used to be." She slowed the horses as we drew nearer to the house.

"Theo seemed better this morning," I said.

"Yes. As if it never happened. I don't know what to think, other than we have to keep a close watch on him. Fortunately, there are a lot of us Barneses." We came to a stop. She bowed her head. "I'm sorry to speak of it again on such a fine day. We should be enjoying the sunshine."

"Don't be. You can say whatever you wish to me. I grew to be a good listener at the orphanage."

She reached over and put one of her hands over mine. "Thank you, Phillip Baker." Just as quickly, she removed her hand. "Would you like to go in with me?"

"Yes, sure. Sit tight. I'll help you down." I got out and sprinted around to her side to assist her. When I had her safely to the ground, she went to the box and chose three books: *Anne of the Island*, *Summer*, and *O Pioneers!* Of them, I'd only read the Willa Cather novel, thanks to Josephine sending it to Walter.

A walkway had been shoveled between the barn and back door of the house. We didn't have to knock. The door flew open to reveal a young woman with skin the color of milk and black curls piled on top of her head. "Josephine, you can't imagine how happy I am to see you. I've been done with all three books you brought last week for two days now." Round green eyes traveled to me next.

"Shannon, this is Phillip Baker," Josephine said. "He's staying with us for the winter."

The winter? I thought it was only through the holidays. I put that at the back of my mind to think about later.

"Come inside. Mam's upstairs with one of her headaches, but she'll be happy to get new books once she feels better."

We walked into the kitchen. A large white sink and a cooking stove took up most of the room. Josephine put her stack of books on a scratched table with spindly legs, one of which had splintered and looked as if it might fall apart at any moment. They needed a sturdy table in here, one with thick legs and a wide top. The bulk of the housework was most likely done in this room: cooking, washing, canning.

Another girl about the age of Cymbeline appeared next. She had fair hair, lots of freckles and the same big eyes as her sister. "Hi, Josephine."

She was introduced to me as Nora.

"Nice to meet you," I said.

"You as well," Nora said. "Other than Josephine, we don't often have visitors."

"We've only just finished the dishes," Shannon said. "Or you would have caught us in the mess."

Nora handed Josephine a copy of *A Little Princess* and snatched *Anne of the Island* from Josephine's stack and twirled around. "I'm so happy for this one. *A Little Princess* was very sad, but I loved it."

"Me too," Josephine said.

Shannon must have noticed my gaze focused on the table. "This old thing's about to fall apart."

"I accidentally knocked the leg with my knee when I got up from the table the other day," Nora said. "I'm so clumsy sometimes."

"It wasn't your fault," Shannon said as she wrapped an arm around her sister's shoulder. "This table's old. Mam found it out by the abandoned mill when they first came here."

"I could make you a new one," I said, surprising myself. "One made of a harder wood. I'm a woodworker." Those sentences should have been in a different order, leading with my qualifications.

"Are they expensive?" Nora's forehead wrinkled as she peered at me.

"I could give it to you for the price of the wood," I said. "The Barnes family's been so kind to me, it's the least I could do."

Josephine smiled at me, and I felt as if I'd just hung the moon. "Papa has some odds and ends lying around. I'm sure we can find the wood at no cost to anyone."

"Mam talks all the time about getting a new one," Shannon said. "Maybe we could surprise her with it for Christmas?" She turned to me. "Could you make it by then?"

I caught Josephine's eye. She nodded, smiling encouragingly. "Phillip?"

We were roughly three weeks before Christmas. It would be tight, but I could do it if I worked steadily. "Yes, I can make one in that amount of time."

"Are you going to open a furniture shop in town?" Nora asked.

"I'd like to," I said. "But I'd need customers first."

"If you made one for us, we'd tell everyone, and maybe you'd get more orders," Shannon said. "Here in Emerson Pass, we prefer to buy locally. No one wants to give city folks any of our hard-earned money."

Lord Barnes had said he would front the cost for wood if I paid him back. If I could set aside my pride and take his help, I might be able to start a business of my own. Everyone needed tables, chairs, chests, kitchen cabinets, and dressers. No one here was doing it. Everything had to be brought in on the train. Making them here, I could do them cheaper than having them sent out from the city.

A plan for my life? One that would ensure my worthiness for the likes of Josephine Barnes? For that, I would do anything. Even taking a loan from her father.

THAT NIGHT we had roast beef for dinner, covered in garlic butter sauce. There were also fluffy rolls and roasted carrots and potatoes. I'd never eaten as well in my life. The Barnes family, jollier tonight than the day before, joked and teased throughout much of the dinner. All tension between Jo and Flynn seemed to have dissipated. Other than Quinn, who glanced with the worried eyes of a mother at Theo, everyone seemed in great spirits.

"Fiona, tell them what Viktor did today at the skating pond," Cymbeline said.

"He had the gall to ask Cym to skate," Fiona said. "Isn't that terrible?"

"I don't skate with my nemesis." Cymbeline buttered a piece of roll with quick swipes. "He's everywhere I am. Just to vex me."

"He doesn't try to vex you," Fiona said. "He just does."

"What did you say when he asked you?" Jo asked.

"I said I didn't skate with boys," Cymbeline said. "Except to race him."

"Then she challenged him to one," Fiona said. "And ordered the rest of the kids off the ice."

"Cymbeline," Quinn said. "You didn't?"

"No one listened to me," Cymbeline said. "Viktor refused to race anyway. Too afraid, most likely."

"You hurt his feelings," Fiona said. "I think you embarrassed him, too. Any of the other girls would have been only too happy to skate with him."

"He didn't seem embarrassed as he skated with every girl there by the end of the day." Cymbeline scowled. "Not that I care."

"I have a feeling that this rivalry is one-sided," Flynn said. "Viktor is taken with our Cymbie."

"Don't say it," Cymbeline said. "Or I'll be sick."

"Flynn, he's three years older than Cym," Quinn said. "Too old to be taken with her."

"You're much younger than Papa," Fiona said, innocently.

Lord Barnes barked out a laugh. "That's different. Mama was already grown when I met her."

"Quite right," Quinn said. "Not sixteen like Cymbeline."

"You needn't worry, Mama," Cymbeline said. "I wouldn't be caught dead with him."

"A girl could do worse," Josephine said. "He's a stellar young man."

"I agree," Quinn said before glancing in my direction. "He was one of my first students, along with the rest of the children in this room."

"They've all grown up so fast." Lord Barnes took a sip of his wine. "So very fast."

"Papa, I'm still young," Fiona said. "Even if I'm no longer the littlest." She turned toward me. "Before the littles came, I was the youngest."

"Spoiled rotten," Cymbeline said.

Fiona nodded solemnly. "I was, too."

"But sweet just the same," Theo said. "Kind of like Addie. Whereas our Delphia takes after Cymbeline here."

"Why does the naughty one have to be equated with me?" Cymbeline asked.

"As if you don't know," Flynn said.

"I can remember the first time I set eyes on the lot of you," Quinn said. "Phillip, on the way here from the train station, I'd fallen out of the sleigh and hit my head."

"Knocked clean out," Lord Barnes said. "Harley brought her here and we put her on the couch."

"When I came to, five sets of eyes were peering at me," Quinn said. "I thought I'd gone to heaven and been met by angels."

"Little did she know then that we weren't exactly angels," Flynn said.

"That quickly became apparent." Quinn raised one eyebrow.

"Phillip's commissioned his first piece of furniture," Josephine said. "Making a kitchen table for the Cassidys. Papa, he'll need your help with the wood."

"We'll go out to the mill tomorrow and pick up what you need," Lord Barnes said.

I warmed under my dinner jacket. I'd wanted to ask Lord Barnes about his offer of wood when we were alone. Would he assume I'd taken his help as a given?

"They desperately need one," Josephine said. "The one they have is about to collapse."

"How are they doing?" Quinn asked. "I've been worried about Moira."

"She was ill with one of her headaches again today," Josephine said. "Shannon asked after you, Flynn."

"How nice?" Flynn asked as he cut into his piece of meat.

"Why's that a question?" Josephine asked.

I glanced his way. He was giving his sister a saucy grin. "Am I supposed to be excited that sweet little Shannon asked after me?"

"She's not so little anymore," Cymbeline said.

"She's very, very pretty," Fiona said. "Everyone thinks so."

"Which you'd know if you ever attended church," Quinn said.

"Last time I saw her, she was in pigtails," Flynn said.

"She's only a year younger than you," Cymbeline said. "I mean, your real age. Not the one you told the army."

"She's sweet, too," Fiona said. "Which is most important."

The sisters were all so different: cerebral, reserved Josephine; tough and feisty Cymbeline; kind and compassionate Fiona. Lord Barnes was a lucky man to have these girls as daughters.

"When you were away, Shannon always asked at church if we'd heard from you," Cymbeline said. "She was genuinely concerned."

"She said she prayed for you every night." Fiona turned to Lord Barnes. "I feel terribly sad for them. They adored their papa, just like I do mine."

"As I do you, sweetheart," Lord Barnes said.

"They wanted to come to the festival," Josephine said. "But Moira wasn't well and they didn't want to leave her alone. That's why they haven't been at church the last few months. The poor girls are missing out on so much."

"I thought you said I would know what she looked like if I were at church?" Flynn asked Quinn.

Quinn smiled. "Don't be wicked."

"Don't encourage Shannon when it comes to me," Flynn said to Josephine. "I have no intention of settling down. I certainly don't want the burden of that farm of theirs."

"Any girl who's praying for my son is good in my book," Quinn said.

"The whole town was praying," Josephine said. "For Isak, too, of course."

"There wasn't a Sunday that Pastor Lind didn't include you in the group prayer," Cymbeline said.

"The prayers must've worked, because here we are," Flynn said with more bravado than I expected he felt. Our battle scars were there whether anyone could see them or not.

"There were so many who didn't return. In towns and cities all across America," Theo said. "The question is—how do we go on, knowing of all the men we left behind? Buried in unmarked graves."

Around the table, silence fell. The weight of what we all knew hung in the air. Life for our generation would never be the same. We carried the memories of our fallen brothers like anchors around our necks.

"We can get Phillip set up in the gardener's shed, can't we, Papa?" Josephine asked, breaking the silence. "It's not used much in the winter."

"Yes, yes. Splendid idea," Lord Barnes said. "When spring comes and everything thaws out, we can see about getting you set up somewhere in town, but for now the shed will serve you well. Like I said, we'll go out to the mill in the morning. You can meet Roy Webber. Decent chap. We'll negotiate prices with him for his finest wood."

"Fine, thank you, sir. I'm very grateful for your help," I said.

"Just be careful and keep your wits about you," Flynn said. "Webber's a good negotiator. When we bought wood for the lodge, he stood fast to his prices. I poured on the charm and even appealed to his sense of patriotism by mentioning our service in the war. He was unmoved."

"He has a mill to run. People to pay," Lord Barnes said. "The man can't be expected to give you a lower price simply because of who you are or even what you've done."

"Yes, Papa," Flynn said. "But I have to try for the best deal I can make. You taught me that."

"True enough," Lord Barnes said with a smile. "You'll be a better businessman than your old papa before long."

"Flynn wasn't trying to get a better deal for business purposes," Theo said. "But because he loves to win."

"Competition's the American way," Flynn said. "Anyway, what does my motivation matter? Winning is still good business."

"Doesn't everyone love to win?" Cymbeline asked. "What else is there?"

"I don't care one way or the other," Fiona said. "I'd rather be loved."

"Then you've won," Flynn said. "Because we love you."

Cymbeline rolled her eyes.

"I'd rather be useful, if it comes down to choosing," Josephine said.

"I suppose I'd choose that one too," Quinn said. "But I prefer to think of it as love in action. We show our love through service to others."

"What about you, Phillip?" Cymbeline asked. "What do you choose?"

I met her gaze, then drifted around to all the faces at the table. They peered at me with such kindness that I was moved to answer from the most honest place in my heart. "I'd love to belong. To something. To someone. To be part of a family." My voice grew husky, so I stopped there before I embarrassed myself.

"What you're speaking of is community and family," Lord Barnes said. "The ties that bind and such. These are the sweetest offerings in this life. My life's work has been building this town and this family and at the end, I'll have no regrets. I'm with you, Phillip."

I flushed warm with pleasure. Although we couldn't have been born into more different circumstances, Lord Barnes and I were alike. We understood what truly mattered. He had it already. I wanted it desperately.

"Theo, you haven't answered," Fiona said. "What would you choose?"

He set aside his fork. "Peace. For myself and the world."

"My darling boy," Quinn said. "From your mouth to God's ears."

THE NEXT MORNING, Lord Barnes and I headed out in the larger of the two sleighs. Overnight, the weather had changed the blue sky to white. As Oz and Willie carried us toward the mill, wide snowflakes dumped from above.

As we drove along, Lord Barnes asked questions about my apprenticeship. I described my experiences as best I could. "It was something of a miracle, sir, if you want to know the truth. After I left the orphanage, I had no idea what I would do. War hadn't yet been declared, and I had no skills, other than a good academic education provided by the nuns . I'd have liked to pursue university, but that wasn't an option for me. I was wandering the streets one day and, to escape the rain, went into a woodworker's shop. He had fine pieces, made from cherry and walnut." I went on to describe Mr. Jenkins's offer of a job. "At first I swept up or assisted him in whatever way he needed. As I observed him working, I started to envision various pieces coming from the wood. It was as if they were being built in my mind if not my hands. A woman had been in the day before when Mr. Jenkins was taking his lunch. She wanted a cabinet like the one she'd had in her childhood home in Sweden. 'To remember my mother by,' she told me. I drew it up on a piece of paper and showed it to her. She asked if I could make it. Of course, I couldn't, but Jenkins had come back by then. He looked at the drawing and told her that he could easily do it for her. But after she left, he asked if I'd be interested in learning from him. He said I obviously had a knack for drawing up what the customer wanted and if I could do that, I could learn to make the pieces, too. I studied under him for two years, learning all I could. When we declared war, I knew I had to go. He gave his blessing and asked that I return to him."

"Why didn't you?"

"I did. He'd died from the flu." My throat ached at the memory. "The shop was all boarded up. I asked around and learned he'd died during the first deluge of cases."

"What a shame. He was a father figure to you, I suspect?"

"Yes, that's right. All my life I've been at the mercy of the good souls who've taken me in, sheltered me, taught me. The nuns, then Mr. Jenkins, and now you."

"I always figure a person attracts what they give out to the world. It's no accident that you've come to us."

"I came because of Josephine," I said. "I hope you know I didn't come looking for a handout."

Lord Barnes chuckled. "Giving you my daughter is much harder than a loan for a business."

I flushed. "I didn't mean to compare them. Josephine is finer than any monetary pursuit. I'd give most anything to win her love."

"That's not up to me. She has her own mind, and I'll allow her to marry whomever she chooses. But from what I've seen of your character thus far, I hope she returns your affection."

"How do you know, sir? If you don't mind my asking. About me, that is."

"You've traveled across the country, risking everything, because of the letters from a girl you'd never met. My wife came here because of a letter I'd written to her about my vision for our first school. I'd imagined her an old battle-ax of a woman—one who would be fine out here in this rough, wild town. When she showed up no older than Josephine is now, I could hardly believe my eyes. She was the prettiest woman I'd ever seen and had the grit of a hundred hungry men. The courage it took for her to leave her mother and sister in Boston and come out to the frontier never ceases to amaze me. She said it was my letter that convinced her to come. The way I described the town and the children who needed a teacher moved her. There's something similar in our stories, don't you think?"

"I suppose there is." I smiled to myself, touched by his confidence in me. "Except that you and Quinn didn't know what was coming. For me, I knew Josephine from her letters. The risk wasn't so great. Other than my soul will be crushed if she doesn't choose me." I said the last part in jest, although it was absolutely true.

We'd arrived at the mill by then. Lord Barnes pulled the horses into the livery and greeted the boy who looked after them while the men were at work. In this rural environment, not many had motorcars, I presumed. Riding horses to work was a necessity.

Smoke rose in a cloud from the mill's building. A conveyer belt moved slowly, carrying logs to the round saws. As we made our way toward the office, the grinding noise of the chains that cut the boards filled the yard.

Lord Barnes and I entered the office to the smell of wood shavings. A stout man with a bushy white beard and eyebrows to match looked up as the door closed behind us. He stood up from his chair. "Barnes, what brings you here?"

"Roy, this is my friend Phillip Baker. He's in need of some wood to make furniture."

Roy came from behind the desk to shake my hand. "Pleasure to meet you, young man."

"You as well."

"He needs wood to build a table," Lord Barnes said.

"In the arts and crafts style," I said. "Clean lines but with practical uses, like storage."

"What do you have for him?" Lord Barnes asked.

"We mostly have firs, pine, and cedar. You can take it home with you now if you'd like."

"Cedar would work for a table," I said.

"Show us the way," Lord Barnes said.

Josephine

For two days in a row I only saw Phillip at dinner. He'd been hard at work in the shed on the Cassidys' table, leaving the house before I'd come down for the morning. During the days, I worked at the library, coming home just after teatime. After dinner, he and I would retire to the sitting room with the rest of my family. I yearned to have him all to myself and ask him a hundred questions. Instead, we were surrounded by my sisters and watchful brothers, not to mention Papa, who seemed to have eyes in the back of his head.

At night, to distract myself from staring at him endlessly, I busied myself by knitting him a pair of fingerless gloves. Working out there in the cold, he needed gloves, but he'd mentioned they encumbered his agility. I'd finished them last night and wanted to give them to him today. Yet I hesitated, shy to go out uninvited to his working space alone. Fiona and Cymbeline were at school. The boys were working with the carpenters at the ski lodge. Papa was at his office. Mama was with the little girls in the nursery. I wished my sisters were here to ask if they'd accompany me. We were a modern household; still, I wasn't sure Papa would like me to be alone with Phillip in such a small space.

I spent a good fifteen minutes moving restlessly around the sitting room. Finally I decided I'd take Phillip a pot of hot tea and casually leave the gloves as well. How ridiculous I was, all this fuss over whether I should go out to the shed.

I went down to the kitchen to ask Lizzie if she'd mind putting a pot of tea together for me. She and Mrs. Wu were both working in their usual harmony. Mrs. Wu was in the middle of peeling a pile of potatoes; Lizzie stood at the stove, stirring a steaming pot of broth that smelled of celery and garlic.

"Good morning," I said.

"Hello, Miss Josephine," Mrs. Wu said.

When she'd first come to us, Mrs. Wu couldn't speak much English, but over the years she'd become quite fluent. She and Lizzie, so opposite in appearance—Lizzie robust and pink-skinned with round features; Mrs. Wu, birdlike and tiny with white hair and a dark complexion—were fast friends. After so much time together they moved about the kitchen as if in a choreographed dance.

Mrs. Wu and her granddaughter, Fai, lived downstairs in our staff quarters off the kitchen. When Li came home, if he ever did, his future was uncertain. His Chinese descent would surely keep him from playing in an orchestra. Papa had influenced the music college to take him by donating generously. But his money could only take Li Wu so far. Li had told me during his last visit home that he knew his escape to school would be temporary, but that he was enjoying every moment while he could.

"Are you hungry?" Mrs. Wu asked.

"No, thank you. I wondered if you'd put together a pot of tea for Phillip."

Lizzie's mouth twitched. "Are you worried he's cold out there?"

"I hadn't really thought about it, but yes, he might be cold." I avoided eye contact and picked up a green apple from the bowl of fruit.

"Looking for an excuse to see him then?" Lizzie asked as she brushed a strand of her graying hair away from her face. In her mid-forties, her face was virtually unlined but recently some gray had crept into her black curls. She and Jasper had married when she was well into her thirties and had their daughter, Florence, about ten months later. Another child was born around the same time as Delphia, but he'd died in childbirth. Lizzie had taken it hard, as had Jasper. His stoic British attitude didn't allow him to show his grief outwardly, but I could see it in his eyes when he thought no one was watching. Lizzie hadn't been herself for at least a year. I'd found her crying down here many times, as had Mama. Eventually, though, she'd gone on, as women have to do.

I looked up from my careful examination of the apple. "Why would you say that?"

"I wasn't born yesterday," Lizzie said.

"Cymbeline says he stares at you," Mrs. Wu said. "With soft eyes. Like this." She widened her eyes.

I laughed. "What was she doing talking about him to you?"

"She wasn't," Lizzie said. "We overheard her talking with Fiona and Fai. Those three gossip all day long."

As did these two.

I took the gloves out of the pocket of my dress. "I made him these."

Lizzie and Mrs. Wu exchanged amused glances.

"He'll like them," Mrs. Wu said. "But not as much as you bringing them to him."

"I'm not sure what you two find so funny," I said. "After I carried on about Walter, who proved to be a cad, I should be ashamed of myself. I mean, really, I shouldn't be bothering with any of this. How can I trust myself? Or anyone else for that matter?" The room suddenly seemed cloying.

"One bad apple doesn't ruin the whole bowl." Lizzie pointed at the fruit. "He came here to win your heart."

"How did you know that?" I asked.

"Cymbeline," Mrs. Wu said. "She has a loud voice. Apparently, she and Mr. Phillip had quite the talk the other morning."

"For heaven's sake. There are no secrets in this house," I said. What else had he said to Cymbeline? That little traitor should have told me. I'd get it out of her later.

"That's the way it should be," Lizzie said. "Secrets are the seeds of unhappiness."

"You're full of analogies today," I said.

Lizzie picked up the teapot from the stove. She refused to use tea bags, calling them newfangled and for lazy Americans. Instead, she made a pot the same way she always had, using a strainer filled with tea leaves. I wandered over to the sink and leaned against the rim. What should I say when I came with the tea? Would he resent the interruption? I'd read that about great artists. They needed long periods of concentration.

"Whatever you're worrying over, don't," Lizzie said. "He'll be pleased to see you."

"Lizzie, am I a fool to be thinking this way about a man we don't know?"

"Not everyone needs to have a fifteen-year courtship like Jasper and me." Lizzie rolled her eyes. "That blasted man."

"Love is good," Mrs. Wu said. "We want that for you."

I wanted it too. I'd wanted it so much that I'd invented a love that hadn't existed.

"You worry too much." Mrs. Wu wriggled her fingers in front of her face. "Will give you wrinkles. See all mine. From too much worry."

"You're beautiful, Mrs. Wu," I said.

"Put your coat on," Lizzie said. "By the time you come back, I'll have this put together. You can go out the back door here." She pointed to the door that opened to steps into the yard.

"I suppose I have the time," I said, joking.

"Not so much time," Mrs. Wu said, "before you're old like me."

RISKING my life by carrying a tray in this weather, I followed the tracks of Phillip's footsteps out to the shed. A fresh layer of snow had partially covered them, and his stride was much longer, so I was afraid to trip and fall. By the time I got there, my shoulders ached from the effort. I caught a glimpse of him through the window. He looked up with a startled expression, then disappeared from view. A second later he hustled out the door and tromped through the snow to me. He took the tray.

"What are you doing?" he asked. "You could slip and hurt yourself."

"I thought some hot tea and a few of Lizzie's scones would warm you."

"They will, but I don't want you hiking out here just for me."

"Nonsense. I grew up here. A little walk in the snow won't hurt me."

"Come inside. It's warmer in there."

I allowed him to open the door for me and passed by him, all too aware of his strong arms and shoulders. The tabletop was perched upon two sawhorses. He put the tea on the crude potting counter. Wood shavings covered the floor. The room smelled of fresh cedar and a slightly acidic smell that must be from the stain.

"Phillip, it's pretty." I pulled off one glove and trailed my fingers over the polished cedar. Light in color with the pretty patterns of the natural wood, it was a work of art. The pieces had been laid out to make it as seamless as possible. "How did you get the wood like this?" The surface felt like silk.

"Fine sanding and then a technique I learned for polishing using a stain." His brow wrinkled. "Do you think they'll like it?"

"They'll love this. It's fine, fine work. They'll be proud to give it to their mother." I turned to look at him. "They've had such a hard year. Losing their father and with Mrs. Cassidy not well. This will be something fresh and beautiful to cheer them."

He crossed over to the cabinet in the corner and held up a partially finished leg. "I don't have the right tools to make anything too ornate, so I'm giving them a simple taper." It was indeed gently tapered, starting fat and ending slender.

"I've only got the one done, but they're going fast compared to the tabletop."

"How will you get it out to them?"

"I'll leave the legs unattached and put them on when we get it into the kitchen. I'm using screws, so they can be taken apart if needed."

"They're going to want new chairs," I said.

"If so, I can make them. Your father was generous with the wood." He gestured to the pile of boards at the other end of the room. "Being back to work in this way feels good. The hours float away."

"I wasn't sure if interrupting you would be welcomed. I'm not an artist like this, but I hate being bothered when I'm reading."

"You think I'm an artist?"

"What other conclusion could I come to?"

He grinned, obviously pleased. "Regardless of what I'm doing, there will never be a time when I wouldn't want to see you. Also, hot tea sounds like heaven."

Shy now, I backed up toward the door. "I'll leave you to it, then. There are scones and butter too."

He put his hands in his pockets and shuffled from one foot to the other. "You could stay. Have tea with me?"

"I'm not hungry, but I'll have a cup of tea with you." I moved over to the cabinet and poured the strong tea into two cups. Steam rose playfully in the drafty room. "Sugar?" I asked even though I knew the answer. He drank his black.

"No, thank you." He took one of the cups and its saucer from my outstretched hand. "Shall we sit? My feet are tired." He gestured toward the bench located under the shed's only window.

Knowing he wouldn't unless I did, I agreed, sitting primly

with my cup and saucer resting on my lap. He sat next to me, watching me as he lifted his cup to his mouth.

I sipped from my own cup, enjoying the bitterness and warmth of the tea. "Oh, I almost forgot. I made these for you." I took the gloves from my coat pocket and handed them to him. "The fingertips are left off so you can still grip."

"Jo, these are great. Thank you."

My stomach turned over as he pulled them over his strong hands. "It's nothing really."

He spread his fingers wide, then wriggled them. "Perfect fit. How did you do that?"

I swallowed, dragging my gaze from those long fingers. "I guessed."

He picked up his tea and took a sip. "I've been thinking about something. I'd like to learn to drive the sleigh. I've never driven horses before, but now that I live here, I should."

"Papa can teach you. Or I?"

"I'd prefer you if I'm able to choose."

"Why do you want to learn to drive?"

"I plan on staying here. A man needs to know how to drive a team of horses. I only hope I'm better suited for it than skating."

I laughed. "Me too, or we might not live through our first lesson."

ONCE A WEEK AFTER SCHOOL, we had children's story time for ages four to ten. I usually read a book with pictures as we sat in a circle on the rug. For the past month, I'd been reading chapters from *The Jungle Book*. The children delighted in the stories, often laughing out loud. Those moments were particularly joyful for me.

Today, as usual, the circle included both my smallest sisters. Even Delphia was quiet and attentive during story hour. Most of the mothers spent the time looking for books to take home while I read, although sometimes they listened, too.

We'd just finished our story time and I'd sent the children off to their mothers to pick out books when I saw Phillip come through the double doors. He took off his hat and looked straight at me, smiling in that way of his that made my stomach flutter. I rose from the small chair where I'd been reading to the children and scurried over to greet him.

"Is it done?" I asked, referring to the table.

"Strapped to the sleigh." He took both my hands and leaned closer, whispering in my ear, "You're beautiful and I missed you."

"Thank you." His eyes upon me seemed to light a fire from within me. It was all I could do to keep my head when he looked at me this way. "I'm ready to go. I'll just go put on my things."

"Harley and the horses and sleigh are waiting out front." A light dusting of snow covered his coat. He shrugged out of his coat and hung it on the rack near the door. I'd put an old blanket underneath to catch the melted snow that would ruin the dark hardwood floors. "But he's going home with your father. Harley gave me a lesson about the horses before we set out. He thinks I'm ready to try driving."

Which meant we would be alone. "I won't be a minute."

Phillip

At the house, Harley and I had tied the tabletop to the sleigh with thick ropes. Afterward, he'd taught me how to brush the horses before outfitting them with their bridles and blinders as he rattled off a bunch of terms such as *turnback*, *hames*, *bearing rein*, *hip drops*, and *tug chains* until my head swam with all the information.

"Get on up there," Harley said as I came down the library steps. "It's now or never."

I got into the driver's seat. Josephine, dressed in a red coat and hat, hustled down the steps toward us.

"Don't worry," Harley said, helping Josephine into the seat next to me. "You'll get it after some practice." He went around the front of the horses and petted their noses. "These two will take good care of you."

"I'll make sure you know what to do," Josephine said, laughing at what must have been a panicked look in my eyes.

Snow began to fall as she took the reins. "I always tuck the excess line under my legs. I don't want them to get tangled around our feet. I'll get us out of town and teach you as we go, then you can try."

"Fine." I was starting to regret my decision.

"We'll see you later, Harley," Josephine called out to him. He gave a wave and headed toward Lord Barnes's office.

"To get them going, just call out a 'Let's go' and jerk the reins slightly." She did just that and the horses broke into a trot, taking us down the street. "There are two styles of driving. One is the way the English adapted from Germany called Achenbach. Papa and Jasper taught us all to do it this way, but Harley and Poppy hold a rein in each hand like Americans. We're all split on our preferred method. I like the American way, but the twins prefer Achenbach. You can decide which you like better after you try them both."

She demonstrated the Achenbach method, moving the reins all the way to the left. Oz and Willie followed her lead and turned out of town toward the direction of the Cassidys' farm. "See there. The horses know what to do." She divided the lines, holding one in each hand. "This way you tug gently on either one, left or right. Same effect."

A whip dangled to the left, near Oz's rear. "I won't have to use that, will I? I don't want to hurt them."

"Not on Oz or Willie," Josephine said. "They're well-trained and know what to do. You really only need those for horses that are slow. Anyway, the whip doesn't hurt them. Not the way we use it, anyway."

On the road, we traveled in the icy ruts made by other sleighs. The horses snorted and increased their pace. "Do you see how much they love it?" Josephine asked. "Harley trained them himself just for this purpose." She didn't wait for an answer. "Are you ready to take over?"

"Not really." From this angle, the horses' back ends seemed massive. What if I lost control and we all tumbled off a cliff? "One thing. What happens when I want them to stop?"

"Tug lightly on both lines. They'll know what that means. Even if I weren't here with you, you would be fine. They know all the routes anyway, so they're practically driving us."

I took the reins, one in each hand. The power of these

magnificent creatures traveled into my hands. Oz and Willie continued at a trot. "Are we going too slow?"

"No, this is fine. We're enjoying the day."

"It's a beautiful day." Josephine was by my side. The bells hooked to the horses' necks tinkled merrily. We stayed within the icy grooves, sliding along easily. The snow fell in lazy drifting flakes as if compelled by the slow, steady rhythm of the bells and stomping of the horses' hooves to meander along rather than rush. The snow-covered bare branches of the aspens that lined the road seemed spun from sugar. Their spindly trunks of white peppered with gray stood straight and tall. A lacy cloth of fresh snow covered the firs and pines.

"You're doing well," Josephine said.

"This isn't as hard as I thought," I said. "I can feel the power of their muscles, yet they're restrained. As if serving us is their only mission."

"They're gentle souls who love us. That's what you're feeling." Josephine let out a sigh and raised her face to the sky. "We can travel along the river. Just turn at the fork in the road up ahead."

I was surprised by this, having no sense of where we were. Out here, the snow and mountains were vast, giving me little to anchor to as far as direction. In the city, everything was marked with street signs. On the Western Front, we'd simply followed orders en masse.

I yanked gently on the reins, and the horses turned left into fresh snow.

"This is a meadow during the warm seasons," Josephine said. "Wait until you see the wildflowers in spring. They're my favorite sight in all the world."

We traveled across the meadow until we reached the river.

"We can start to follow the river here, which will take us to their farm," Josephine said.

The river was not frozen over like the pond. Instead, batches of snow and ice were scattered over the surface in a patchwork design. Rich brown winter cattails sprang up in clumps along the bank.

"Balm for my soul," I said. "All this."

"Yes. For me too. I'm glad you feel the same."

"It's enough to take away all the images from the war I carry with me."

She reached over and brushed her knuckles against my cheek. Even through her gloves, the warmth of her skin penetrated mine. "I wish you didn't need a balm. I'd take every one away if I could."

A lump formed in the back of my throat. I took her hand to my mouth and gave it a light kiss before letting it fall back to her lap. "If I could look at your face every day for the rest of my life, that would be enough."

A smile lifted the corner of her pretty mouth. "You might just have the power to make me forget what a fool I was to fall for such lines."

"In this case, it's not a line." I glanced over at her.

"I'm beginning to believe that you're truly as good as you seem to be."

"I'm a good man," I said. "But that doesn't mean I'm worthy of you. I can't give you what your father's been able to provide. Not yet anyway."

"Would you believe me if I said I have every faith in you?"

For the second time in as many minutes, my throat ached. A buzzing started between my ears like the happy hum of honeybees. "You make me believe it, too."

In the distance I spotted the stark white farmhouse. It looked lonely and too small here in the vastness of the meadow and the white mountains on either side of us. A plume of smoke was the only evidence of living people.

"I'm excited for them to see what you made." She practically knocked me out of the sleigh with her radiant smile. My heart surged with love. What would I do if she ever turned me away?

I'd fallen into the well that was Josephine, and I might drown if she didn't return my feelings.

I SUCCESSFULLY HALTED the horses in front of the house. No sooner had I gotten Josephine out than both Shannon and Nora barreled out of the house.

"Is it done already?" Nora asked.

"It didn't take as long as I thought," I said. "Is it all right that we brought it out here?"

"Yes, yes," Nora said.

"We'll give it to Mam early. We'll have it for the holiday preparations, Nora."

Nora squealed. "I hadn't thought of that."

A woman with a shawl wrapped around her shoulders came out to the porch. "What have you done, girls?"

"Mam, we have a present for you," Nora said, squealing again. "A new kitchen table."

"You've brought it on the sleigh?" Mrs. Cassidy came down the steps and moved toward us.

"Yes, the legs aren't attached yet," Josephine said. "Shall we bring it into the kitchen?"

"Yes, please," Shannon said.

I wasn't sure how to get it inside with only these small women, but I had underestimated Josephine. She was small but mighty, as was Shannon. They each took an end. We carried it inside with a blanket covering the top. I would need to turn it over to put on the legs and didn't want to scratch the top. Nora and Mrs. Cassidy followed, each with two of the tapered legs.

We eased it through the front door and down the hallway to the kitchen. "What do we do with the old one?" Josephine asked.

"We'll set this one aside and I'll get the other one out of here."

We gently set the tabletop against the hallway wall. I rushed back outside to get my tools and then took the legs off the old table. It was so thin and light that I was able to take it out to their shed with little effort. The girls were helpful by following with the legs.

"Dad never liked to toss anything," Shannon said. "So we should probably save this in case we want to do something with the old wood."

"I'll think about what I could make with it, if you'd like," I said. "I might be able to make end tables for you. But for now, just keep it dry."

I followed them back into the house. Mrs. Cassidy had put on a pot of coffee and was huddled with Josephine near the stove.

"Yes, I'm having a good day," Mrs. Cassidy said as I came in. "The headaches come suddenly and without warning, but usually only last a day."

Josephine formally introduced me to Mrs. Cassidy. I plucked my hat from my head. So focused on the table, I'd almost forgotten. "Nice to meet you."

"You as well."

We brought the tabletop into the kitchen, and I assembled the legs using the screws. I had it all put together in less than ten minutes. The girls helped me turned it over as Josephine snatched the blanket out of the way.

Mrs. Cassidy's hands covered her mouth as she exclaimed, "Oh my, it's pretty." She held out her arms. "Girls, how did you pay for this?"

Josephine shook her head. "Never you mind that. Consider it a gift from the Barnes family and our new, very talented friend."

After embracing her girls, Mrs. Cassidy dropped into one of the chairs. "This is such a thoughtful thing you've done, but I don't know how we can possibly stay here on the farm. Without my husband, we don't have much chance for survival." She turned to Josephine and me. "Years ago, my husband decided to add cattle that we could sell to the butcher shop in addition to our milkers. Right before he died, we lost five of them to a disease. I don't know how or why they got sick. Or how to save the rest if it comes to that. Without the sale of that beef, we didn't have any meat to sell to the Higgins brothers for their shop. I couldn't pay our farmhand, so he left. The barn roof partially collapsed after the last snowfall, and I've nothing for the repairs." She wiped under her eyes with one of her apron strings. "I've sent a letter home to Ireland. I have a brother who might be able to take us in."

"Mam, no," Shannon said. "This is our home."

"Even before we lost your dad, I wasn't sure we'd make it. Without him, I'm sure we can't." Mrs. Cassidy's weary tone told me how defeat had rendered her incapable of seeing any hope. "And I'm not well. There's debt." She placed her hands over her face. "So much debt, just piling higher and higher." She dropped her hands and directed her gaze once more at us. "We lost our bull last year and Dorrin had to take out a loan to replace him, which put us behind. That's been our story for years. We're always on the brink of losing everything. Your dad believed in taking risks. But he didn't foresee dying on us at age forty-five. I can't do it without him. These girls have worked tirelessly to save everything, but it's not fair to them. They're bright and should be at school learning how to get out of this kind of life. I've failed them."

"Mam, no. You're brave and good," Nora said. "We've done what we had to do to keep the farm. That's all we want."

"We can't go to Ireland without Alma," Shannon said. "When she's done with her nursing school, she'll be able to help with money."

"Not enough to run a farm," Mrs. Cassidy said. "Anyway, she promised Alexander Barnes that she would come back here and be a nurse for the town. That was the agreement we made with him when we took the tuition money."

"She's our sister," Shannon said. "We can't leave her here and go to Ireland to be with family we don't even know."

Nora had started to cry silently. My heart ached for her. She didn't want to lose more of her family.

"Show Miss Josephine your hands," Mrs. Cassidy said.

Shannon put out her hands. A defiant look came to her eyes. "I'm not ashamed of working hard."

"Nor I." Nora held out her hands for us to see. Tears streaked her thin face.

Both sets of hands were red and chapped. Broken and bloodied calluses marred the palms.

"They're doing the work of two men," Mrs. Cassidy said. "Do you see why we can't stay? If I sell the farm, I can pay back the debt and maybe have enough for fare home."

"I didn't know how bad it was for you," Josephine said. "You should have come to Papa for help. If he'd known, he would've done whatever it took. Mama will be furious to think of you out here feeling helpless and alone. This is not how we do things in Emerson Pass."

"I can't ask your father to help us," Mrs. Cassidy said. "It isn't right."

"What's not right about it?" Josephine asked gently. "Don't we hear every Sunday about what the Lord expects from us? What kind of Christians are we if don't help our neighbors?"

I knew what to do then, as if God had reached down to speak to me directly. "Ma'am, I could help you. I'll be your farmhand. With instruction, of course."

"Thank you, but as I said, I don't have the money to pay anyone." Mrs. Cassidy's gaze dropped to her lap. I knew as sure as I knew my own heart that she was ashamed of being poor and at the mercy of charity to survive. Worry had caused her headaches. If her financial situation improved, so would her health. Grief and desperation made it impossible for her to get better. I must convince her to allow me to help. "The Barneses have invited me to stay in their home until I can find a place of my own, which at this rate will be a while. They've been very kind to me. I'd be honored to repay them for their kindness by helping you. I don't have a lot of experience on farms, but I'm sure these girls can teach me."

"Yes, we can show you what to do," Shannon said. "Nothing hard, but it requires strength."

"And grit," Nora said.

"I've a bit of that." The furniture shop would have to wait. This was what I was meant to do for now and a way for me to pay the debt of kindness owed to the Barneses. "Please, Mrs. Cassidy, allow me to do this for you. Someday, you'll show someone the same kindness and they'll pass it along."

"Yes, that's it exactly." Josephine's eyes shone with gratitude and affection—all directed toward me. To evoke that expression again, I would have worked a hundred farms for a hundred years. "He's learning to drive the horses. Papa will lend you the smaller of our sleighs to come over to the farm."

"I can repair the barn first," I said. "That I know how to do."

"How many cows do you have left?" Josephine asked.

"Only two," Shannon said. "And the bull."

"Hardly a herd," Mrs. Cassidy said with a bitter edge to her voice. "I told your dad the same thing when he moved us here, but he was as stubborn as they come." Despite the regret in her words, I detected love too.

"America is about dreams," I said, surprising myself. "We can't give up on them, even when things are hard."

"Dreams don't feed hungry daughters," Mrs. Cassidy said. "We're running out of supplies, and it's not yet Christmas."

The girls were both thin. I hadn't thought about it much, assuming that girls that age tended to be slender. Now, however, I looked at them with more care. Nora had a pinched look to her face, as if she were gritting her teeth against hunger. Shannon's cheekbones were too prominent. She was seventeen, already grown, and yet had no evident curves. Compared to Cymbeline, who was two years younger but robust and glowing with health, Shannon would appear sickly.

The nuns had made sure we were never hungry. Some of the children who came to us over the years had shared tales of near starvation on the streets of New York. They'd had a hungry look in their eyes even after months of being well-fed at the orphanage. I could remember one boy who slouched over his food as if shielding it from a predator.

"For now, we'll focus on repairing the barn and getting that bull to do his job," Josephine said briskly.

Nora giggled as she wiped away her tears.

"We're not sure how that's done," Shannon said. "Dad didn't tell us anything about...how all that works."

"Poppy's coming home soon from her apprenticeship with the veterinarian," Josephine said. "Perhaps she'll have some ideas for us."

"Mrs. Cassidy, will you allow me to come out tomorrow?" I asked. "Even if you were to sell the farm, you'll get more for it with a good roof on the barn."

She looked up at me with tired eyes. "I can't turn down the offer, and I thank you kindly."

Josephine

Phillip went out to inspect the barn. We left shortly thereafter, worried about keeping Oz and Willie out in the cold for too long. Phillip had promised to return at first light. I planned on sending him with some staples, such as flour and lard.

With Phillip driving the horses, I had time to think. Phillip couldn't repair that roof on his own. The twins would have to help. Viktor and Isak Olofsson might be able to spare some time as well as the Cole brothers, Noah and Roman. All the old gang from our first year at the school were as bonded as a group of people could be, having survived the day that Louisa Kellam's father had come for Mama. She'd taught us that we were stronger as a team. We proved her right that day when we jumped and hog-tied him before he could finish choking Mama. I shivered, remembering. I could still see the roster of that first class in my mind. Mama, known as Miss Cooper to us then, had called out to us from it every morning.

Class of 1910, Emerson Pass, Colorado
Teacher: Miss Cooper
Martha Johnson, Age 16
Elsa Johnson, Age 14

Josephine Barnes, Age 13
Poppy Depaul, Age 13
Isak Olofsson, Age 11
Alma Cassidy, Age 10
Theo Barnes, Age 9
Flynn Barnes, Age 9
Louisa Kellam, Age 9
Viktor Olofsson, Age 9
Noah Cole, Age 8
Shannon Cassidy, Age 8
Roman Cole, Age 7
Nora Cassidy, Age 6
Willa Cole, Age 6
Cymbeline Barnes, Age 6

THINGS WERE DIFFERENT NOW. Most of us were grown. Three had fought in the war. Martha and Elsa were married now with babies of their own. Alma would soon be home from nursing school. I'd opened our library. Poppy was studying under a veterinarian so she could come home and be of help to the farmers and townspeople with beloved pets. Before she went away to finishing school, Louisa had assisted her adoptive mother with church duties. The Cole brothers and their uncle had opened a café in town.

I could still see how we'd looked back then, however, just by closing my eyes. What a scared little bunch we'd been. Papa's dream to have a school to educate us had come true. It still made me proud to think of what he and Mama had built together. But now some of our gang were in trouble, and we needed to come to their aid.

"I can hear your mind turning," Phillip said.

"I was thinking about that barn. You'll need a village of men. With some help, you can finish it within a few days. By yourself, it could take weeks."

"True enough."

"I don't want you up there on your own in the middle of winter. You could slip and fall. Break your neck."

"You care about my neck?"

"Perhaps a little." I glanced up at him. What a neck it was, thick and strong, albeit covered with a scarf at the moment. I had it memorized. More than once I'd wondered what it would feel like to trace the area from his ear to the base of his throat with my fingertips.

The snow had stopped and the world was in the quiet, still state that came afterward.

"I was thinking about the first year we were all at school together," I said, changing the subject. "All the boys from that year will want to help with the barn. I'm going to organize the women, too. We'll raise money and get them a milk cow."

"How?"

"By throwing a Christmas party at the house. With cakes and dancing and punch."

"How does that raise money?" he asked.

"Because we'll have a donation jar. Placed somewhere discreetly so as not to be gauche. In the invitations I'll say it's for the Cassidy family during their time of need and encourage them to donate what they can. I'll ask Papa to match the total at the end of the night."

The afternoon had dimmed, but we were close to home. I could see the lights from our house.

Without my prompting, he easily steered the horses into our driveway. "Dancing, huh?"

"Yes, do you like to dance?" I asked.

"Depends on who my partner is. If it were you, for example, I should like it very much."

"I'll save you at least one."

He laughed. "Only one?"

"Or two. I'll probably be very busy running the party."

"Would you rather do that than enjoy yourself? Being useful, as you say."

I thought for a moment. "I never think about it that way. Before this, there was never anyone I cared to dance with."

"Before this? Does that mean before me?"

I flushed despite the coolness of the air on my cheeks. "Yes, that's what it means."

Our merry bells and stomping of the horses' hooves stole the quiet as we slid over the slick tracks toward home.

"We went out to the Cassidys' farm today," I said at dinner.

"And?" Mama asked.

"They're not well. Actually, it's worse than I thought," I said. "I should've done a better job of seeing what was happening out there." I shared with them what we'd learned of their plight, including Mrs. Cassidy's idea that they return to Ireland.

"With Alma away at nursing college, the younger girls have been doing all the chores by themselves. Despite their efforts, the farm's falling into disrepair. They've not enough to eat. The girls look gaunt and exhausted."

"I had no idea they'd lost that many cows," Papa said. "We've not been good neighbors or friends. I should've been over there to see them."

"I'm ashamed," Mama said. "Moira's always been private. I'm sure asking for help didn't feel like something she could do."

"Speaking of help, Phillip's offered to work out there for them, starting with the barn." I smiled at him from across the table. My hero with the pure heart smiled back at me.

"How thoughtful of you, Phillip," Mama said.

"I can help," Cymbeline said.

"You have school, darling," Papa said. "But I appreciate the sentiment."

"Flynn and I can help," Theo said. "We're at a standstill on what we can do at the lodge and ski area until the snow melts."

"Certainly. We'll go with you tomorrow," Flynn said.

"I thought Viktor and Isak might be of help too," I said.

"They'll be willing to help without question," Theo said. "We'd all do anything for the Cassidys. We all go back a ways now, don't we?"

"I wish we'd known sooner," Flynn said. "I hate thinking about them feeling alone out there. That's what community is for."

"Not every place is like this," Phillip said. "I wouldn't have believed it to be true until I came here and saw it with my own eyes."

"Indeed. This was my intention when I dreamt of the future here." Papa beamed at us from his place at the head of the table. "I'll rest easy knowing we passed that value on to you children, which you, in turn, will pass on to yours."

"What can I do?" Fiona asked. "I'd like to help too."

"I have an idea of what you and the rest of the women in our group can do," I said. "Throw a party." I presented my idea for a gathering to raise money for the Cassidys. "We'll have it here at the house. Desserts and punch and dancing. We'll invite all our old schoolmates and whomever else we'd like, with a gentle suggestion that whatever they can spare would be appreciated, no matter how small."

"Li Wu will be back from school in a few days," Fiona said. "He and I could play the music for dancing."

"Splendid idea," Papa said. "What a treat for everyone to hear him play."

"And you, too, Fiona," I said. There would be much merriment with the two of them playing together.

"To make a dance floor, we'll have to move furniture around in the parlor," Mama said.

Our parlor was at the back of the house. Other than Fiona, who practiced at the piano in the formal room, none of us spent much time there. However, whenever we had a party or other grand occasion, we had it in there. We'd never had a dance before, but why not? I could already imagine the couples twirling to the music.

"We'll put the desserts on a table here in the dining room," Mama said. "And the sitting room can be for anyone who wants to talk quietly."

We all started chiming in on ideas for the gathering, excited to have a plan to help the Cassidys. I agreed to handwrite the invitations and deliver them at church this coming Sunday.

"I'd like to go out and see Moira tomorrow," Mama said. "I'll have Lizzie put a basket of food together."

Phillip

There were five of us that morning to repair the roof of the barn. The Olofsson brothers, strong as a pair of oxen, had readily agreed to come. We started by assessing the damage. The trusses had not been strong enough to support a roof heavy with snow and had splintered or broken in half, which had caused the roof to collapse. After determining what we needed, Flynn and I took the cargo sleigh out to the mill and purchased thick pieces of fir to replace the broken ones. We also made an order for shingles and plywood, which we would come for the next day.

When we returned, Josephine and Quinn had come and gone with sandwiches and thermoses of hot tea for our lunch. We ate on the covered front porch of the farmhouse sprawled out on low-slung chairs and the porch swing. I'd just finished my second sandwich when Shannon came out from the house.

"I can't thank you boys enough," Shannon said. She had an apron on over a faded dress. Her curls were swept back in a messy bun at the nape of her neck.

The men all ripped off their hats and jumped to their feet.

Flynn stared at her for a second longer than was polite. "Shannon, you've changed since the last time we saw you."

"I know, I look awful. This place has robbed me of my youth." She smiled and gestured toward the barn. "I've practically turned into my father. All bones."

"My brother simply meant that you were a girl the last time we saw you," Theo said.

"Yes, that," Flynn said.

"It's wonderful to see you all," Shannon said. "Doesn't it seem so long ago we were all students together?"

"It does," Isak said. "A lot's transpired since then."

"Again, thank you for your hard work. I've been despairing of late. Mam's talking about returning to Ireland. Nora and I can't bear to think of leaving our sister and all our friends. Whatever you can do to help us stay here—I'll be indebted for life."

"We'll do whatever we can," Flynn said.

"And you must ask for whatever you need," Theo said. "Our families are forever united. Don't forget that, all right?"

"I won't make that mistake again," Shannon said.

"Did Josephine tell you about the party?" Flynn asked.

"Yes." Shannon's eyes sparkled. "Something to look forward to, even though I have nothing to wear."

"You could wear what you have on," Flynn said. "You look fine to me."

She flushed and gave him a shy smile. "Flynn Barnes, have you become charming in your older years?"

"Haven't I always been charming?" He grinned, still staring at her.

"I seem to recall an incident with a frog in my lunch pail."

"That wasn't me, I swear," Flynn said.

"It was definitely him," Theo said.

"We'll have to settle this later," Shannon said. "I've housework to do. Good luck this afternoon. Please don't hesitate to knock if you need anything." She bobbed her head, then slid back into the house.

"I can't believe that's little Shannon Cassidy," Flynn said, shaking his head. "All grown up."

Isak nudged Flynn's shoulder. "You might've been a little obvious."

"Nah, I'm charming. Didn't you hear her say that?" Flynn asked.

We all laughed as we traipsed down the stairs and headed back to work.

IN THE LATE AFTERNOON, we called it a day, all of us wanting to get home before dark. The Olofsson brothers left together in their sleigh for town. I was about to take off with the twins when horses appeared on the horizon.

"It's Josephine," Flynn said.

"Who wants to bet it's not one of us that she's come for?" Theo said.

"I'll take that bet," Flynn said.

"She's teaching me how to drive," I said, sheepishly.

"Sure, that's the reason," Flynn said.

"Enjoy your drive," Theo said.

They got into their sleigh and were off, passing Josephine in the driveway.

She came to a halt in front of me. "I thought you might fancy a drive. It's such a lovely afternoon."

"You know my answer will always be yes," I said as I climbed in beside her.

The sun was low in the sky, making gold streaks between the trees as we set off down the driveway.

"Let's go home through the meadow," she said.

"Sure."

We chatted for a few minutes about the barn and our progress. I made her laugh by describing Flynn's reaction to Shannon.

"Do you think they could be a love match?" she asked, sounding incredulous.

"Why not? She'd be lucky to have a fine man like your brother." All her money problems would be over, but I didn't say it out loud for fear of offending her.

"Flynn recently claimed he's going to be a bachelor all his life," she said.

"Men have been known to change their minds."

We came upon a grove of aspens, white against the blue backdrop. "Nature's sculptures," I murmured.

"Aren't they, though?"

We continued to travel across the meadow until we came to the bank of a creek. I turned the horses so that we trotted along the edge of the water. The frozen creek was icy blue.

"Do stop for a moment, won't you?" Josephine asked. "It's such a peaceful scene. One of my favorites on the property. I always thought a cottage would be just right here by the creek."

I tugged on the reins and called out to the horses to stop. The snow-covered meadow spread out in front of us in one direction. Across the water, the landscape changed to a thick forest. In the distance, over the meadow, smoke rose from the Barnes home.

Josephine pointed into the forest. "Our friends the Coles live through there. They own the café in town."

I'd seen the young men hustling around the café through the windows as I walked by one day. The Coles were dark-skinned men who would not have been able to own a business in the white parts of New York City. But here, things were different. Although most of the town appeared to be of European descent, it seemed no one here cared that the Coles didn't look like them. There was the Wu family, too. Mrs. Wu and her granddaughter, Fai, seemed as comfortable in the Barneses' household as Lizzie and Jasper. Josephine had told me that Lord Barnes had sent Li Wu to music school. I'd wanted to ask Josephine about both families, but hadn't wanted to seem as if I disaproved.

"This is one of my favorite spots, no matter what time of year. This is one of the deepest and widest parts of the creek that runs through our property. In the summer, we swim there. As you can see, it's frozen over now."

"I hope you haven't brought our skates," I said.

She laughed and tugged on her scarf, exposing a small portion of her neck. "It's not safe to skate here. The ice is unpredictable because of the depth of the water. It can crack and break. Falling under the ice is most likely death."

I shivered. "You won't have to tell me twice. That sounds horrid. Do the children know not to go near?"

She turned from the scenery to look me. "Yes, they know. Mama and Papa forbid them to walk on it, and even Cymbeline obeys."

The sun had lowered farther, casting a gold tinge over the snow. Above, the sky had turned the dark blue of winter twilight.

Her eyes sparkled as she watched me.

I moved closer to her and brushed my thumb on the inward curve of her cheekbone. "This light becomes you, beautiful Josephine."

She blinked but didn't move. "Phillip?"

"Yes?"

"Have you ever kissed anyone before?"

Startled by the question, my gaze slid toward the creek before coming back to her. "One time." A nurse before I left for the war had kissed me, surprising me so thoroughly that I'd just stood there like an oak tree for a few seconds before turning on my heel and running away as fast as I could. She was not to my liking. Too loud and brash and smelled sour. The woman sitting next to me now smelled nice. Very nice.

"Who was she?" Josephine asked.

I hesitated for a second in an attempt to decipher her tone. Would she think ill of me if I confessed to a kiss with a woman I didn't know? However, I'd committed to telling her the truth and shouldn't stop now. She'd forgiven my intrusion into her privacy by reading the letters. This would be a minor offense. "I never knew her name. I met her right before I shipped out. I was out with a few of the boys I'd trained with. She and several of her friends had joined us at a bar, and we all carried on until the sun rose." I grimaced, remembering how we'd spilled out into the street, blinking in the morning light. She'd thrown herself into my arms and kissed me, then wished me luck. "She told me I should have a kiss before going overseas and possibly dying. I guess she decided that was her responsibility. She had breath that smelled of onions."

"Onions?" Josephine's eyes widened. "That doesn't sound pleasant."

"It wasn't. But I don't suppose all kisses are unpleasant. Not that I've had any other experience to test it against. I should like to. With you, most of all. I'll look forward to the day you give me permission to do so." I smiled and brushed my thumb along her delicate jawline.

My smile faded as her expression turned mournful. After spending so much time together over the last week, I was able to interpret her facial expressions. A slight downturn of her mouth told me she was sad.

"I kissed Walter," she said, as if I'd asked. "Many times."

My chest tightened. I didn't want to know. Not how many times or if she'd found his kisses pleasant. The thought of his mendacious mouth on hers was more than I could stomach.

She looked down at her lap. "When I believed he loved me, I thought it was fine. We were to be married. At least that's what I thought. Now that I know the truth about him, I feel spoiled. Dirty."

My heart softened, jealousy forgotten. She shouldn't feel bad for being tricked. It was all him. "No, no, you mustn't think like that. He was the one in the wrong. Anyway, those are only old-fashioned ideas, handed down from our puritanical beginnings. You're a modern woman. There's no reason you should be ashamed."

Her mouth curved upward as she looked up at me. "You sounded very smart and worldly just now."

"I'm not, but I'd like to be smart. For you." I held up my hands. "But I'm afraid my cleverness is in these, not here." I tapped my temple.

"You don't have to be anything other than yourself. Not for me or anyone else. You're kind, which is the most important thing to be, but intelligent too. I admire you."

My chest warmed at her compliments. "Me? How so?"

"You're a survivor. All the obstacles in your way and yet you're here helping others."

"You and your family inspired my generosity. It's I who admire you."

She was quiet for a moment. A sparrow darted from one bare branch to the other.

"When I think how he strung me along, I'm filled with shame," she said. "I wonder how you could think well of me when I acted so foolishly."

"As a man who's yearned for love and family for as long as I can remember, I can easily understand how one see things inaccurately. The desire outweighs your better instincts. Anyway, it's him I think ill of. When I see what he could have had with you, I can't think of a bigger fool."

She raised her gaze to mine. "I should have saved a first kiss for someone who deserved it."

"You could forget all that and start over. No one has to know but you and me. We could both start at zero kisses."

Josephine went back to staring at her lap. A flush had risen to her cheeks, making her even more beautiful than the moment before. "And who would be our first kiss then? Each other?"

"I'd not discourage you from that idea." Oz and Willie nuzzled noses as if to show us how.

She smiled again and slowly turned toward me. "I never thought I'd kiss anyone ever again. And now here you are. Honestly, I don't know if it's another case of me being in love with love, but your feelings for me are thrilling."

"Is there any part of you that thinks you could love me, not the idea of love?"

"How does one know, though?" Her nose wrinkled. "I'm scared to make another mistake."

"I could kiss you if that would help you decide."

Her eyes widened, and her lips parted slightly. Was that an invitation? I'd wait to hear the words from her rosy pink mouth. Making a mistake and scaring her away was my greatest fear at the moment.

"Are you asking permission?" she asked.

"Yes. May I kiss you?"

"You may." She lifted her chin and closed her eyes. "Go ahead."

I laughed. "There's no need to be stoic about it. You have to at least pretend you want me to."

She giggled as her eyes flew open. "I do. I'm just not certain how it works with you. With—"

I held up a hand to cut her off from whatever she was going to tell me about Walter. "Don't say it—I don't want to hear anything more about him or his kisses."

She sobered and dropped her chin, shaking her head. "I'm sorry. You're right. Not another word."

"Look at me, beautiful Josephine."

A giggle erupted. "I'm suddenly nervous."

I leaned forward, not thinking this time, and cradled her face in my gloved hands. The world went away as I kissed her sweet-tasting, yielding lips.

Her mouth parted slightly to allow me to delve further, which I did. After a few seconds, I withdrew to look at her. She stared back at me with wide eyes. "Was it all right?"

"I can't be certain." Her face broke into a smile. "Shall we do it again to decide?"

Josephine

Kissing Phillip was like nothing I'd ever experienced. I'd enjoyed the kisses from Walter, but this glorious feeling that reached into my toes was something altogether different. The rest of the world faded away, and it was only the sensation of his mouth against mine and the woodsy smell of him. An ache for more reverberated throughout my body.

He parted from me at last. I had no idea how long we'd kissed. It could have been seconds or years.

"That was...magical," he said.

I nodded, too breathless to speak.

"I guess kissing isn't something one needed to practice beforehand," he said.

"That wasn't like the others." Walter's had been quick and chaste, merely a brush upon my lips. Had he not felt anything for me? No passion? And what of me toward him? Nothing he did, kissing or otherwise, had ever evoked this kind of desire. "I had no idea what it was supposed to be like, but I do now."

"I hoped it would be this way, but having nothing to go on but the onion kiss, I wasn't sure."

We laughed like two children, free and without inhibition.

Like two people who'd not seen the horrors of war or the loss of parents or even the embarrassment of betrayal. Was this what love did? Eradicate the past? Or at the very least push it aside to make room for a new life? "Phillip, I didn't know."

"Know what?"

"That a man was supposed to look at me the way you do. If I'd known that, I wouldn't have wasted those years on Walter. What if you'd never come? I'd have gone my whole life not knowing what this feels like."

"It wasn't a waste." He brushed his mouth against mine but didn't linger. "If you hadn't written Walter all those letters, I wouldn't have known you. I wouldn't have known to come here."

I looked up at the sky. The light was beginning to fade into the gloaming. We would need to go if we were to get home before dark. "I'd like to stay forever in this moment, but we should get back to the house before Mama worries."

"One kiss before we go?" He peered at me, bolder than ever before. We'd moved into a new level of intimacy. He felt more sure of himself with me and I with him. No longer would I question myself in regard to Phillip. This was a good man. An honest one who saw me as a gift. He was not like Walter. This was clear to me now in the fading light. I would no longer chastise myself but simply thank God that he'd granted me another chance to choose the right man this time.

"One more." I smiled at him as I answered his request for another kiss. Had I ever known what it was to smile from my belly, as if it started there and worked its way out to my mouth?

He kissed me again, this time with one arm wrapped around my waist and pulling me close against his chest.

"There's never been a girl like you, Josephine Barnes. Not in all the world."

"They say no one snowflake is like the other."

"If you were a snowflake, you'd make all the others jealous."

"Are you sure it's me who has a way with words?" I asked.

We laughed as he told the horses it was time to return home at last.

WHEN WE ARRIVED BACK to the house, pink-cheeked from the cold and warm from our kisses, I was surprised and overjoyed to hear the sound of Poppy's voice coming from the sitting room. I quickly took the pins from my hat. "Poppy's here," I said to Phillip. "Come meet her."

"You go and say your hellos first," he said. "I'll hang up our coats."

I thanked him and then ran into the sitting room. The moment I saw Poppy, sitting between Fiona and Cymbeline on one of the couches, I froze. Her hair. She'd chopped her long brown hair into a bob that fell just below her jawline. "Poppy, what have you done?"

"She cut her hair off." Cymbeline's eyes shone with obvious delight. "Doesn't she look modern?"

I rushed across the room as Poppy rose from the couch. "It's...it's all gone." My hands covered my mouth as I tried not to cry.

Poppy put her hands out in a gesture of peace. "Jo, don't be mad. A lot of the girls in the city are bobbing their hair. It's very Parisian."

"The fashion magazines say so too," Fiona said.

Poppy had her bob styled in bumpy waves that flattered her strong jaw and big brown eyes. Still, I mourned the shiny tresses I'd brushed and braided so many times when we were young. Her thick hair had been spectacular. Like Jo in *Little Women*, her crowning glory.

"But...but...why?" I asked.

"It's so much easier this way," Poppy said. "I was up every morning at dawn and often called out to a farm in the middle of the night. This allows me to get up and go without any fuss."

I didn't say so, but wasn't a braid or a bun just as easy?

As if I'd said it out loud, Poppy continued with her argument. "Anyway, all that hair was giving me headaches. You don't want me to have an aching head, do you? You're much too kind for that." She flashed me a puckish smile, knowing it and her words would melt me. We'd known each other for too long.

"Jo, she was having headaches," Cymbeline said, chiming in from the couch. "Isn't that awful?"

I shot my sister a withering look, which she completely ignored. The gleam in her eye told me she was already planning her own dance with a pair of scissors.

"I know what you're *both* doing," I said. "Playing on my sympathies."

"Is it working?" Poppy asked. "Please say you forgive me. I've been so worried to show you."

"Of course I forgive you. It's your head anyway."

"That's right. Her head," Cymbeline said.

"Cym," Fiona said. "None of this is your business."

"Poppy's my friend too." Cymbeline crossed her arms over her chest. "I can have an opinion, and I think she looks worldly and sophisticated and not bound down by the patriarchal society."

I laughed as some of my irritation with my sister subsided. "Cym, where do you get these ideas?"

"From books, as you well know," Cymbeline said. "Books in your library, I might add."

"In fact, it did feel as if I were cutting off a lot of expectations about how I should be," Poppy said. "I feel more myself now. Free and independent."

"She has her own job." Cymbeline's voice rose in pitch. "Think about that. She won't ever have to rely on a man."

"It's true," I said. "I'm awfully proud of you."

"She boasts about you to anyone who'll listen," Fiona said. "We all do."

Poppy smiled at us all in turn. "Oh, you lovely girls, I'm glad to be home. I've missed you all more than I can say."

Truly, who was I to say anything? Poppy was living in a man's world of muck and mud while I pampered my precious books in a warm library all day. However, Cymbeline was still a child with no idea of how her impetuousness could get her into trouble. Someday she might like to have a man. A concept she was so disdainful of now might at some point be attractive. I couldn't wait for the day she fell in love and understood that not everything is a race or a competition. Loving someone would change her, soften her. I hoped, anyway.

"We've missed you," I said to Poppy. "Now give me a hug."

We embraced. The muscles in her arms and shoulders tightened around my waist. "You're so strong."

"Wresting around farm animals will do that to a girl." She let me go and took her place between the girls.

As I sat across from them, I further studied Poppy. In addition to the cutting of her locks, she had a new air of assurance and confidence. She wore a light blue traveling suit that flattered her small but sturdy stature. Only a few inches over five feet, she often reminded me of the quarter horses she loved so well—small, strong, and graceful.

I'd worried growing up that she felt caught in the shadow of the Barnes girls. Had she felt envious at times? If so, she never let it show. Still, her brother was our employee. Although Mama and Papa had always made sure to include the Wu children and Poppy into whatever parties or treats we had, the reality remained. We were rich, and they were not.

Whatever the case might have been back then, here in front of me now was a woman of the world. A professional who would make such a difference in our community.

"You're the luckiest person in the whole world," Cymbeline said. "Working outside all day. Not having to care about manners and staying clean and pretty."

"You can be both strong and pretty, you know," Fiona said. "Like Poppy."

"Thank you, sweet Fiona," Poppy said. "You've grown up since I saw you last. You're becoming a great beauty like your sisters."

Fiona beamed. "I am? Do you think I'll be a lovely young lady like you and Jo?"

"I've no doubts," Poppy said.

"For heaven's sake, who cares?" Cymbeline jerked to her feet and went to stand by the fire. "All this talk of beauty is utterly boring."

"I didn't mean you weren't pretty too," Fiona said, looking stricken. "But you're not all grown."

"I know, goose," Cymbeline's eyes softened. "I didn't take it that way." In the firelight, her skin glowed with health and vitality. "As far as that goes, you all look beautiful."

"I agree. And Josephine Barnes, you're all sparkly and flushed." Poppy narrowed her eyes. "I might even say you have the look of a girl in love. Your sisters have been telling me about your house guest. Have you been out with him?"

Just then, Phillip appeared in the doorway.

"There he is now. Phillip, come meet Poppy," Fiona said.

He walked toward us, a strained look on his face. "I'm not presentable, as I've been working all day, but I'll say hello."

"It's nice to meet you, Phillip," Poppy said.

He bobbed his head. "You as well. I've heard a lot about you."

Poppy investigated him with her wise brown eyes, either unwilling or incapable of hiding her curiosity. I'd not written to her of his arrival, knowing that she would soon be home and I could tell her all about it in person. What would she think of my scandalous ways once I told her my feelings? Falling for the friend of my former love? Not really, I reminded myself. He was a fraud. She didn't yet know, though, unless my sisters had told her.

"I shouldn't like to know what she's told you," Poppy said. "Jo and I have known each other since we were small girls. She knows everything about me. The good, bad, and embarrassing."

"She knows all mine too," I said.

"There aren't any of Jo," Poppy said. "Of all of us, she was always the good one."

"We all know it wasn't Cymbeline," Fiona said, teasing.

"Fiona, you're supposed to be on my side." Cymbeline nudged her playfully on the shoulder.

"We had more than one scrape," I said. "Mostly because of Flynn and Cym."

"Vastly exaggerated for comic effect," Cymbeline said.

"We had fun during our escapades," Poppy said. "Even if there were a few times we got in trouble."

"Phillip, come sit with us," Fiona said. "There's tea left."

"I'd love to," Phillip said. "However, I'm too dirty from working on the barn to sit with such fine young ladies. If you'll excuse me, I'll get cleaned up. I'll see you all at dinner."

Fiona grabbed a few of the tea sandwiches from the tray and put them on a plate for Phillip. "Take these for your room. You're probably famished."

"Thank you, Miss Fiona," he said with a polite bow of his head. "You're very thoughtful to think of it."

She smiled up at him. "You're welcome."

He nodded at me and then headed toward the door. My hand impulsively waved, as if I had no control whatsoever.

BEFORE DINNER, all five of the Barnes girls gathered in the bedroom with Poppy. My littlest sisters had already had their meal and were in their flannel nightgowns cuddled under the covers in one of the twin bunk beds. Fiona was fixing Cymbeline's hair at the dressing table. Poppy and I were side by side on the window seat. Addie and Delphia had been flooding a patient Poppy with questions for a quarter of an hour.

"Did you help make the animals feel better?" Addie asked. "Were they often sick?"

"They weren't always sick. Sometimes they were having babies and I had to help them."

"What kinds of animals?" Delphia asked. "Did you ever see a kitten?"

"We mostly looked after pigs, cows, sheep, and horses. Sometimes we were called out to help with a beloved pet like a dog and cat." Poppy widened her eyes and spoke in a menacing voice. "And one time a naughty rooster."

"Like Doodle?" Addie asked. "He's very naughty. Sometimes he chases me."

"Doodle is a nice boy compared to Red," Poppy said.

"That was his name?" Delphia giggled.

"Yes, for his temperament," Poppy said. "Red like hot peppers."

"What did he do that was bad?" Delphia's eyes sparkled with curiosity. A little too much, as if she were gathering ideas.

"He pecked the farmer and his wife and chased them away whenever they came to get the eggs," Poppy said.

"But why?" Addie asked.

"Red saw it as his job to protect the hens. But that meant the farmer couldn't get any of the eggs because of that naughty cock-a-doodle-doo. One day Red pecked their little girl's hand and caused her to bleed. That's when they called Dr. Miller and me to come help."

"What did you do?" Addie asked.

"We advised the farmer to establish dominance. Roosters are very prideful. Red had to be taught that the farmer and his wife were in charge."

"Pride is a sin," Fiona said as she placed a comb in the back of Cymbeline's hair.

"Even for a rooster?" Delphia asked, sounding disappointed.

"I'm afraid so," Poppy said.

"Did it work?" Addie asked. "Did they tame him?"

"In this case, they weren't able to. No matter what they did, Red wouldn't stop attacking people. Finally, the farmer decided it was too dangerous for his little girls and they had to send him away."

"To where?" Delphia asked.

Poppy hesitated before answering. "I'm not sure. Perhaps they sent him away to another farm."

"Probably into the pot," Cymbeline said.

"Why was he so mean?" Addie asked.

"He was just extremely protective of the flock of hens," Poppy said. "It's the way some breeds are. Red saw everything and everyone as a threat to his hens."

"I feel sorry for him," Fiona said. "He couldn't help how he was made."

"I did too." Poppy smiled as she looked around the room. "I've missed you all very much."

"We missed you," Fiona said. "Jo's been practically bereft without you."

"It's true," I said.

"It's good to be home," Poppy said. "But being away was worth every homesick moment. I'll be able to help our farmers and ranchers here in Emerson Pass now. I've learned a lot."

"Speaking of which," I said, "the Cassidys recently lost five of their cows. When you're settled, I'd like to take you out there and see if you can figure out what happened to them."

"I'll be happy to," Poppy said. "I'm grateful to Lord Barnes for sending me to apprentice under Dr. Miller. Although Miller wasn't exactly welcoming at first. I don't know what kind of favor he owed Lord Barnes, but he sure didn't want me there."

"Because you're a girl." Cymbeline scrunched her face into a scowl. "We have to bow down in gratitude simply for being allowed the chance to work for free."

"Cymbeline." Fiona's lashes fluttered as she chastised her sister. "Be nice."

"I don't want to be nice," Cymbeline said. "I want to do

things. Be someone important. Not push out babies for the rest of my life."

"I do understand," Poppy said. "However, the reality is it's harder for a woman to do much besides be a mother, nurse, or teacher."

"Was it awful for you?" I asked.

"Did Miller treat you poorly?" Fiona asked.

"I hope you gave it right back to him," Cymbeline said.

Poppy grinned. "Let's just say the first time he saw me tame a wild colt, he stopped muttering about training a girl. From then on, he wasn't friendly but respectful."

"You could teach him a thing or two about horses," Cymbeline said.

"He knew the insides of horses," Poppy said. "But I know their souls and what they respond to best."

"I'm proud of you," I said, squeezing her hand. "What an accomplishment."

"Now, tell me what's been going on here," Poppy said. "What have I missed?"

My sisters started rattling off answers one after the other.

"Jo has a beau," Fiona said.

"And has stopped moping around after that awful Walter," Cymbeline said. "Who turned out to be a fraud."

"We're having a party with a lot of cake," Delphia said.

"The party's for the Cassidys," Fiona said. "They're having a hard time and Jo's arranged for a party to raise funds so they won't lose their farm."

"Phillip made a pretty table," Addie said. "And the twins are opening a ski area where you go down a hill really fast on wood sticks."

"My goodness, I've missed a lot," Poppy said. "But let's start with Jo's beau." She turned to me. "Tell me everything."

Phillip

A routine developed to my days, making time gather speed. In the mornings, the twins and I set out together to the Cassidys' farm. After a few days, with the help of Viktor and Isak, we finished the roof of the barn. The rest of the week was spent doing additional repairs and other chores. In the late afternoons, Josephine arrived in the small sleigh so that I could drive us home. These excursions served two purposes. One, my driving was improving, as was my kissing of Josephine. Two, we talked, laughed and always stopped at our spot by the creek for a few kisses.

With each passing day, my feelings for her deepened. I wanted desperately to marry Josephine Barnes. But what could I offer her? I didn't have my own home. Thus far, I only had one paying customer for my furniture. Pastor Lind had asked for a new pulpit, one worthy of his growing congregation. As I worked on the piece in the late afternoons and into the evening, it became clearer to me just what a daunting task opening my own shop would be. It might take years.

"What is it?" Josephine put her fingers against her mouth, as if worried she'd done something wrong. "Something's troubling you. I can see it in your eyes."

"I'm thinking about the future. Our future."

"What about it?"

"Do you see us having a future together?"

She looked up to meet my gaze, grazing my cheekbone with her fingertips. "I think you know the answer to that. I wouldn't be here right now if I didn't."

"I've no home to offer you. And an uncertain future."

"When the time comes, Papa will help us."

"What sort of man would that make me?" I searched her face for answers, but the thin wintery light cast shadows. I couldn't quite make out her expression.

"Money isn't everything," Josephine said.

"Spoken from one who's never wanted for anything."

She stiffened and turned away.

"I'm sorry," I said. "I didn't mean it to sound unkind."

"It's true. I've had everything. Every creature comfort. I must seem spoiled to you."

"Not at all." I struggled to find the right words. "You're gracious and hardworking. I'm not good enough for you. That's the trouble."

"A confident man believes in himself and his capacity to make his dreams come true. You believe in your talent and drive, don't you?"

"Yes, I do. But not everything is up to me. There are circumstances out of my control."

"And you think I don't understand that?" Her voice was soft as a feather but as brittle as the ice that clung to the branches of the trees.

I spoke the next words slowly, knowing they could make her angrier. "I think you've had help. And I've had little. That's all. I'm starting with nothing. I'm frightened to fail you."

She jerked her head up to look at me. "The only way you'll fail me is by being timid. If I'm the one you want, then you must do whatever it takes to make me yours."

"My desire isn't in question. I want to be part of your family. But I have to earn it."

Her chin lifted slightly as she stared me down. "Is it me you want or my family?"

I flinched, surprised. Did she believe it was only her family that attracted me? Could she possibly think it was the money, like stupid Walter? "You, Jo, above anything else. Without question your family's an additional blessing. I'd be lying if I said the last few weeks hadn't been the best of my life, in part because of the way they've welcomed me into your home. I love pretending to be a big brother to your sisters. The camaraderie with the twins is the type of friendship any man craves. Your father's attention and advice are an answer to prayer. But without you, Jo, they're just a family I care about very much. It's you I want. Don't ever mistake that." I reached out to her, taking both her hands. "I know you're doubtful because of what happened with Walter. I can't blame you for being so." I tapped my chest. "But me? I traveled across the country on my last dime to see if what I thought was true." I hesitated, unsure what to say next. "It's just that I want the very best for you, and I'm not sure I can give it to you."

"This feeling I have for you—if you were to betray me—I would be devastated. This isn't like with Walter. I made him into something he wasn't. You, though, you're real and true. I'm in love with you, Phillip Baker."

"You are?"

"Yes. I was convinced I'd hardened myself to love until you came to me with your big heart. If you walk away because you're poor, *my* heart will be broken."

Her words melted me. "What do you want me to do?"

"Ask Papa for permission to marry me. Allow him to help you come up with a plan for your business or some other kind of employment. Take a loan from him if you have to. Don't let your pride ruin this chance we have for happiness."

"All I've had is my pride," I said, smiling.

"Now you have me. And the rest of my loud, interfering, maddening family. I'd rather live with you in a shack than in a mansion with anyone else."

I kissed her again, my heart full.

"Are you sure this is what you want?" I asked.

"I'm sure."

"I'll ask your father for permission," I said. "If he says yes, you will too?"

"Phillip, yes. I've said it already."

"All right, all right," I said, laughing at the impatience in her tone. "You must remember, I'm a man and therefore slower than you."

"Isn't that the truth?" Her face broke into a smile. She looked eight years old for a moment, delighted by a gift.

"What if he says no? What do I do then?"

"He won't. Papa wants me to be happy. He'll help us get started if we need him."

I hoped she was right. If she had read him wrong, then I didn't know what I would do to convince him to take a chance on me. The truth was simple. I was a man with no fortune whatsoever asking for the hand of an heiress. These matches were not supposed to happen. I could only hope that the wild country where he lived was also in Lord Barnes's blood.

As we set out toward home, I prayed silently. *God, send me a miracle.*

At the Cassidys', the twins and I spent the morning mending a fence and replacing decaying wood in the stalls. The Olofsson brothers weren't able to join us, and I'd picked up tension between the brothers. They usually joked and sparred during our work but today the twins were quiet.

When we broke for lunch, they didn't seem as jubilant as I felt. We'd finished up the last of the work for a family who needed us. Given their big hearts, it surprised me they weren't more excited to have completed what we set out to do.

Leaning against the side of the sleigh, we ate our sandwiches and drank hot tea from the canister Lizzie had sent. The bright midday light made the snow almost blinding, so we stood with our backs to the sun.

"I'll go inside and let the ladies know we're done for now," Flynn said.

I expected Theo to tease him about Shannon, but he didn't say anything or even nod in acknowledgment.

I waited until Flynn was inside before I turned to Theo. "Is anything wrong between you? You've hardly spoken a word all day."

Theo sighed and set his empty cup back into the lunch basket. "We've had a fight. A terrible one."

"I'm sorry to hear," I said. "Is there anything I can do?"

"The only way you could help is to take over my part in the ski venture."

"I'd hardly be qualified," I said, lightly, knowing he was joking. Yet was he? "Do you not want to do it?"

"I want to go to university like I always planned. Flynn has this way of getting me caught up in his schemes. Now I'm trapped. He can't run the ski business without someone more analytical and detail-focused. He's to be the public part of the business, dealing with people, while I run the operations." He rubbed both of his temples with his fingers, as if his head ached. "But I have to tell you, I hate every moment of it. The whole thing is dreadfully dull, and we fight over fundamental aspects of how to run the business. I'm not sure our relationship as brothers is worth the strife. We may end up completely estranged."

"What would you rather do with your life?" I couldn't imagine a better thing than to run a business with a brother.

"I want to be a surgeon."

"A surgeon?"

"During the war, I learned some techniques from the medics. They taught me how to do simple sutures, set broken bones, clean wounds. I could be useful doing this kind of work. Skiing is fine for fun, but it's not my life's work. Flynn's always wanted to be outside. The minute he saw the ski mountains in Europe, it was like a light went off inside him. He found his purpose over there. So did I. Unfortunately, they don't match up. I've been doing some soul-searching. Wandering into the snow while sleepwalking isn't right. It's time for me to do what I want. Not doing so is going to kill me. I know it to be true. I told him this last night, and we fought. Going my own way feels like a betrayal to him."

I'd already let my mind wander to dangerous places as I listened to him. I would be the perfect partner for Flynn. I had the math skills and detail orientation to run the business while Flynn charmed guests and created an atmosphere of leisure and fun. I yearned to say all this, but I knew better. They would think me ridiculous to offer up such an idea with no experience whatsoever.

Theo continued. "Flynn's reasoning isn't completely selfishly motivated. If it was, I might be able to argue against his ideas. He believes the only way Emerson Pass survives into the future is to have a business that creates work. We have to provide a place where wealthy people want to flock. A place for rich families who have income to spend on luxuries like ski vacations. Papa agrees with him. As it stands now, there aren't many more opportunities for new businesses that haven't already been taken. A town can't thrive without a larger business to build around and create jobs. The mill isn't enough. Not unless we want to sacrifice every tree on these mountains. This town is ripe for tourism. Not just the ski slopes but ice-skating as well."

I'd never heard Theo say this many words at once.

He abruptly stopped, however, when Flynn reappeared. His expression remained dour.

"Everything all right inside?" I asked.

"Yes, the ladies said to thank you," Flynn said. "I don't want to go home yet. What should we do?"

"We could stop in town and see if your father needs anything done back at home," I suggested.

As if he hadn't heard me, Flynn turned toward the northern mountain. "I'd like to show you the lodge, Phillip. Would you like to go out and see what we've done before we head home?"

"Sure, if we have time."

"I'll hitch up the horses," Theo said.

"What is it, brother?" Flynn asked Theo. "What's wrong with you now?"

I didn't know what he thought he heard in Theo's tone, as he sounded benign to me. These two knew each other's subtleties like their own reflections.

"Nothing," Theo said. "We'll do whatever you bid us to."

"It was a *question* not a *bidding*." Flynn's eyes flashed with temper. "You're finding fault where there is none."

"No fault?" Theo asked. "No fault, other than you've done this our whole lives."

"Done what? Suggested we do things other than sitting in our room reading endless books instead of living?"

"Is that what you think I do?"

"If it wasn't for me, yes," Flynn said.

"You're a donkey's ass, you know that?" Theo strode toward the barn where Oz and Willie waited.

Unsure what to do, I made myself busy packing up the remnants of our lunch.

"Sorry you had to hear all that," Flynn said.

"Not at all."

"He wants out of this whole thing." Flynn squinted as he looked up to the sky. "Believes I pushed him into it, which I suppose I did. I get excited about something and always want him with me. He has other plans. Ones that don't include me. Growing up, that never occurred to me. I thought we'd do everything together."

"You two have a bond that goes deeper than most brothers," I said. "Which complicates matters sometimes."

"I didn't know he was resentful until recently." He took off his cap and ran his hands through his hair. "And now this. I don't know what to do here."

"Let him go." I blurted it out without much thought. "Hire someone to manage the business. I'm sure there are a lot of men who would jump at the chance."

"I want a partner. Someone with stakes in the game."

Theo came out of the barn leading the horses. The twins didn't speak as they worked in tandem to hitch Oz and Willie, each taking a horse. Their movements were almost identical. Yet there were profound differences in their dreams and desires. I hoped, for their sakes, that this didn't become a permanent divide. No business was worth losing your brother. Having none of my own, I knew that in a way most couldn't. Parting ways would be difficult, even for Theo. But perhaps it was necessary for them to become the men they wanted to be.

FIFTEEN MINUTES LATER, we came to a stop in front of the lodge built from logs. I squinted into the light, taking in the mountain. The slopes had been stripped of trees for two ski runs that snaked down the mountain in snowy rivulets.

Flynn hopped out of the sleigh. "By this time next year, skiers will be speeding down these runs. Isn't it a beauty?" Flynn asked, pointing to the gear-and-pulley system for the ski lift. "That takes you up to the top. You won't even break a sweat. Come on, Phillip. We'll show you the inside."

I followed him into the log building. Theo trailed behind us, but joined us just the same.

The large rectangular room was as rustic on the inside as out. Crevices between the logs had been closed with cement. "You can't imagine how long it took us to strip these logs," Flynn said, sounding proud. "The Olofsson boys helped us but even so, it took us the better part of the spring."

"They look great," I said, feeling as if I'd been asked to comment on a man's child.

Flynn strutted around, showing me where the bar would be that would serve warm beverages and sandwiches. "Tables will be there." He pointed to the area closest to the windows. "Where people can eat and drink or just relax and warm up before going back out again."

"We wanted to serve beer," Theo said. "But with Prohibition, it won't be possible."

"Still possible," Flynn said. "If my puritan brother looks the other way."

"I don't want us shut down for breaking the law." Theo glared at Flynn. "But my criminal-minded twin refuses to see reason."

"You know as well as I do that the bar in town will serve homemade brews and liquor in secret." Flynn pointed to a trapdoor on the floor. "We have a basement for just this purpose."

Was his plan to serve alcohol downstairs or make it? Regardless, I didn't think interfering in their argument to ask would be welcomed at this time.

"What do you think?" Theo asked me.

"I...I don't know. The new law will most certainly be violated. I don't think people will give up their liquor just because the government tells them to."

"Especially out west," Flynn said.

"Whatever you decide, you'll need to be united." I inwardly cringed, waiting for one or the other to start arguing again.

"But what do you think, Phillip?" Flynn asked. "We want to know your opinion. Break our tie."

I really didn't want to share my thoughts, but I did anyway. "I don't know much about the tourist business, but I'd think serving liquor would be profitable. As long as you didn't get caught."

"See there, he's reasonable," Flynn said.

"If we didn't get caught," Theo said. "Which is not guaranteed."

"You could put systems into place," I said. "Ways to dump the liquor or hide it if the cops show up."

"Or we could just buy off our sheriff," Flynn said. "Everyone knows Lancaster's a crook anyway."

"The only thing we agree on," Theo said. "Lancaster is no better than the criminals he puts away."

"Perhaps you could agree to set this argument aside for now," I said. "It's not really important that you decide right away." To distract them from further strife, I gestured around the room, rattling off ideas of how things could be laid out, including where to put the fireplace. "What matters more is the atmosphere. If you want to attract rich tourists, then you should decorate with women in mind. For those who don't ski, they might like to spend the afternoon here. You'll want a roaring fire, don't you think? I could build a special mantel, maybe with etchings of bears and deer or something indicative of the area? Definitely soft couches where people can rest after a long day of skiing. For that matter, have you thought about having an inn on the property? Otherwise, where will the tourists stay?"

They were both staring at me as I turned back to look their way. "Have I overstepped? I apologize. This project has my blood pumping."

"No, don't stop," Flynn said. "What other ideas do you have?"

"Maybe not an inn," I said, thinking out loud. "But something grander and bigger, like they have in Europe? Do you know the ones I mean? You also need an activity that could bring them here in the summers."

"Fly-fishing," Flynn said under his breath. "We could advertise it as a fishing vacation. People could stay for a week. I'd take them out to the best spots."

"Sell the gear here," I said, unable to keep the excitement out of my voice. “Waders, flies, the whole bit. Same with skis and clothing. That way you have more revenue than just the slopes.”

Flynn and Theo exchanged a look.

“This is what I was talking about last night,” Theo said. “The kind of enthusiasm and ideas that I don’t have but should. You need a partner as driven and excited by this enterprise as you are.”

“Are you thinking what I’m thinking?” Flynn asked his brother.

Theo’s expression changed from combative to contemplative. “It’s fairly obvious. The answer to all our problems is staring us right in the face. Phillip has an obvious affinity for this kind of work. His strengths complement yours.” He turned toward me. “Phillip, you need a livelihood if you’re going to support Jo.”

“This solves it all.” Flynn grinned. “I’m a genius.”

“But...but I’m not qualified. I know nothing about skiing.” Despite my protestation, my stomach fluttered with excitement.

“Who cares? You have business sense. That’s what we need.” Flynn placed a hand on my shoulder. “What do you say, old boy? Would you like to be my partner?”

“I don’t have any equity to buy my way in.” This fact deflated me. There was no way I could be an equal partner.

“I’ll lend it to you,” Theo said. “You’re doing me a favor by getting me out of this, so it’s the least I can do. As you become profitable, you can pay me back slowly.”

“‘Getting me out of this’?” Flynn asked, repeating Theo’s words back to him. “Is it really that bad to you?”

“The thought of being able to attend university is a huge weight off my shoulders,” Theo said. “I need to go my own way. Anyway, Phillip’s going to become our brother once he marries Jo, so it’s still in the family.”

“If your father says yes,” I said.

“You know he will,” Flynn said. “We know, anyway.”

“We’ve never seen our sensible, serious sister quite so happy,” Theo said. “And for that, we thank you.”

"All right then, do we have an agreement?" Flynn asked. "Should we shake on it?"

We did so. In the firm grip of the twins' hands, my life seemed to unfold before me. God had granted me my miracle. Was it possible I was getting what I'd wanted for so long? A family. Good, honest work. And the woman of my dreams.

Josephine

After breakfast, Poppy and I went out to the Cassidys'. When we arrived, Shannon and Nora were in the barn feeding the cattle.

"They're so thin," Poppy whispered to me.

"It's been a hard time for them. Which is why I'm glad you're here to help." In my normal voice, I shouted out to them, "Girls, I have a surprise."

They turned in tandem to look at us. Both the girls wore overalls and men's rubber boots. Their hair was covered with scarves, like peasant girls.

Nora squealed. "Poppy, is it really you?" She set aside her pitchfork and ran to us.

"Yes, I've returned," Poppy said.

Shannon put her shovel against the wall and approached. "I'm a mess or I'd hug you. We must look a fright." She placed her hand over the scarf. "But we have chores all day long."

"Don't be silly. I've been away too long for you not to hug me." Poppy embraced both girls. "I'm very sorry to hear about your dad."

Shannon's eyes teared up. "Thank you. He didn't suffer. Heart attack."

"We can be grateful for that," Poppy said. "He was a kind man. I remember how encouraging he was to me when I left for training. I promised him I'd bring back whatever knowledge I could."

"He spoke highly of you until the day he died," Shannon said. "My sisters and I teased him that he wished he'd had a daughter like you."

"Your hair looks like a magazine cover I saw," Nora said, shyly.

"You look different, but I guess we do too," Shannon said. "Dressed like boys."

"I think you look strong and independent," Poppy said. "Which is to be admired. Now, tell me about the sick cows you lost."

I left them to it and went inside the house to take the basket of food Lizzie had prepared. When I reached the front door, I knocked and waited for Mrs. Cassidy. Soon, she arrived, opening the door and greeting me with a smile.

"Come in, lass. You've brought more food? I'll never be able to repay your family for their kindness."

"Nonsense. We're neighbors." I set the basket on their new kitchen table. The room smelled of coffee. Dough for bread was rising in a bowl near the stove. "How are you feeling today?"

"The doctor came out a few days ago and gave me some powder to take when I feel one of the headaches coming on." She spoke faintly, as if worried to bring one on by speaking too loudly.

Pale and wan, her color looked no better than the last time I'd come. "Has it helped?"

"I haven't had a headache since. Isn't that just the way?"

I suspected that having the men repair the barn and the other chores had eased her mind, which in turn helped the headaches.

"Please, sit. Would you like coffee?" Mrs. Cassidy wiped her hands on the front of her apron. "I've not much else to offer."

"No, thank you. I've had enough this morning." I sat at the table in one of the rickety chairs. One of the legs was shorter than the others, making it wobble as I shifted to look at her. "Poppy's out with the girls. I brought her to see if she can figure out what happened with your cattle last summer."

"I do hope she can. Shannon's worried herself sick about the remainder of the herd." She sighed as she sat across from me. "My poor girls have the weight of the world on their shoulders. I wish I'd had a son to take some of their burden."

"You should be proud that they're doing the work of a man."

"I am, truly. However, 'tis not the life I'd hoped to give them when I left my mother country."

"Are you still thinking of returning to Ireland?"

She shook her head as she glanced out the window in the direction of the barn. The light through the glass made it so the fine lines around her eyes and mouth were visible. Mrs. Cassidy was so young to have lost her husband. The last year had aged her. "The girls are vehemently opposed to the idea. Since they've taken on their father's duties, I can't argue. If they're willing to do the work to stay, then who am I to argue? Anyway, all our friends are here. The last few weeks have certainly made me see how much community matters. I wish I'd reached out sooner."

"Speaking of which, I have a question for you." I laid out the idea for the party. "It'll be a fun event to celebrate the season but also provide some financial relief to you."

Mrs. Cassidy wiped her eyes with the corner of her apron. "Oh, you good people. I can't thank you enough. Having people into your home, just for us? I don't know what to say."

"Perhaps someday you'll be in the position to do for others. That's how it is, isn't it? Sometimes we're in the position to help. Other times we need help."

A worried look replaced the one of gratitude. "The girls and I don't have anything we can wear. Nothing that wouldn't embarrass us."

"Mama is about your size. And my sisters and I have a few dresses to spare."

"I don't know. That's too much."

"Please, let us do this for you. For your girls. Don't they deserve a fun evening where they can get dressed up and dance?"

"Yes, when you put it that way, I can see you're right. I can't deprive them of it." She dabbed at her eyes again. "May I speak to you about another worry?"

"Of course. Anything."

"My Shannon has developed a crush on your brother Flynn. I'm afraid she'll make a fool out of herself. A girl like mine isn't likely to attract a Barnes."

I covered my mouth briefly as it twitched into a smile. "Mrs. Cassidy, you underestimate your daughter's inner and outer beauty. She's indeed caught the eye of my brother. It's not only her who's smitten. We were afraid you'd think him too much of a rascal for your daughter."

"I've known all you kids from when you were small," she said. "I remember him as a little boy. How sweet he was to the little ones."

"True. He has a big heart, even if sometimes he causes trouble."

"He's brave, too. My daughter would be lucky to have him."

"Well, now that we've got that settled, you and I should agree not to interfere. If they think they have our approval, it might cool the entire process."

We were interrupted when Poppy and the girls entered the kitchen.

"What do you think, Poppy?" Mrs. Cassidy asked. "What's killing our cows?"

"It's the acorns that have done it," Poppy said.

"Acorns?" I asked.

"Yes, acorns." Poppy gestured toward the window. "There are all these oak trees just outside your fences. They drop their acorns and the cows eat them, not knowing they're poisonous—gives them the very symptoms your girls described to me. We had a similar case last year on one of the ranches."

"What do we do?" Mrs. Cassidy asked.

"You're going to have to cut down the trees unless you want it to keep happening," Poppy said.

"Or pick up a thousand acorns a season," Shannon said. "We have enough to do."

"Once the snow melts, the boys and Phillip can come out and help you fell the trees," I said. "It'll be good firewood, anyway."

"I can't thank you enough," Mrs. Cassidy said. "We can't afford to lose any more."

"This should take care of it," Poppy said. "And I'll be around in the spring to check on them."

Mrs. Cassidy started to cry again as she rose to her feet. "How can we ever thank you?"

"Keeping your girls here is enough thanks," Poppy said. "Give it time, your circumstances will improve. I'll be here whenever you need me and for the rest of the community. I have to make Lord Barnes proud that he sent me to Dr. Miller."

"You already have," I said.

"WHAT DO YOU THINK, JO?" Flynn asked as he plopped down next to me on the couch in the sitting room. Theo stood with his back to the fire, watching me with glittering eyes.

They'd spent the last few minutes pitching their idea to bring Phillip into the ski and tourist business. Initially, I'd not been sure. Phillip's passion had seemed to be in woodworking. Running the operations of a ski lodge and the mountain seemed wrong somehow. However, the more I listened to Flynn describing how Phillip had lit up with excitement while banging out ideas had me rethinking my position.

"Do you think he'll be happy?" I asked. "Or is he doing this for me?"

"You make him happy," Theo said. "Whether he's doing it for you or not seems irrelevant."

"I disagree," I said. "If he does it for me, eventually he'll come to hate it and resent me."

"Like Theo's done?" Flynn asked.

We were all quiet for a moment. The truth of his statement couldn't be denied.

"I'm sorry, Theo," Flynn said after a few more moments of awkward silence.

"Don't be." Theo gave him a weary smile. "You've given your blessing for me to start down my own path. We can put aside our resentments, can't we?"

"Yes, of course, brother," Flynn said before turning to me. "Don't you see, Jo, that this is an answer for all of us? We're all getting what we want, including Phillip."

Theo nodded. "He's genuinely excited, and he has an affinity for business."

"He wants to be part of a team," Flynn said. "Family, brotherhood. All the things the three of us have taken for granted."

"As long as he's sure," I said. "A man doesn't like to feel obligated to his wife's family. The loan worries me."

"Ah, Jo, don't worry so much," Flynn said. "All will be well."

I looked into the warm eyes of my brother. Of the three of us, he was the one who didn't worry, instead plunging into everything with unbridled sureness that everything would work out to his advantage. Perhaps his approach was better than Theo's and mine, fretting over every decision? Whatever the case might be, I would go along with whatever Phillip decided. He wanted to make a path for the two of us to marry, which I wanted too. I hoped that he wouldn't have to give up too much of his pride and dignity in order to do so.

Theo moved from the fire over to sit on my other side. He

placed his hand over mine. "Jo, this is good for all of us. I truly believe it with all my heart."

Flynn took my other hand. "Jo, please say you approve."

"I approve." I smiled at them both in turn. "May God help us all."

"Amen," my brothers said in tandem.

I WOKE in the middle of the night from a dream. I sat up and turned on the bedside lamp. My heart pounded and my nightgown was damp with perspiration. Several deep breaths later, I slipped from bed and shed my flannel gown. Shivering, I crept over to the dresser and pulled out fresh nightclothes. Instead of going back to bed, I went to the window. The night was clear, with a full moon hanging in the sky.

Edges of the dream came back to me. I'd been dreaming of my mother. She'd been standing over me with a knife while I slept. In the dream, I'd opened my eyes just before the knife plunged into my chest.

"What are you doing?" I'd asked her as my hand wrapped around her wrist.

"Theo," she said. Then I woke.

Theo. Regardless of my brothers' agreement, Theo was in trouble. Would giving up his part in the business help? I hoped so.

A flicker of light near the barn caught my eye. I pressed closer to the glass. A silhouette of a man standing at the fence. Theo. He was outside. Sleepwalking?

I threw on a coat and stuck my feet into the boots I wore to the barn and headed out of my room and down the stairs.

I tore out of the house. The walkway to the barn slick under my feet, I ran as fast as I could, slipping once and breaking the fall with my bare hands. Only vaguely aware of a stinging pain on my palms, I got up and started again. By the time I reached the barn, Theo had turned toward me.

"Theo, are you all right?"

"Jo, what are you doing?"

He seemed lucid enough. His eyes were open, and his voice sounded normal.

"What are *you* doing?" I asked in response.

"Taking a midnight stroll. What did you think?"

"I thought you might be sleepwalking."

He shook his head. "No, I'm fine."

I drew closer, still unsure about his state. "Why would you be out here at this time of night?"

"I couldn't sleep." His cheeks glistened under the moonlight. Damp from tears, I realized.

"Oh, Theo, what's the matter?"

"I can't shake the memories, Jo. That's all. And nightmares. Sometimes I'm afraid to fall asleep."

I plunged my hands into my coat. Cold had crept up my bare legs. "No one knows what to do for you."

"I'm not sure there is anything. Other than for me to delve into a purpose. Some way for me to focus on something other than the past."

"Is that why you're so keen on university?"

"Partly, I guess."

"What's the other part?"

"I don't know how to describe it, really. This feeling all the time...like I want to crawl out of my own body."

I looked up at the sky. The stars twinkled back at me, encouragingly, but I couldn't draw on their light tonight. The darkness surrounded me. My little brother was hurting, and there wasn't a thing I could do to help him.

"If I could become a doctor and save people, then perhaps God would forgive me for the things I did over there. The lives I took."

"Theo, you were only doing what was asked of you."

"I'm a man for whom what's asked of me is too much to bear. The others didn't think of our enemy as men. But I did, Jo. I could imagine their mothers, like our Quinn, waiting for their return. Praying on their knees every night for their return. And I took that from them. These wars, fought for what? Men who want more territory to rule? Who pays the price? Mothers, wives, sisters. All for nothing."

I couldn't argue with him. These were thoughts I'd so often contemplated while my brothers, Isak, and Walter were over there. Even now, knowing what Walter had done, I mourned his loss and those of all the men and women all over the world who'd paid the ultimate price. And as my brother said, for what?

"I wonder sometimes," Theo said, "if what we were fighting for is even true?"

"The fight for freedom for all?"

"Yes, but are we really free?"

"For those of us in countries ruled by democracy, I suppose we're as free as we can be.'"

"I don't feel free. I feel chained by these demons in my mind." He brushed a layer of snow from the top of the fence. "I used to think if I could just get home, I'd be all right. Stay alive. That's all I thought about. Now that I'm here, I realize that living wasn't the only thing I should have worried about. I should have been more concerned over what lasting damage I would bring home with me."

"Yes, I see that now too. I was the same, praying only, 'Bring them home.'"

"Flynn says he's fine, but I know different. Isak too. None of us will ever be the carefree boys we were before the war."

"I'm not sure any of us can ever be like we were as children. The war changed us here at home too. But Theo, even before that, we had tragedy and hardness inside us. You and I haven't been innocent since Mother died."

"Even before that. Her strangeness and violence."

"The girls were too young to remember, and Flynn, well, he

has a way of directing all his energy into the current moment. But the two of us, we were the ones who suffered."

He turned his head to look at me for a moment before returning his gaze to the blanket of snow. "Yes. You and me."

"Yet I feel as helpless as I ever did. When you came in that day after finding Mother, I knew in my heart that you would never be the little boy you were supposed to be. She robbed you of it. I hated her for that."

"Do you still hate her?"

"I try not to think of her at all."

"I have more pity for her than I did before—understanding and empathy. I'm frightened I'm becoming her." His voice shook as he uttered those last words.

"No, Theo. You're not like her. I remember her better than you. You're not mentally ill. You're haunted by your experiences. Horrible ones at that. It's not the same thing." I wanted desperately for him to believe me. As I stood there watching a myriad of emotions cross his face, I didn't know if he ever would. Or could, for that matter.

"I don't know what to do, Jo."

I searched for the right thing to say, feeling as if my next words were the most important I would ever say. Papa had said to me once that our only purpose in life was to discover how we could best serve others with our particular talents. "Theo, of all of us, you're the smartest. You've always been the scholar of the family. Become a doctor. Help people. Purge the demons with service to others."

"Papa's been telling that to us all our lives. I think that sentiment is what made Flynn determined to enlist. His brawn, you know. Fighting against the bad with his muscles."

I smiled, thinking of my physically gifted brother. "He did what he had to do to feel as if he was giving what he could to the world. Now it's your turn to do the same."

"I have a confession to make."

"What is it?"

"There's another reason I've been angry with Flynn."

I waited.

"Louisa's in love with him. The girl I want, wants my twin."

My heart sank. Poor Theo. "How do you know?"

"I found a letter she wrote to him during the war. He never told me about it, knowing how I felt. I'm trying not to feel jealous, but I can't help it. He got everything I wish I had."

Phillip

The night of the party, I stood in front of the mirror fiddling with my tie. The twins were already dressed in their formal evening suits and were sprawled on their beds.

"I'm hoping Shannon's feeling nothing but warm things for me and will dance with me all night," Flynn said.

A knock on the door drew our attention.

"It's Cymbeline," came the voice on the other side of the door. "I need to come in."

"Enter at your own risk," Flynn called out to her.

The door opened and Cymbeline appeared. She wore a light blue dress with shimmery capped sleeves. Her hair was fixed in a sophisticated bun, with shiny tendrils framing her face.

"Can you believe Mama's making me wear this dress?" Cymbeline put her hands on her hips. "I look like that blue pincushion she has in her basket. And look at my hair. Jo made it all...all...womanly and grown-up."

"What's the matter with that?" Flynn asked. "You look pretty."

Cymbeline stomped her foot. "I don't want to be a pincushion. Fiona got to wear a normal dress instead of this formal thing."

"She's only thirteen," Theo said. "I thought you'd be happy to wear a grown-up dress."

"I'm not. All the boys from school are going to laugh at me when they see me this way."

"I don't think laughing is quite what it'll be," Flynn said, frowning. "As a matter of fact, it's best if you stay with one of us throughout the night."

"I agree," I said. "You're much too pretty. We'll have to watch you like a hawk."

She lifted her chin, looking very haughty. "I shan't allow any of them to put me in a compromising position. I'll sock them in the nose."

If she hadn't looked like an angel with her alabaster skin and shining brown hair and full mouth, she might have a chance of intimidating the boys. But Flynn was right. The boys were not going to be laughing at her, nor would they be scared of her. At sixteen, she was already a great beauty, even more evident in the lovely dress. The boys of Emerson Pass didn't have a chance.

"Don't worry, Cymbie, we'll take care of you," Flynn said. "No one's going to mess with our little sister."

She marched up to him and shoved him in the chest. He fell backward onto the pillows and burst into raucous laughter. "You know I hate it when you say that. I do not need anyone to take care of me, especially my brothers."

"All right, don't hurt me, Cymbie," Flynn said as he put up his fists as if to protect his face. "We'll throw you to the wolves if that's what you want."

"Great. That's exactly what I want." She crossed her arms over her chest and glared at him. "And stop laughing at me."

"I'm sorry, but you're too funny," Flynn said. "I can't help myself."

"Calm down, little sister," Theo said. "You'll wreck your hair."

She twirled around to face him. "Do you think I give one fig about my hair?"

"Well, you should." We all turned to see Josephine in the doorway. "It took me a good amount of time to tame that head of hair of yours. I won't appreciate you ruining it before the party even starts."

I tried not to stare, but my eyes were glued to Jo. She wore a soft lavender dress and long white gloves that came to just below her shoulders. Her hair was fixed in an elaborate twist that I'd never seen before but emphasized her eyes and elegant neck.

"You." Cymbeline pointed at Josephine. "You and Mama have conspired against me."

"To make you a proper young lady? I can't say we haven't." She gestured for Cymbeline to come to her. "Now, come here, my little tiger girl. We're to go down together. Papa's request."

"I'd rather spend the night with the animals," Cymbeline muttered to herself.

From behind Josephine, Fiona appeared, then ducked under Josephine's arm to enter the room. "Oh, you all look especially nice tonight. Isn't it wonderful we can all be together to have fun but also help the Cassidys?"

"For heaven's sake, Fiona, you're impossibly cheery," Cymbeline said. But the edge had left her voice. I'd noticed before that Fiona had the ability to calm her sister with just her presence. She looked sweet in a sailor-collared dress in the same blue as Cymbeline's dress but cut just below the knees. A wide white bow tied back her hair.

"Shall we go downstairs en masse then?" Flynn asked. "The original five plus our esteemed guest?"

"Where are the little ones?" I asked.

"They're already downstairs with Mama," Fiona said. "She said they could have cake and stay for a little while."

"I hated when they had parties with all the cakes and cookies and we weren't invited," Cymbeline said.

"Remember the time we sent you up in the dumbwaiter to try to steal some treats?" Theo asked.

"And you got stuck in between the floors," Flynn said. "Which might be the funniest thing that's ever happened to us."

Cymbeline scowled. "Of course I remember. How could I forget? I thought I'd be in there until I perished from lack of food and water."

"She thought we left her in there to die," Josephine said to me. "But we'd only gone for help."

Cymbeline flashed an evil grin and rubbed her hands together. "While they were gone, I spent the entire time thinking of all the ways I was going to haunt them when I came back as a ghost."

"What was one of them?" Flynn asked.

"I was going to drip water on your faces while you slept," Cymbeline said. "Another was to take your things and hide them and laugh as you tried to find them. Eventually, I'd make you think you'd gone loony. It was all part of my master plan."

"An evil mind at work," Theo said.

"No, she would never really have done those things," Fiona said. "Even as a ghost."

"Our little princess always sees the best in people," Theo said.

"Even when it's not true," Flynn said.

"To think I actually missed you two while you were gone," Cymbeline said.

Josephine laughed as she took Cymbeline's hand and tugged her toward the doorway. "Come along, wicked one. Let's go have fun."

We all followed behind. Theo had given Fiona his arm and they shared a special smile as they walked into the hallway. That left Flynn and me. He held out his hand for me to shake. "Don't be shy tonight. Josephine loves to dance."

"Thanks, I'll do my best."

"That's all we can do, brother."

Brother. I liked the sound of that.

THE PARLOR HAD BEEN TRANSFORMED into a festive fairyland of twinkling lights. The crystal chandelier cast sparkles that danced on the walls. A Christmas tree decorated with real lights filled the room with its spicy scent. Furniture had been moved aside to make way for dancers. A table on the far end of the wall was covered with treats: cakes, cookies, pies, and candy. From a large glass bowl, Lizzie scooped red punch into champagne flutes and set them in tidy rows on the table. Mrs. Wu, whom I'd never seen outside of the kitchen, came up with a stack of plates and silverware. Fiona went straight to the piano to organize her sheet music.

"Have a punch," Josephine said to me. "Enjoy yourself. I have to play hostess for the next bit."

Guests began to arrive, seemingly all at once. Fiona and Li played one merry Christmas tune after the other as the room filled. Jasper and Lord Barnes were back and forth, answering the door, taking coats and escorting folks into the formal room. Josephine and Quinn made sure everyone had a drink or something to eat. I stood in the corner near the tree watching it all.

Theo came to stand with me, pointing out who was who and giving me brief details of how they were connected to the family. He stiffened when Pastor Lind and his wife, Pamela, came through the doors with a young woman between them. She was petite, like Josephine if not a bit taller. Dark blond tresses were set in attractive waves and pulled back to the nape of her neck. Large blue eyes darted immediately our way.

He turned to face me with his back to the door. "That's Louisa. She must be back from finishing school. I haven't seen her since I left for the war." His voice had turned raspy during this description. "She's prettier than when I left," Theo said. "Which I didn't think was possible."

"Will you go say hello?" I asked him as quietly as I could while pretending to look around the room with no particular interest on anyone or anything. "She's looking this way."

"I can't. I wouldn't know what to say. The last time I saw her I made a complete blunder."

"How so?"

"I declared my undying love and asked if she'd write to me while I was away."

"Why is that a blunder?"

"She burst into tears and ran away," Theo said. "That was before I knew she was in love with my brother."

"No, really?"

"Yes, really," he said. "She wants someone like him. Quick and strong."

"Why do you say that?"

"She had a hard time until Pastor Lind and his wife took her in as their own when she was nine years old. Her father had hurt her, torturing her with horrible games like chasing her through the woods with a shotgun to teach her how to be tough."

"How awful." My stomach turned at the thought of anyone doing such a thing to an innocent child.

"As the years went by, living with the Linds, I saw her flourish. She lost the scared look in her eyes, like she was waiting for the next punch."

We'd had a few children at the orphanage who had come from violent homes. They had had the wary look of an abused animal, watchful and suspicious. Any loud or abrupt movement made them jump or instinctively cover their faces.

Louisa was making her way directly toward us. "She's coming right over to us," I said under my breath.

"What? Are you sure?"

He had no more time to ask questions. She was upon us, giving me a shy smile before touching her fingers to the sleeve of Theo's jacket. "Hi, Theo."

He turned toward her, acting surprised to see her. "Hi, Louisa. Are you home from school?" He kissed her gloved hand.

She nodded, ducking her chin modestly. "Yes, I've graduated finally. I now know all the forks and can walk across the room with a book on my head."

"Allow me to introduce you to our friend Phillip Baker." He put his hand on my shoulder. "Phillip, meet Louisa Lind."

She turned to me. "Pleased to meet you."

"Pleased to meet you as well." I took her offered hand and bowed my head in greeting.

"Is Flynn here?" Louisa asked Theo.

Right away asking after Flynn. My sympathy for Theo deepened. To be the one not chosen was never easy, heightened when your rival was your charming, popular brother.

Theo spoke quickly without seeming to breathe between sentences. "He's around somewhere, talking with Shannon Cassidy last I noticed. Would you like punch? Either of you? I'm going to have some with some whiskey."

"I'd love a punch," Louisa said.

"Me too," I said.

"I'll be right back." Theo didn't wait for a response, charging across the room toward the punch bowl.

I cleared my throat. What did I do now? I had a good mind to give her a tongue-lashing. How insensitive to ask after his brother, given their last interaction.

"You've been staying here at the Barneses'?" Louisa asked.

"Yes, I have."

"How is Theo? Does he seem all right?"

I didn't know how much she knew about his mental state, and I didn't want to be the one who spilled family secrets. "He seems fine to me." *Other than being lovesick over you*, I thought.

"Mother said he didn't seem himself when she saw him in town at the festival. I've been worried about him."

She was worried about him? As a friend, I supposed. "I understand you all go way back."

"Yes, we were all together at school when we were younger. The twins and Isak went off to war and everything seemed to change overnight. I miss the old days when we were all still children."

"Time does keep on, doesn't it?"

"Too fast. Other than while they were away. Time seemed to have slowed as we waited for the hideous war to be over and return our boys to us. Then, I was sent away to school just as they were about to return. I've longed to see all of my old friends but especially the twins. Their family is special to me."

The twins? Or just Flynn? "They've been very good to me."

"Mother said as much." She looked up at me with friendly eyes but also ones that I could easily imagine wary and questioning. The years had not completely restored her innocence. She'd known cruelty and terror. They still lurked beneath her finishing school shine. "She also told me what you and the others have done out at the Cassidys'. We appreciate your efforts."

I smiled down at her. "It's the least I could do for a community that's welcomed me. I've never really had a home."

"I was never at an orphanage, but I know what you mean."

Theo returned with glasses of punch for Louisa and me.

"Are you happy to be home?" Theo asked her as he handed her the glass.

"More than I can say. After being in Chicago, I'm even more certain I prefer the country to the city."

"I think Phillip here feels the same way."

I chuckled, nodding my head. "As long as I'm not run out of town, I'm here for good."

"I hadn't known how special it was until I was no longer here. One doesn't know what they have sometimes until it's gone." Her brow wrinkled as she peered into her punch.

Theo watched her lift the glass to her mouth and take a sip.

"Father tells me you and Flynn have taken out a path of trees from the mountain for skiing?"

"That's right. We're copying slopes we saw in Europe."

"I do hope it won't bring too many people. I like our sleepy town the way it is." Louisa's gaze traveled across to the doorway as Flynn entered the room. "There he is," she said under her breath, as if she'd forgotten us entirely.

I stole a glance at Theo as he downed his drink.

Louisa raised her hand in greeting as Flynn approached.

"Hello, Louisa, welcome home," Flynn said as he kissed her hand.

She'd flushed pink. "Thank you. You as well. Did you get my letters?"

His face, in direct juxtaposition to Louisa's, paled as he shot a guilty look in Theo's direction. "Sure did. Thank you."

"I thought maybe they hadn't arrived since I never heard back from you," Louisa said.

"Um, right. Sorry about that. I'm not much of a letter writer," Flynn said.

Her gaze returned to her drink as she spoke just above a whisper, clearly trying not to cry. "I should go say hello to some of the others. Have a nice night, gentlemen."

She scurried across the room and out the door, leaving the three of us in awkward silence.

"I'm sorry," Flynn said. "I didn't ask for her to write."

"It's all right." Theo downed the rest of his drink. "I know how it is."

"I didn't want you to find out, especially not like this." Flynn spoke softly. "I'm sorry."

"I already knew. I saw the letters."

"Oh. Damn, I'm sorry. I feel like a heel."

"It's not your fault," Theo said. "You're naturally charming and funny. I don't stand a chance."

"She's just one girl," Flynn said. "Look at all the others right in front of you."

"Easy for you to say," Theo said. "You could have any of your choosing."

"Why her, anyway?" Flynn took a flask from his pocket and took a swig.

"Why does anyone fall for anyone?" Theo held his glass out. "Give me some of that, will you?"

Flynn poured from the flask into Theo's empty punch glass. "Forget her. She's not in her right mind if she chooses me over you." Flynn said this lightly, obviously trying to cajole Theo out of his dark mood.

"Sure. Whatever you say." Theo took a sip of whiskey, then coughed. "I'm going outside for some air." He put up a hand as both of us seemed to be about to offer to go with him. "Alone."

We both watched him cross the room and walk out the door.

"What am I going to do about this?" Flynn asked.

"I'm not sure. I feel terrible for both of them. She's obviously got it bad for you."

"Right. Great. I can't seem to win with my brother lately."

Josephine floated over to us, rescuing me. "What's wrong? You both look like a storm's hovering over your heads."

"Theo and Louisa," Flynn said.

"Oh, that," Jo said.

"She asked me why I hadn't answered her letters," Flynn said. "Right in front of Theo."

"How insensitive," Jo said.

"Agreed," I said.

Shannon Cassidy appeared. With her hair fixed and wearing a beaded green dress, she looked like a different girl than the one I'd seen a few days before at the farm.

Flynn lit up like the Christmas tree at the sight of her. He took both her hands. "You look...just...beautiful."

She smiled and made a little curtsy. "Thank you. I feel like the queen of England tonight."

"You look like it was made for you," Jo said.

"Thank you for the dress and all of this." Shannon's eyes glimmered with tears. "I won't ever forget this night for as long as I live."

Fiona started a waltz on the piano.

"Dance with me?" Flynn asked Shannon.

"Yes, sure."

He took her hand and they went out to the floor, joining a half dozen other couples.

I looked over at Josephine. "May I have this dance?"

"Yes, you may." Her smile weakened my knees. Hopefully I'd be able to remain on my feet.

I escorted Jo onto the dance floor, then tucked one arm around her slender waist and took her hand in the other. I'd not felt the whole of her against me before. It was all I could do not to scoop her into my arms and carry her upstairs. "Have I told you how beautiful you are tonight?" I asked close to her ear.

"Not yet." She peeked up at me. I missed a step.

"I'm sorry," I said. "I'm a clod when it comes to dancing."

"You're not."

"It's that your presence causes my legs to go slightly numb."

"Isn't that only in romantic books?"

"I can tell you with certainty that it is not."

"Oh, Phillip, I adore you." She sighed as she rested her cheek against my chest. "I could stay this way forever."

"Some nights should last forever," I said.

"But they won't, will they? The morning will come whether we want it to or not."

"When a moment's shared between two people, it can always be resurrected. One day, we'll be sitting on the porch, old and gray, and I'll say, 'Jo, do you remember the night we first danced together?'"

"And I'll say, 'Yes, you were dashing in your evening suit and I liked the scent of your shaving soap.' What will you say back?"

"That there's never been a more beautiful woman in the history of the world than Josephine Barnes."

"You're a charming older man. I can't wait to meet you in the future." She giggled. "Will we really ever be old and gray? I can't imagine being anything other than what we are right now."

"If we're lucky, we'll live a long life together and have many stories to tell our children and grandchildren about our love story."

"I hope so," Jo said.

"A lifetime of wonderful memories, if I have my way," I said.

The song drew to a close, but we remained wrapped together swaying gently until the notes of the next song began. We needed only the music made from the mingled beating of our hearts.

Josephine

Several days after the party, I stood on the ladder in the library, shelving returned books on the upper stacks. I hummed a tune, happy with the outcome of our party for the Cassidys. We'd raised enough money for them to live comfortably through the winter and to replace several of the cattle they lost with babies come spring.

The morning had been busy with patrons gathering books for the Christmas holiday, and I hadn't had a chance to put away books. We would be closed tomorrow for Christmas and throughout the holiday weekend. People didn't want to be left without a good read. Outside, the sky seemed to press close. A blizzard was coming. I hurried, not wanting to stay later than necessary.

Fiona had come into work with me today to help with the rush. Phillip was to arrive just after four to take us home. We'd be home and safe by the time the storm hit.

What a month it has been, I thought as I put away the last of the books. A whirlwind of emotions, beginning with the sting of betrayal, but quickly and completely replaced by falling in love with Phillip.

Fiona had begged me to bring her in with me, as she was

bored at home without school to occupy her. I had her in the back office, working on the numbers. Papa had recently shown her how to keep books and budget. He'd suggested I let her practice her new skills with the library budgeting for the upcoming year. Since I detested this work, I was only too happy to have her help. I'd have Papa look it over to make sure her findings were accurate.

From the top rung of the ladder, I saw that the last of my patrons, Mrs. Rory and her daughter, June, were waiting for me at the checkout desk. "I'll be right there, Mrs. Rory."

"Thank you, Miss Barnes."

I carefully climbed down the ladder and scurried over to assist them.

"Sorry to keep you waiting," I said. "I didn't notice you there."

"It's no problem at all," Mrs. Rory said.

"How are you today, June?" I asked. "Are you bored at home without school like Addie?"

She nodded, peeking up at me with shy eyes.

The Rorys and their daughter, June, lived here in town, just on the other side of the church. They'd come from back east somewhere. Her husband worked at the train station. June and Addie were in the same grade at school.

We made small talk as I listed the books in my log. June continued to stare at me, with one small fist wrapped in the material of her mother's wool coat.

"These are all good choices." I pushed the stack of books across the desk. "*The Five Little Peppers and How They Grew* is a favorite at my house."

"Addie's my friend," June said. "Did you know that?"

I smiled down at her. "I did, in fact. Would you like me to tell her hello for you?"

"Yes, please. And tell her I can't wait for school to start back up again. We sit together at lunch."

"I'm delighted to hear it," I said. "Now off you go before the storm comes."

"How do you know a storm's coming?" Mrs. Rory asked.

"The sky," I said. "Just has that feeling to me."

She thanked me, and they hurried out the door. For the next fifteen minutes, I tidied up loose ends. Outside, the sky had darkened and snow began to fall. I felt a sudden urgency to get home. *Don't fret*, I told myself. We'd be fine as long as the wind didn't start up as it sometimes did.

I set out to tidy up the chairs and tables, humming to myself to keep from worrying about the incoming blizzard. Would Papa have had the same instinct about the blizzard and sent Phillip to fetch us early? We might have to stay at his office for the night. He always had some food stashed away and bedding just for this purpose. There was always plenty of firewood for the stove, so we would be warm there.

Was I worrying too much? I had this strange feeling of foreboding. *You're being silly*, I thought. *Everything's fine.*

I went to the back-facing windows and peered outside. The snow was more like ice, and the wind had picked up, slamming against the side of the building.

When the bells over the front doors rang out, I turned around, expecting Phillip. I'd forgotten to lock the front doors, so preoccupied with the weather. I froze, staring. For a moment, I couldn't comprehend the vision before me. It was not Phillip as I'd expected but someone else. *No, it can't be. Not him.* No. I was seeing things. I shook my head and blinked. But when I opened my eyes, the sight before me couldn't be denied. My head grew light. I stumbled forward, grasping the back of a chair to keep from falling.

It was not Phillip in the doorway but Walter Green. A living, breathing Walter Green.

Phillip

A half hour before I was to leave for town to pick Jo and Fiona up at the library, I knocked on the door of Lord Barnes's study. It was now or never. My stomach turned as I waited for him to answer.

"Yes, who is it?"

"Phillip, sir. Could I have a word, please?"

"Yes, yes. Come in."

I opened the door with damp fingers. "Excuse me, Lord Barnes, for the interruption."

He sat in a leather reading chair next to a roaring fire. A book lay facedown on his lap. I'd interrupted his reading time.

"Is this a bad time?" I asked.

"Not at all. What's on your mind?"

I'd not been in Lord Barnes's study before now. Josephine had told me it was his private sanctuary and that only Quinn was ever invited to sit with him. A simple, manly room with dark green furniture and a skinny mahogany desk. Lamplight against dark paneling cast a cozy yellow glow. This was Lord Barnes's sanctuary from the world and a busy household. *I should be brief*, I thought. He would want to get back to his book.

"I wanted to ask you something."

"I was about to partake in a whiskey. Would you care for one?" Lord Barnes asked.

"Thank you, sir. Shall I get them?"

"Please." He put a feather bookmark in the novel on his lap and set it aside.

"I'm sorry to interrupt your reading time." With shaking hands I managed to pour whiskey into two glasses without spilling.

"Not a problem. I'm assuming you have something important to speak with me about." His eyes twinkled at me. He must know why I'd come. I breathed a little easier. He wanted me to ask. He would give his permission. Jo and the boys had been right.

"Yes sir." I handed a glass to him and waited for him to invite me to sit in the twin chair next to him.

"Sit, please."

I did so, then took a swallow of whiskey. The alcohol burned my throat. I coughed and tapped my chest with one fist.

"You're not really a whiskey man, are you now?" Lord Barnes peered over at me, clearly amused.

"Not really, no."

"The first time I ever gave Quinn a glass, she went into a coughing fit and declared it the worst thing she'd ever put in her mouth, or something to that effect. Terrible of me, but it made me laugh."

I placed my glass on the small table between us.

"What can I do for you, young man?"

I swallowed. The whiskey wanted to come back up. "I'm here to ask for Josephine's hand in marriage."

"I see." Lord Barnes studied me without blinking.

"I understand I might not have been your first choice."

"Why should I say yes, then?"

"Because I love her like no one's ever loved a woman. I'll cherish her and take care of her better than anyone can because of it. I'll do whatever it takes to provide a good life for her. She gives me something to fight for. I know I may not seem good enough for her." I cleared my throat. "In fact, I'm *not* good enough, as you well know. But for some reason she loves me. Just as I am. I've come to her with nothing, but it won't stay that way for long. If all goes well out at the ski area, that is."

"I have great faith in you and Flynn."

"You do?

"Without question. Your solution is a good one, as long as you really want to do it. What about your woodworking?"

"That can become a precious hobby," I said. "Something I can do for our family."

He narrowed his eyes as he observed me. "I do believe you're sure."

"I am, sir."

"You've made all of my children happier by coming to us. Theo is free now to do as he wishes, with the blessing of his brother. You have my permission to marry Josephine."

"Oh, well, thank you, sir." My chest expanded with joy and relief. "I'll do you all proud, I promise."

"Did you think I would say no?"

"I wasn't sure."

"Put your mind at rest," Lord Barnes said. "I hope this change will be what Theo needs."

"I hope it will too, sir."

Lord Barnes was quiet for a moment, sipping from his whiskey glass. "It all goes so bloody fast, young man. One moment, they're little boys in knickers. Next thing you know, they're marching off to war. Or marrying a young man with great promise."

"Thank you, sir."

"I only hope I've given them what they need to make it in life. Not financially but emotionally. My Theo." He turned away, looking into the fire. A deep sadness came to his eyes. "I worry about him. All the time."

What could I say that wouldn't sound trite? I didn't know

how it was to have raised babies into young men. I didn't even know what it was like to be someone's beloved child. What would it have been like to have a father like Lord Barnes, championing your every move, loving you without conditions? "Sir, if I may say so, they've been lucky to have you as their father."

"That's kind of you to say. Sometimes, I wonder. I second-guess every decision, imagining what would have happened if I'd done this or that or the other thing."

"They're all good, kind people, sir."

"Yes, this is true. If this is the measure of a father, then I've done well."

"I'd say so, sir."

"Those years my boys were away, there was a pressure on my chest all the time. The same question rolled over and over in my mind. Would my precious sons come back to me?" Lord Barnes spoke softly. "For the first year of their lives they slept curled around each other like they must have been in the womb." He turned toward me, his eyes glassy. "I used to stare at them for minutes at a time, marveling over the miracle of their perfect fingers and toes and almost envious they would always have each other. I felt quite alone at the time. My first wife, you know."

"Yes, I understand."

"One day when the twins were about a month old, I found Josephine next to their cradle. She was three at the time—my little angel girl with hair so blond it almost looked silvery and eyes that seemed to have lived a thousand years. She looked up at me and said, 'Papa, how come I don't have another one of me? It makes me feel lonesome.'"

"What did you say?" My chest ached at the thought of Jo as a small child.

"I said I understood exactly what she meant. That I, too, envied them. Then I pulled her into my lap and assured her that I loved her very much. She nestled into my chest and, in the way children do, gave me her whole weight. She trusted me with her life. I can still remember the sweet smell of her hair and the weight of her. We sat like that, watching the babies sleep, until she lifted her face to look into my eyes. 'Papa, I'll be a good big sister, won't I? Even though I'm jealous?' I stifled a laugh at her earnest expression and assured her that she would. She was, of course, loving her brothers when her mother couldn't." He shifted so that his torso faced me. "Phillip, there was always something lonely about her. Perhaps because she was the older sister to twins and felt left out. Or because her mother was incapacitated. Her sisters, born three years apart from each other, have always been close, perhaps because they're opposites. Until Quinn came, Cymbeline and Fiona were more like Jo's children than her sisters. Even after that, she always had a distant, longing look in her eyes. I'd catch her staring out the window sometimes, as if she were waiting for someone to arrive.

"And then, one day you did. I knew the moment you walked into this house that you were the one for my Josephine. You were the one she'd been waiting for, even if she didn't know it. She's different with you. Lighter. Joyful. That longing in her is gone. She's given you her full weight, young man. A gift like no other."

My eyes stung as I gathered myself. "If I may, I'd like to say that I, too, had a longing for someone. This chronic loneliness that only went away when I read Jo's letters. I don't know why or how, but we fill that empty space for each other."

"For that, young man, I shall be forever grateful that you arrived on our doorstep declaring your love for a girl you knew only through letters. She wrote those letters to the soul mate she's wanted all these years. God intended for you to have them. There are no accidents that way."

I bowed my head and, to my utter dismay, started to cry.

Lord Barnes put a hand on my shoulder. "Ah no, son. No tears today. You've had enough of those for a lifetime. You're a Barnes now. You'll never be alone again."

His kind words only made it worse. I buried my face in my hands and willed the tears to stop. Before I realized what was happening, Lord Barnes had lifted me to my feet and taken me into his arms. I should've stiffened and drawn away like a man, but in that moment I was a boy again. A boy no one wanted. A boy who craved the arms of a father.

"It's all right, dear boy." Lord Barnes patted my back. "All that's behind you now. We want you. All of us. Even stuffy old Jasper likes you, and he doesn't like anyone."

I laughed through a sob before drawing away. "I'm sorry. I don't know what's come over me."

"You've been alone for too long a time, that's all." Lord Barnes put both hands on my shoulders. "Don't ever be ashamed to show Josephine what you're feeling. A wife likes to know what's inside a man's head. I've learned that from Quinn. They're less afraid of emotion than us."

"Yes sir. All that said, perhaps my bursting into tears could be kept from my future wife."

He laughed as he let go of me. "I hope you will come to me if you ever need anything. Advice. Or just to talk."

"Thank you, I will."

"Now, there's one thing I have to discuss with you. You'll want your own nest to make your own family."

I hung my head, immediately ashamed. "I thought I'd rent a place for us in town."

He poured another finger of whiskey in his glass. "I don't think that will be necessary. I've set up a savings fund for all of the girls for when they marry. Quinn wanted me to. If something happened to me, they'd still have a dowry. Even without your income, Jo has more than enough to live modestly for years to come, as well as build a house if you so choose."

"I don't know what to say."

"There's one stipulation."

"Yes?"

"If you have it in your heart to take pity on your father-in-law, I'd be most grateful if you'd build a house on our property. Any spot you want, as long as I can see your light from my windows. It's the only thing I'll ever ask of you."

"Lord Barnes, I'd be very happy to do so. In fact, I have a feeling I know where Jo will choose."

He sighed, seemingly relieved. "Thank you for taking pity upon me. I promise not to interfere too much. Although we'd love to have you for Sunday dinner." He grinned as he waved his hand around. "Only every so often, of course."

"It'll be our pleasure."

He snapped his fingers. "I almost forgot. I have something for you." He strode over to the desk. "When Josephine was born, my father and mother sent a ring that they'd had in the family for years. They asked that I give it to her when she married. It belonged to my mother's beloved aunt, also named Josephine."

He handed me a small velvet bag. I untied it and pulled out an emerald ring surrounded by small diamonds. "Sir? Are you certain?"

"Will she find it too old-fashioned, do you think?"

"She's old-fashioned too. I think she'll love it."

"Use it to propose to her," he said. "I want my little girl to have a moment to tell her children about. She's been such a good daughter all these years, and I want her to have it all." Now it seemed to be Lord Barnes's turn to cry. "Look at me. Sentimental old fool." He dabbed his eyes.

A soft knock on the door followed by Quinn's voice interrupted us. "May I come in?"

"Yes, darling, Phillip's with me."

She entered, eyes sparkling in the lamplight. "Has it happened?"

"How did you know?" Lord Barnes asked.

"You know there are no secrets in this house," Quinn said. "Even Delphia knew."

Lord Barnes chuckled. "I've given him the ring."

"When will you do it?" Quinn asked. "I promise not to say a word."

"What about tonight?" I asked.

"You could take her for a sleigh ride," Quinn said. "That would be romantic."

I shook my head. "No, I want to do it in front of her family. That's what she would want."

"I do believe you're right," Quinn said as she held out her arms to me. "I'm so very happy. You're the answer to my prayers. Welcome to our family."

For the second time that evening, I let myself give in to the embrace of a parent figure I'd wanted for so long.

Josephine

I gripped the back of the chair and stared at the ghost before me.

"Aren't you going to say hello?" Walter asked as he crossed the room toward me. Yes, it was his voice, low-pitched and smooth. He was thinner than last I saw him, and his golden hair darker. Even thus, he was as beautiful as my memory. His features seemed carved from the finest stone into a statue of a Greek god.

"Walter? I thought you'd died."

"I didn't." He grinned and held out his hands as if it were the most ordinary thing that he'd been gone missing for two years and was now in my library. "Are you glad to see me?"

"Were you captured?" My mind tried to sort through how this could have happened. If that was the case, the army would have known, wouldn't they? "I don't understand. You were dead."

"No, not exactly dead." His light blue eyes that had once melted my resolve flickered up to the rafters. "The details are uncertain but I'll tell you best I can."

I waited, watching him with great intent, hoping to tell if he was saying the truth or not.

"During the battle, I was hit and went down, then passed out. I'm not sure what happened, but I woke to find myself surrounded by dead bodies from both sides. My shoulder had taken a gunshot, but I was able to get to my feet. My unit had left. In pain and disoriented, I started walking. I had no plan or any idea what direction I was headed. For days I walked and saw no one. Finally, exhausted and near starvation, I collapsed. The next thing I knew, I woke in a Swiss hospital. I couldn't remember any of what had happened to me. That came later, after the war. I didn't know who I was. Somewhere along the way, I'd lost my tags. The Swiss people took pity on me and allowed me to stay at a sanitarium. When the war ended, I still had no memory of anything, so I stayed."

"But how did you get to Switzerland? Surely someone would have seen you and either captured you or helped you?"

"Like I said, I can't remember anything. The nurses said I came in on one of their ambulances. For years, I had no recollection of who I was."

"And then suddenly your memory returned?"

He smiled, and my stomach turned. That smile. I'd been susceptible back then, but now my stomach knew that he was a liar. "It took a long time, but finally it returned. I knew I had to come home for you. There was some trouble with my paperwork, given that the army thought I was dead, so my way to you was long."

Stunned by this information, I took a second to gather myself. "This all seems unbelievable."

"Doesn't it, though? But it's all true. Every bit." One corner of his wide mouth twitched. He stepped closer. "Aren't you pleased to see me?"

I moved behind the chair. My heart thudded in my chest.

Quick as a cat, he moved around the chair and picked up both my hands and kissed each one in turn. "I can't believe it's really you."

I snatched my hands away. “Why didn’t you write after your memory came back?”

Without blinking, looking directly into my eyes, he answered with great urgency in his voice. “I did. At least twenty times since my memory returned.”

“I didn’t get them.”

“I can’t imagine why they wouldn’t have arrived. I was afraid this was the case, as I knew you’d write to me if you’d gotten them. I wished I’d had your letters many, many times in the last few months. The ones you wrote me during the war so that a piece of you was still with me. They’d have helped me survive as I worked out how to get here. Do you remember all the things you said in your letters? I read them over and over back then. I’ve never had anyone love me that way. I’ve never loved anyone but you, Jo.” He drew nearer. I caught the scent of whiskey on his breath. Had he had whiskey during the dinners we’d had together? I couldn’t remember now. “It’s finally time for us to be together. You look as beautiful as ever. Maybe more so, if that’s possible. Tell me you’re not married.”

“No, Walter, I’m not married. Even so, it’s too late for us. Too much has happened. I’m in love with someone else.” The desire to have him gone surged through me, followed by fear. I didn’t want him here. How would I get rid of him? Did I tell him about Phillip, or would that make it worse? Why had he come after I was finally happy? And this tall tale of amnesia? I didn’t believe it for a second. Had he deserted his post? I already knew him to be a liar. Perhaps he saw his opportunity to desert and took it.

“Don’t say so, Josephine. Please. I didn’t mean to be away for so long. The moment I remembered who I was, I knew I had to come find you. I knew you’d wait for me. You said so in your letters.”

“I did wait. Even after I thought you were dead, I pledged my eternal love to you. I told my family I was a spinster, having loved only you. I thought no one could measure up to you. All these years, I lived on the memory of those two weeks we had together."

"See, I knew you'd be here. I knew my faithful Jo wouldn't let me down. What an epic love story we are." He smiled as he placed his hands on my shoulders. His expression turned tender. Only now I could see the skillful way he rearranged his features to what he thought I wanted to see.

How had I not seen how fake he was, how practiced in the art of deceit?

He caressed my cheek. I jerked away. I didn't want his touch. Not the places where Phillip had touched me. My heart belonged to him now.

He continued on as if he hadn't noticed my rebuke. "We can finally start our life together. Your family, are they well? I'll finally get to meet them. You can't imagine how I've longed to see you. I couldn't bear the thought of you with someone else. My greatest fear was to find you married." He picked up my left hand. His eyes filled as he brought my hand to his mouth. "I've dreamt of this moment for so long. The thought of you waiting here for me was all that got me through. You'll marry me now, won't you?"

I yanked my hands from his and backed up a few inches. "And my photograph? Do you still have it? Wouldn't that have sustained you during these long months of separation?" I baited him just to see how quickly he could lie.

The corners of his mouth turned down into a frown. "My love, I dropped it somewhere along the way. I've lost more than a lifetime of sleep wondering where it went. If only I could remember the time after I was shot, I might be able to pin down when I lost it. Then at least I could imagine it lying somewhere in France. Waiting for me, just as you did."

Triggered by the lie about the photograph, a blind fury came over me. "What about the others? The other women who thought you loved them? The ones who thought they were your one and only? Did you lose their photographs, too, or did you leave them behind in the same box where mine was?"

"What other women?" He stared at me with blank, innocent eyes.

"I know the truth. I know I wasn't the only one who thought you'd return to them. Have you been to see them first? Am I your last stop? Did you work your way west? Were they all married so you came here for one last chance? Your despicable lies pile up one after the other, Walter. I know my photograph wasn't with you as you promised." I held up a hand. "Don't bother to try to defend yourself. I know everything. Every single thing out of your mouth has been a lie. You were only interested in my wealth."

"How could you possibly know that?" His voice turned menacing. A glittering anger shot from his eyes. This was the real him. *I'm seeing him for the first time*, I thought. *This is the real man. Dark and twisted. Conniving.*

"Know about what? The other women? Or about how you found women with money and then seduced them with your charm?"

"All of it." He spat the words out as if they were venom.

"Where have you really been all these years? Have you seen all the others first? Am I your last chance?"

His jaw clenched.

I was right. I was his last stop. His last chance to be taken in by an unsuspecting woman. The others had moved on, perhaps married already. He had to come to see if I was still available and charm me into believing whatever lies he'd come up with about his whereabouts.

"Answer my question." He wrapped his hands around my shoulders and shook me. "How do you know this?"

My limbs went numb as the anger drained from me. I'd provoked him. He was dangerous. A cornered animal. Who knew what he might do?

Fiona. She was in the back. *Please stay in the office*, I prayed.

He tightened his grip on my shoulders and dug his fingers into the spot just above my shoulder blades.

I yelped with pain.

"How do you know about them?" he asked.

"How does that matter?" The words came out angry when it was really fear that seized me now.

"The only men who knew about the other women served with me in France, and most of them died in the same battle I escaped from. Who survived to tell you this?" His eyes had changed since he walked through the library doors. Instead of playful, they were wild. They reminded me of a feral cat we'd once found in the woods.

"Did you run away? Is the amnesia story a lie like so many of your others?" I couldn't seem to stop myself.

"Shut up," he said, spitting.

"How could you walk away from your fellow soldiers? You left them there to die to save yourself."

"One measly man doesn't win a war."

"One cowardly man."

"I told you to shut up." His hands moved to my neck and pressed into my windpipe for a second before loosening the grip slightly. "You don't know what it was like over there. The terror and the absolute lack of hope. I saw a chance for survival, and I took it. Anyone in my situation would've done the same."

"No, some men had reasons to come home. Women who loved them who were waiting, praying on their knees every night. If you'd loved someone, you would have done whatever you could to get back to them, even if it meant fighting through one more battle. You're a coward and a liar."

He tightened his hands around my neck. I pressed into his wrists with my nails, but it didn't deter him.

"Tell me who told you or I'll kill you right here and now."

Black dots floated before my eyes. I would not die this way. The truth might buy me some time. "Phillip."

His eyes widened in shock. He loosened his hands from my

neck. Before I could bring my own hands to massage the area he surely bruised, he smacked my cheek with the palm of his hand so hard that I fell to the floor, landing heavily on my left arm. I cried out as he yanked me up by my hair. *Please, Fiona, do not come out here,* I begged silently.

"Phillip? How do you know him?"

"He came here to bring me the letters I sent you," I said. "And to tell me the truth about the man I thought I loved."

"Phillip Baker. The snake. I should've known. He used to listen to me read your letters and wish they were sent to him. Not that he could ever get a girl like you for real."

"Not true. He's worth a thousand of you."

"How dare you. Do you have any idea of the kind of trash he is?" He knocked me to the floor once more, this time with a blow to the other side of my face.

I cowered as he hovered over me. "Please, just leave me alone. Go find some other innocent who'll believe your lies."

He fell onto his knees. "Where did he go? Phillip, where is he?"

"How should I know?" Instinct told me to keep it to myself.

He opened his mouth, then shut it, as if trying to think what to say next. "His father died in prison. Did you know that?"

"That's not true. His parents died of yellow fever."

He went still. "I wonder why you'd believe him and not me?" He spoke between gritted teeth. "After everything we went through. He lied to you about his father. Who knows what else?"

"He didn't lie. He would never lie to me."

His eyes narrowed into mean, snakelike slits. "For God's sake, you're in love with him? Aren't you? I can hear it in your sickly sweet tone. The one you used to use only for me."

I tightened my lips together and jutted my chin out in a way I hoped looked more rebellious and courageous than I felt.

He snapped his finger and thumb together. "Oh, I see now. He's here in town, isn't he? I should've figured. The moment he thought I was dead, he started making plans for how to win you over, starting with telling lies about me."

"Phillip doesn't lie. He's incapable. He didn't plan to even tell me about your lies because he didn't want to hurt me. But he couldn't let me go on believing you were this wonderful man, so the truth spilled out of him."

Walter rolled his eyes. "Jesus, girl, I guess he figured you out as fast as I did."

"What does that mean?" I knew better than to engage with him, but I couldn't stop myself.

"You're gullible and easy to manipulate. The little princess who lived in her daddy's tower all her life has no idea about what it's like to have to scrape your way through. You've never had anything bad happen to you in your ivory tower. Which makes you the perfect target."

"Phillip will be here any minute. You should go."

"No. You're coming with me." He yanked me to my feet.

"Why? What do you want from me?"

"What I've always wanted, you stupid girl. Your money." He lifted his jacket to reveal a pistol in a holster. "Be quiet and you won't get hurt. If your rich daddy gives me what I want, I'll let you go. You can marry sad little Phillip and live happily ever after."

"Where do you think we're going in this weather?"

That seemed to give him pause. "Someplace to hide you. I need to think."

He dragged me toward the back door. I prayed silently. *Please, God, take care of Fiona. Don't let her follow us. Wait for Phillip, Fiona. He'll know what to do.* With her keen musician hearing, she would have heard the entire conversation. I imagined her in the office frightened, likely hiding under the desk. She would be afraid for me but wouldn't know what to do. What if she decided to chase after us? *No. Stay put. Tell Phillip what you learned.* It was better for her to be a quiet witness than confront this crazed man with a gun. I had an idea then. She needed to know Walter had a gun.

"I'm not afraid of your gun," I shouted.

"You should be."

He tossed me out into the cold. I didn't realize until the door shut behind me that I had no coat or hat. The snowstorm was in full force. I'd freeze in these temperatures without outerwear. I hoped he had a warm, dry place in which to keep me captive.

Phillip

I knew the moment I pulled around to the back of the library that something was wrong. Fiona was squatting near the back steps with her arms wrapped around her middle. The light that hung over the door illuminated her pale face as she lifted her gaze to the horses and me. "Phillip, Phillip, help." She rose to her feet and ran toward me.

I jumped from the sleigh. She stumbled into me, shaking and sobbing. I took hold of her shoulders. "What's happened?" Hard, cold dread settled in my stomach. "Is it Josephine?"

"Yes, he took her. A man. He was here and he took her."

"Who took her?"

"Walter. Walter Green."

"Fiona, what are you saying? Walter's dead."

The words spewed from her in a heated rush. Words I would never have expected. Words that terrified me. "No, he's alive. He ran away from the war to Switzerland, but now he's come for Jo. He said he'd lost his memory but it came back and that's when he decided to find her again. When Jo said she didn't want him anymore, he started yelling and I think he might have hit her because she cried out and now he's taken off with her. He has a gun, Phillip."

"Where did they go?" I fought against a rising panic. *Stay calm*, I ordered myself. *This is like the war. I must go to the place in my mind where my thoughts are disengaged from my actions. Be a soldier. Do what needs to be done*. "Tell me everything you remember." The snow fell in hard pellets, and the wind pushed into us. Josephine had said there were many different kinds of snow. This was the bad kind. A layer had settled on Fiona's hat and coat.

"I didn't see where they went. They were already gone when I came out from the back. But there are tracks." She pointed to two sets of footprints, quickly being covered with fresh snow. I could see them only as far as the light from the porch allowed.

"They're on foot?" I asked, as if it weren't obvious. Where did he think they could get on foot? I released Fiona and we both followed the tracks as far as they went. They disappeared at the street, hidden in the slush made from sleigh blades and wagon wheels.

"What does he want?" I asked, more to myself than Fiona. "Why would he come here after all this time?" Where had he been the past few years? How had he managed to fake his death? All these questions tumbled into my mind and out again to be replaced with the cold reality. He'd taken Jo, and I didn't know where.

"Money." Fiona said this matter-of-factly. "That's why he's really here. He wants Papa to give him money."

I silently cursed. Of course that's what he wanted. He'd not come for Jo out of some insane love but to save himself. My mind quickly worked out his motivations. I knew what he wanted and how he would have approached the situation. If he had indeed had amnesia, which I doubted, he would have quickly come to the conclusion that he needed money and that it was time to put his plan into action. But what had gone wrong that he came here?

This would have been his last choice because of the location. He saw himself as a fancy man about town. A city dweller. However, the other women were probably already married. I remembered addresses from the eastern states on their envelopes. He would have chosen the easiest route first. If those women had rejected him for whatever reason, he would have had no choice but to come out here and try with Josephine. But he'd found her unwilling to fall for his lies now that she knew the truth. Once he'd discovered that, out of desperation, he would have gone to his final move. Kidnap her for ransom. Would he hurt her if he didn't get what he wanted? We'd both killed during the war. Would he see it as the same? A battle for a way of life?

"Phillip, what do we do?" Fiona asked as she wiped under her eyes with the tips of her gloved fingers.

"I've got to find them." They couldn't have gotten far. Emerson Pass was a small place. Given my reasoning, however, the best thing to do might be to return home and wait for his request. Again, he would do what was easiest.

"Fiona, do you know how to get into your father's office? I want to call home and tell them to come join us in the search."

She nodded. "Yes, we all have a key in case we ever get stuck in town during a blizzard. We can go now. It's faster than driving back home."

We ran back to the sleigh. Willie and Oz whinnied upon our return, as if they, too, knew the urgency of the situation.

The office was only a few blocks away. Both Fiona and I searched right and left as we drove down the main street of town, hoping for a hint of where he'd taken her. We passed the boardinghouse. "Do you think he would be staying there?" I asked. "Maybe he took her there."

"They would know Jo there," Fiona said. "They'd know something wasn't right if she was there with a stranger."

He'd have taken her someplace hidden. Like a barn or an empty attic. In this weather, they couldn't have gotten far. Once I called the Barneses' residence, I was going out to look for them.

THE MOMENT I hung up from the phone call with Lord Barnes, I headed toward the door. "Fiona, stay here with the door locked until your father arrives. He's coming in with Jasper, the twins, and Harley. We'll find her, don't worry."

"Wait, take this." Fiona picked up a kerosene lamp from the desk. "We keep this in case we ever lose our lights." With quick movements, she removed the glass top and lit the cloth wick from a match she'd found in one of the drawers. "Please, be careful."

"I will. Now lock this door behind me and get the fire built up. I don't want you cold."

The moment I walked into the blinding snowfall, I realized how foolish it would have been to go out without the lantern. Night had fallen, and visibility was terrible. The horses were still hitched to the sleigh and standing just outside the office door.

However, I decided to stay on foot for my initial search. They had to be somewhere in town. There was no way they'd gotten far walking. But where were they? *Think*. Where would conniving Walter be inclined to go? *Always the easiest way.* He'd not have wanted to walk long in this ice, which fell now in slants and stung my cheeks. He would find a haven somewhere here in town.

He had a gun. Would he threaten someone else with it and take over their house or shop? I scanned the street for lights. The shops were all dark. Everyone had gone home for Christmas Eve suppers.

And then, what felt like a miracle happened. The festive bulbs hung over the pond turned on, filling the square with light. *Fiona*, I thought, *clever little thing.* The switch was located just outside Lord Barnes's office. I should have thought of it myself.

Feeling more confident now, I surveyed the other side of the street. A flicker of light came from the tailor's shop window. Not the usual electric bulbs that lit the shop but more like a flicker from a candle's wick. Upstairs, in the Olofsson family living quarters, the windows were dark. Why would the lights of their apartment be off this time of day? Isak had mentioned how his father often worked right up until suppertime, enjoying the quiet while Mrs. Olofsson prepared the meal upstairs.

Had he been working when Walter walked in with Josephine? Mr. Olofsson wouldn't have hesitated to invite them in, even if the shop was closed and she were accompanied by a stranger. He knew and trusted her. Once inside, had Walter pulled out his gun and forced them both upstairs? Did he have them all tied up? And were the boys home at the time? If so, did he have them too?

They had to be there.

I had no gun. Storming into the place without a weapon would be foolish. Lord Barnes and Harley would bring their pistols. Should I wait for them or barge into the place myself?

"Phillip." Someone whispered my name. I turned, searching for the origin. Isak crouched in the small alleyway between two buildings, hiding behind an empty barrel. He gestured for me to follow him.

I hustled behind him through the alleyway to the back of the building. He'd either escaped or suspected, as I did, that not all was right at his parents' shop and home.

The moment we were out of the alley, he told me what he knew. "Both my parents were downstairs trying to finish a job before it got too late, and I'd offered to put supper together. I happened to be at the upstairs window when I saw a man escort Josephine into my father's shop. He was trying to hide it, but I could see he had a gun at her back. The moment they disappeared inside, I heard a scuffle, like bodies thrown against a wall, and a man's voice shouting. My brother's not home, and I didn't want to go down there only to be captured as well. I shut out the lights, hoping that would be a clue to anyone who knows we live above the shop, and came down the back stairs to the alley as quietly as I could. I ran to the sheriff's office, but Lancaster wasn't there. I tried the saloon, assuming he was there, but then remembered it's not open because Pastor Lind pressured them to close for the holiday weekend. It's like a ghost town here tonight. I was about to start running for the nearest house when I saw you."

"Lord Barnes, the twins, and Harley are headed into town. I called them from his office. Fiona had a key." Realizing I was babbling, I took in a deep breath. As quickly as I could, I told him what Fiona had heard. "I don't think he means to harm them, just to get money from Jo's father."

Isak nodded. "With the weather like this and no one else open, what other choice did he have but to hold them all inside until he can get what he wants?"

"Quinn and the rest of the girls are waiting at home to answer the phone in case he calls," I said. "Where's Viktor?"

"I don't know. He was supposed to be home an hour ago—he was working out at the mill today, and Roy usually drops him off on his way home." He took off his cap and ran his hands through his hair. "I'd never seen that man before. I know everyone here."

"I know him. He's supposed to be dead. That's Walter Green."

"How is it possible?"

"He somehow escaped France and went to Switzerland or somewhere. Honestly, I don't know."

"What do we do? Wait for Lord Barnes?" Isak asked.

Before I could answer, the sound of a gunshot echoed through the quiet night. Without thinking, I took off running through the alley until I reached the street, vaguely aware that Isak was behind me. Another shot rang out. When we reached the street, I stopped dead in my tracks.

Viktor, with Jo in his arms, stumbled through the door of the tailor's shop. He had a gun in one large hand, poking out from under Jo's skirt. Blood covered the front of her dress. Ice shot through me. *Please, no. Not this. Please, God, no.*

I finally reached them. Through the open door, I saw directly into the shop. Mrs. Olofsson knelt over the prone, bloodied body of Walter Green. Mr. Olofsson ran out the door, shouting that he would get the doctor.

Viktor dropped to his knees with Jo still in his arms. It was then I knew it was not Jo who had been hit but Viktor. He was bleeding from a wound in his shoulder. His blood had spilled onto Jo's dress.

Viktor set Jo down, then slumped over onto the street and spread out lengthways as if he were simply taking a nap. I grabbed Jo and held her against my chest.

"I'm all right," she said. "Viktor saved us."

Isak sank to his knees beside his brother. "What happened? Viktor, talk to me. Are you all right?"

Josephine knelt beside them. "He wrestled for the gun, and it went off...hitting him in his shoulder. But he was able to get the gun from Walter after that. Viktor shot him squarely in the chest."

From inside, Mrs. Olofsson said in a shaking voice, "He's dead. The man's dead." She stumbled as she ran out to her sons. "Viktor, Viktor." Tears ran down her face. "Do something, Isak."

Isak tore through the fabric of his brother's shirt. The angry red wound bled profusely, but the hole was neat. I went down on my knees and lifted his shoulder. With my fingertips, I searched for the wound on the other side. It was there, thank God. "The bullet went through. This is good."

"You were so brave," Jo said, stroking Viktor's hair off his forehead. "You're going to be all better. Your dad's getting the doctor. He'll be here soon."

Viktor groaned, but his eyes fluttered open. "Am I hurt?"

"A little, but you're going to be fine," I said.

"I don't feel a thing," Viktor said.

"Liar," Isak said.

"Mrs. Olofsson, can you bring out some cotton fabric?" I asked. "Something to stop the bleeding. Two pieces."

She nodded and ran inside.

Viktor's face was as white as the snow. "I shot him, Isak. He had the gun on all of them. I was in the back but he didn't know, so I sneaked in on him. Tackled him...and then..." He drifted off, closing his eyes.

"He's going into shock," I said.

Mrs. Olofsson handed me a strip of white fabric. As gently as I could, I pressed into the entrance and exit wounds. Poor Viktor moaned.

"We should bring him inside," I said. "Where it's warm."

Isak and I each took a side and lifted him to his feet as Viktor groaned in pain.

"I'll get that bastard out of our way." Josephine sprinted indoors. With both hands around his ankles, she dragged Walter out the door and onto the sidewalk. How she'd done that, I couldn't say. Perhaps the heightened emotions had given her super strength.

"I don't want him near Viktor," Jo said. "He's trash who deserves to be out on the street."

"Here, bring my boy to the window seat," Mrs. Olofsson said.

Blood from Walter sullied the normally pristine front of the shop. A smear of it from where Jo dragged him outdoors was impossible not to step in. Our boots made a sickly sticky sound as we crossed over to the window seat.

Viktor moaned once more as we helped him lie across the seat. His muscular legs were too long and dangled over one end.

Mrs. Olofsson knelt by her son's feet, weeping. "My sweet boy, please be all right."

Josephine took over pressing into his wound with the fabric. She looked up at me. "How did you find us?"

"Fiona heard everything."

"Where is she?" Josephine asked me. "I hated to leave her, but I had no choice."

"She's locked in your dad's office. She's fine. Very brave, in fact."

Outside, the sound of bells and the whinny of horses told me Lord Barnes had arrived. I went out to greet them. Lord Barnes sprang from the sleigh. His expression turned to panic when he saw the blood. "Phillip, is she hurt?"

"No, no. It's Viktor. He's been shot in the shoulder. He killed Walter." I gestured toward the body.

Lord Barnes looked as if he might faint. I put out a hand to steady him. "The doctor's on his way. It's a shoulder wound, but the bullet went straight through." I told them what I knew. "Then Jo dragged him out here. I've never seen a woman that strong in my life."

Dr. Neal rode up on his horse. Harley offered to take care of the animal so the doctor could go directly inside. Lord Barnes said he'd go across the street to his office and call the undertaker.

I stood with Isak and Harley outside, all of us stomping our feet to stay warm. Josephine came out to stand with us. She immediately started shivering. I took off my coat and wrapped her up, then put an arm around her shoulder to draw her close to my side. "Are you all right?" I asked.

She rested her head against my shoulder. "I am now. I'm so sorry for all this. Isak, the last thing I wanted was for anyone to get hurt because of my poor judgment. I'm mortified and so very sorry."

"Not your fault," Isak said, gruffly. "I'm glad Viktor was there and that things went the way they did."

"I've never been more frightened in my life," Josephine said. "Your poor mother and I were huddled together, both of us shaking like a leaf. Walter paced back and forth while holding the gun on us, muttering to himself. He had no plan. The shop was the only one with a light on. Then, all of a sudden, Viktor tore out of the back of the shop." Josephine gave us a tremulous smile. "He barreled right into Walter, with no fear and like a bear. They struggled for what seemed like an hour. The gun went off, hitting Viktor in the shoulder. Despite that, Viktor had the foresight to bite Walter's hand. Walter dropped the gun, and like lightning, Viktor grabbed it. Shot him right through the chest." She pressed her fingers against her mouth for a second before continuing. "I'd never seen anyone die before. He looked surprised for a moment and then crumpled to the ground. The light faded from his eyes and then went blank."

"We've seen it like that too," Isak said.

"Too many times," I said as I squeezed her tighter. "I don't know how I'll ever repay Viktor."

"I know what he wants," Isak said, smiling. "He's besotted with your Cymbeline. She's all he ever talks about."

"Truly?" Jo asked.

Isak nodded. "All about how Cymbeline did this and that and isn't she perfection—that kind of thing."

"Oh dear, that's worrisome." Josephine peeked up at me.

"Why?" Isak asked.

"She thinks of him as her nemesis," Josephine said. "He's angered her by being so good at the things she wishes she could do."

"Well, you know what they say about that?" Isak asked, raising his eyebrows. "Strong feelings one way might indicate there's more there than what she's admitting to."

Lord Barnes returned, bringing our discussion to a close. Seconds later, the doctor came out to ask if we might help Viktor into the sleigh and take him over to his medical office. "I'll keep a watch on him tonight. Strong young man like this will be up and about in no time." Dr. Neal explained that he'd given him a few tugs of whiskey for the pain and cleaned and sewn up the wound. "He'll be fine as long as there's no infection, which is less likely in my clinic."

Viktor was sitting up with his mother by his side when we came inside to help. His color had greatly improved. He gave us a goofy grin.

"Hello, boys. Don't look like that. I'm fine. Doc gave me some whiskey and I'm feeling no pain." His words slurred slightly.

"You gave me a scare, little brother," Isak said as we helped him to his feet.

"Nah, I'm too dumb and tough to die," Viktor said.

With Mr. and Mrs. Olofsson trailing behind, we escorted Viktor into the back of the sleigh and tucked blankets around him. "You'll come with me?" Viktor asked Isak.

"I'll be there the whole time." Isak climbed in beside him.

Dr. Neal came outside and walked over to the sleigh. He held up his hand to show us a bullet. "Found this lodged in the front of the counter. Went clean through you, Viktor, thank the good Lord above."

Isak took it from him. "We'll keep that as a memory of how brave my baby brother was tonight."

"Yes, yes," Mrs. Olofsson murmured as she wrapped her arms around her waist.

"Mother, please, go upstairs and rest," Viktor said. "You've been through enough."

Mr. Olofsson took his wife's hand. "I'll take her up and make her something hot to drink."

"We'll come see you in the morning," Mrs. Olofsson said.

"He'll be home in the morning if all goes as expected," Dr. Neal said. "This is merely cautiousness on my part."

A smaller sleigh driven by Cymbeline came speeding down the road. She slid to a stop and jumped to the ground, then grabbed Jo into her arms. "Jo, thank God. I was scared to death." She let go and gasped when she saw Walter's body on the ground. "Is he dead?"

"I shot him," Viktor called out gleefully from the sleigh. "Saving your sister."

"What? Viktor?" Cymbeline's gaze darted to her supposed nemesis, then back to her sister. "Is it true?"

"He's a hero," Jo said.

"What are you doing here, young lady?" Lord Barnes asked.

She appeared not to have heard her father. As if in a daze, she walked over to the sleigh and climbed inside. Then, in a move no one saw coming, she leaned close and kissed him on the cheek.

"Cymbeline," Jo said, under her breath. "What're you doing?"

"Cymbeline Barnes, get out of there this instant," Lord Barnes said.

Cymbeline ignored him. She seemed only to have eyes for Viktor. "Does it hurt?'

"Not now. Doc gave me medicine and whiskey." He gazed at her with the eyes of a man in love. "You're very pretty."

"Thank you, Viktor. Not for the unnecessary compliment but for saving my beloved Josephine. From this moment forward you shall no longer be my nemesis."

"I was your nemesis?" Viktor touched his cheek where she'd kissed him.

"Of course. How could you not know that?" Cymbeline's forehead wrinkled in obvious confusion. "We've been enemies since the dawn of time."

"Impossible," he said. "You're not my enemy."

"What are you talking about?" Cymbeline asked crossly. Had she forgotten her pledge only moments before?

"I can't be your enemy." He gave her a boozy, loving smile. "I love you with all my heart and soul. Someday, you'll be my wife."

Cymbeline jumped from the sleigh so fast it was as if her skirts were on fire. Seconds later, she'd gotten into her own sleigh, turned the horse around, and headed down the road toward home.

"Did I say something wrong?" Viktor asked with a longing look at the back end of Cymbeline's sleigh.

Despite everything we'd been through that night, the whole lot of us burst out laughing. Even Lord Barnes.

Josephine

The party must go on, even after an abduction by your former—formerly dead lover. Dinners for the entire week of Christmas in our house were grand, jolly affairs, and this year would be no different. By the time dinner was ready, I'd bathed and dressed and promised myself for tonight, at least, I would put aside all thoughts of horrible Walter. This time of year was magical to my little sisters, and I didn't want to ruin it for them.

We sat around the dining room table for our feast. My littlest sisters, sitting on either side of me, looked adorable in their matching red dresses and bows. Cymbeline and Fiona sparkled in dresses made in the same shade of deep blue. All the men were in evening suits and bow ties. Mama wore a beaded gold dress that glittered under the chandelier.

I took both my baby sisters' warm hands in mine as we all bowed our heads for the family prayer.

"Thank you, Father, for the bounty we're about receive," Papa said. "And for our special guest at our table tonight, Phillip Baker. Thank you for sending him to our family." His voice cracked as he said the next part. "Thank you for keeping my

Josephine safe today and for Viktor. In your name we pray, amen."

After a chorus of amens around the table, Cymbeline and I got up to serve us our first course. The staff had cooked the meal, but they were enjoying dinners with their families tonight. Mama couldn't bear to have them away from their loved ones during holidays. She remembered her own father having to work through every Christmas.

After dinner, all the staff and their little ones would come for caroling and cake. Mama's mother and sister, Annabelle, and her husband, Clive, would come too. Papa would pass out presents to the children and holiday bonuses for the adults. I always looked forward to our festive evening, made even more so this year with the presence of Phillip.

The first course was a savory squash soup and one of Lizzie's buttery rolls. I took the platter of rolls around while Cymbeline served the soup. When we were done, I sat back in my chair. I glanced across to Phillip, seated between Cymbeline and Fiona. He smiled at me with such love that it gave me a lump in my throat. I looked down to grab my spoon and gasped. There was a felt bag where the soup spoon should have been.

"What's this?" I looked at Papa, assuming it was something from him. "Do we all have one?" I scanned the table. My brothers had goofy expressions on their faces. Fiona bounced in her chair. Cymbeline wouldn't look at me at all. Mama gave me a gentle smile.

"No, darling, this one's just for you," Papa said. "And it's not from me."

Phillip rose from his chair and went around the table, stopping in back of Addie's chair. My sister, as if rehearsed, jumped from her seat to sit with Delphia. Phillip moved Addie's chair out of the way, then picked up the bag and withdrew something into the palm of his hand. He dropped to one knee. My hands flew to my mouth. This was the moment. It was happening. In front of my entire family. I started to shake, not from fear or cold as I had earlier but from pure excitement.

Phillip held up an exquisite emerald-and-diamond ring. Where had he gotten such a thing?

"Josephine, your father's been saving this for you. It's from his great-aunt Josephine and is to be given to you upon your engagement. By the grace of God, I'm the man who gets to offer it to you."

My gaze darted to Papa. He nodded and smiled.

"Josephine, I've loved you from the first time I set eyes upon you. You're everything I've wanted all my life. A place to call home. Will you be my forever home? Will you be my wife?" Phillip smiled up at me. "Please say you will."

"Yes, I will marry you."

He slipped the ring on my finger as my family clapped and cheered.

"You may kiss her," Papa said. "Since you're officially engaged."

"As if they haven't already," Cymbeline said.

"Cym, hush," Fiona said.

Phillip leaned close to brush his lips against mine. "Thank you for making me the happiest man in the world. I'll not let you down."

"I know you won't." I touched my hands to the sides of his face. "I trust you with my heart. With everything."

When he stood, Delphia said, "Phillip, you may sit next to Jo now since you're engaged." She blinked her big blue eyes to show us all what a sacrifice she was making before sliding from the chair and heading to the one formerly occupied by Phillip.

I gazed down at the ring on my finger. "I've never seen this, Papa. I had no idea."

"It was a secret," Papa said. "A surprise from the past and a reminder of how much you've meant to this family. Your sacrifices and the good example you've always set for your younger brothers and sisters has never gone unnoticed. Your mama and I are so very proud of you."

Tears spilled from my eyes at his kind words. "It was easy to be good with these people as my siblings."

"Not that good," Cymbeline said.

"Speak for yourself," Fiona said, smiling sweetly.

Mama raised her glass. "Shall we toast our lovebirds?"

We all clinked glasses and then dived into our soup.

"When will the wedding be?" Addie asked.

"What will your dress be like?" Fiona's eyes grew even bigger than usual. "Aunt Annabelle will make it for you, won't she, Mama?"

"I don't think we could stop her," Mama said. "When would you like to marry?"

As soon as possible, I thought to myself. "What do you think, Phillip?"

"Whatever my bride wants is what I want."

I placed my hand on his knee. "Should we have a winter wonderland wedding?"

"Wait until spring," Cymbeline said. "So you can have it outside in the yard with all the flowers in bloom."

"I'd like to walk you down the aisle at the church," Papa said. "The first of five."

"Yes, Papa. I'd like that too," I said.

"Can I be the flower girl?" Delphia asked.

"How do you know about flower girls?" Mama asked.

"A book." Delphia dipped her spoon back into her soup as if the answer were so obvious it wasn't worth asking.

"A spring wedding *does* sound lovely," Mama said. "And would give Annabelle time to make your dress. She has a lot of clients these days."

Spring sounded far away.

"And we'll want to get started on your cottage right away," Papa said. "Our wedding gift to you."

"But Papa, you've already done too much," I said.

"When a daughter gets married, it's expected that her father will give a dowry to her groom. I already made a deal with Phillip that it has to be within walking distance."

"So you're not really getting anything for free, old boy," Flynn said. "All of us breathing down your neck night and day."

"I can't ask for anything more," Phillip said. "I look forward to each and every one of you being in and out of our home whenever you wish."

"You say that now," Cymbeline said with a shake of her head. "Just wait. You'll see how annoying we all are before long."

"I think he already knows," Theo said.

Everyone laughed as we continued on with our soup. I barely tasted it, though, so blissful with the man I loved by my side. A spring wedding. Yes, that would be perfect, even though I wished it wasn't months and months away. Having a ceremony and reception we'd remember all our lives would be worth the wait. And really, who was I to disappoint Mama and my sisters? Or deprive Papa of walking me down the aisle? Sensible, dependable Josephine would have to take second place to this giddy, frivolous one.

I looked around the table once more, taking in the faces of my precious family. We'd all been through so much together, but when I looked back, I would remember the good moments rather than the hard ones. This one had to be at the top of the list.

Josephine

The morning of my wedding, I sat on the window seat of the bedroom I'd shared with my sisters for most of my life. Birds chirped and sang from the trees. Cymbeline and Fiona had risen before me and were already downstairs. Faint music of Fiona at the piano accompanied by Li's violin drifted up to me as they practiced for the festivities. On the lawn, Jasper, Harley, and my brothers were arranging tables for the reception. No one could put together a party quite like the Barnes family.

"Good morning, darling."

I turned to see Mama in the doorway. She had a tray with coffee and breakfast rolls.

"Good morning, Mama. Why aren't you downstairs for breakfast?"

"Two reasons. I had to have myself a little cry, and I wanted to spend a little time with you before it's time to get you into your dress."

"Why're you crying?" I asked, alarmed. "Is Grandmother all right?"

"Oh, yes, she's fine. Looking forward to today. As is my sister. She thinks your gown is the prettiest she's ever made."

"What's made you sad?"

"Not sad, more sentimental." She set the tray on the dresser and poured a coffee from the silver pitcher into a cup. Immediately, the nutty aroma filled the room. "I'll miss you, that's all. You've been such a friend to me."

"Mama, I'm only a few minutes away. You can walk over to see me any time you want."

She let out a sigh as she fluttered her hands in front of her damp eyes. "I know. But it's the end of an era. My oldest baby flying from the nest."

"Oh, Mama. I'll never fly too far."

"You're such a dear to put up with my nonsense. Anyway, don't mind me. I've come with breakfast. Lizzie's afraid you might be too nervous to eat, so she's sent your favorite rolls with a dish of butter and some fresh strawberries. If you recall, she was a wreck the morning of her wedding."

"I'm not a bit nervous." I smiled, remembering how Lizzie had paced this very room in her wedding dress before it was time to go to the church. "I'm simply deliriously happy."

"I didn't think you would be. I wasn't nervous for my wedding, either. As I recall, I couldn't wait to marry your dad, and the rest of this brood, as far as that goes. The sooner the better. Do you want coffee? I've just realized I poured you a cup without asking."

"I'd love some." I rose to fetch the steaming cup from the tray. She took a cup for herself, and we settled on the window seat together. Wearing a white silk dressing gown and robe and her hair in a braid down her back, Mama looked no older than a schoolgirl.

"Is there anything you'd like to ask me? About the wedding night, that is?" Mama asked this while looking out the window. A flush of pink dotted both cheeks.

"I don't think so." I'd grown up with animals. I knew the basic idea of what happened between a male and female. "I've spent a lot of time in the barn."

She laughed, which came out sounding more like a hiccup. "Oh dear, all right. I suppose that would inform you of the technical aspects of...things. However, I wanted to mention that it's not usually blissful the first time and that you shouldn't give up. You'll feel some pain, but that's normal for your first encounter. The second time will be much better."

It was my turn to blush. I'd had plenty of time over the last few months to imagine what it would be like to finally be in Phillip's arms. Waiting had been excruciating. Every kiss made me yearn for more. However, I hadn't known that it would hurt the first time. "I didn't know that it would be painful. Thank you for that information."

"That's just it. No one tells you these things and then the night happens and, well, the not knowing is often worse than the reality. I didn't want you to be scared."

"I assumed it must be nice or women wouldn't keep having babies."

She laughed, less tightly this time. "Quite right. And there's absolutely no reason to feel ashamed for enjoying yourself. I wanted to tell you that too."

"Thanks, Mama."

She patted my knee. "All right, then. As long as you don't have any questions, I'll leave it be."

"I can't think of anything else." I wanted to ask many things, but I held back. Would I know what to do? For that matter, would he know what to do? Would he still like me without a pretty dress covering my body? How long should I stay in the bathroom to change into my wedding night gown?

She took my hand. "I can see all the questions in your eyes, dear one. Please don't worry. You and Phillip will find your way together. When you love someone as you love Phillip, the body knows the course."

"How did you know what I was thinking?"

"I was a young bride not so long ago."

Tears came to my eyes as an image of my parents on their

wedding day a decade ago flashed before me. "You saved us, you know, when you came here."

"Ah, no. You're the ones who saved me," Mama said. "You can't imagine how scared I was that day I stepped off the train."

"I can remember that day too," I said. "Not long after, the five of us started plotting how to make you our mother."

Mama dabbed at her eyes with her lace handkerchief. "You children and your father have made me a very happy woman. Even though I would never have imagined seven children."

"You've never made any of us feel that we needed to be anyone but ourselves," I said. "We've all felt loved as if you'd given birth to us."

Her gentle brown eyes glistened as she reached for my hand. "You've been the best big sister any of the girls or boys could ask for. I hope this big, messy family hasn't made you wish for no children at all."

I glanced out the window. Addie and Delphia were doing cartwheels between the tables, not exactly helping but at least occupying themselves. Cymbeline had a pile of cut roses on one table and was meticulously trimming their leaves and putting them into vases. My brothers and Phillip were in the process of erecting a dance floor out of boards. Harley and Viktor were loading the church piano from the back of a wagon—Papa's solution to my request for an outdoor reception. Later, Fiona and Li would play for us.

I turned back to Mama. "I'd like to be the heart of a family like you are to us. What could be a better use of my life?"

"When you're someone's mother it goes far beyond the word *usefulness*. There's really no way to describe the immensity of a mother's love or of what she'll do for her child. Your heart becomes entangled with their joys and sorrows. You question yourself each and every day if what you're doing is the right thing. You send boys off to fight a war and pray on your knees every night that they'll return to you in one piece or at all. You stay up all night with a sick child, wiping their brow when they're delirious with fever. You watch as your beautiful adult daughter gives her love to the wrong man. All the time, you worry. Will they survive? Will they be happy? And then some days, like this one, your heart is overjoyed to see that same beautiful daughter about to marry the man meant for her. For a day, at least, you're at peace. Until the next when you wake worried about one of the others. But it's all worth it. Every minute. Because no one ever loves you like your mother, and to have the privilege of loving another human more than yourself is the greatest gift God gives. It's the closest thing to what he feels for us, you know?" She paused, taking in a deep breath. "I guess that's what I wanted to say—why I was crying this morning. I'm proud of the woman you've become. More than I could ever say."

By now I was crying too. She took me into her arms, and I leaned into her embrace as if I were still the child I'd been when she first came to us. As I had then, I marveled at how such a small woman could have so much strength. "Thank you for giving me the chance to be a child."

Mama withdrew from me and reached into the pocket of her robe. She placed a small rectangular box in my hand. "I have a gift from Papa and me. He wanted me to give it to you before the ceremony for your 'something new.'"

I took the box from her and lifted the lid to see a string of gleaming pearls. "They're beautiful."

"Every girl these days wants a string of pearls, isn't that right?" Mama asked with an anxious lilt to her voice. "Do you like them?"

"I love them. I'll wear them proudly today."

"All right then, enough of this." Mama stood, smoothing her robe with her hands. "Merry's asked if she might help you dress today. For old times' sake."

"How sweet. Tell her I'll be waiting."

She gestured toward my gown, which hung on a hook on the door. "The next time I see you, you'll be in your dress. Now eat some breakfast. We can't have you fainting in the middle of the ceremony."

THE CEREMONY SEEMED over before it had begun. Papa insisted on driving us home in his motorcar, followed by the guests in their own cars. Everyone beeped and cheered as we paraded down the main street of town. Onlookers stopped and waved and clapped. Embarrassed by the attention but also touched, I waved back to them.

My groom beamed down at me. "What a town we have here."

From the front seat, Mama nodded. "Isn't it wonderful? The whole town cheering you on as you start your new life together."

We drove down the dirt road until we reached the entrance to our property. I let my gaze linger on what would be my first home as a married woman. My brothers, Phillip, and the Olofsson brothers had spent every free moment since the snow melted to build it for us. White with black shutters and surrounded by a field of wildflowers, the house seemed as if it had always been there. We'd chosen the spot of our first kiss on which to build the house in which we would raise our family.

"I can't wait," I whispered to Phillip.

He kissed my gloved hand. "For what, darling?"

"Everything. Every moment of the rest of our lives together."

"Ah, then, I agree."

OUR ENTIRE FAMILY and our friends cheered as we entered through the back gate of Papa's garden. My sisters were at the front of the crowd and rushed toward us to bestow hugs and kisses, except for Addie, who hung back, watching me with her big eyes. I knelt, careful not to let the bottom of my dress touch the grass.

"What is it, little love?" I asked.

She wrapped her arms around my neck and whispered in my ear. "Besides Mama and Papa, I love you the best. Will you forget me now that you're married?"

"Never," I whispered back. "You can come see me whenever you wish."

Her small body shivered as she clung to me. "Thanks, Jo."

"I love you very much. Don't forget that."

"I won't." She gave me one last squeeze and then scampered over to stand with the rest of my sisters.

Phillip and I clasped hands as, one by one, people came to congratulate us. Last in line was Viktor. His shoulder had completely recovered since that winter night when he'd proven his true valor. No one would ever have known by looking at the strapping young man that just months before he'd bled all over my dress.

"Viktor," I said as I held out both hands. "You're looking well." He wore an impeccable summer suit made by his skilled father. His tie matched his light green eyes.

"Thank you, Josephine. I'm hopeful my presence doesn't remind you of a dark day."

"Never. You're a reminder of the finest parts of us."

Phillip held out his hand, and the men shook. "I'll never be able to repay you for saving my Josephine."

"No payment necessary. It was my honor."

Out of the corner of my eye, I caught Cymbeline watching. Since the night she'd kissed Viktor, Flynn had teased her unmercifully. The more Flynn asked her when she would be marrying the fine young man, the angrier she became, insisting it had only been a moment of relief over my well-being. I thought otherwise, but knowing my obstinate sister as I did, I kept it to myself. The more we insisted she liked the boy, the less likely she would be to admit it. For her and Viktor's sake, I didn't want to ruin their chance at happiness.

We moved on to the dining portion of the afternoon. Lizzie

had made mountains of food: fried chicken, potato salad, strawberries and cream. Our wedding cake was a vanilla cream and decorated with rose petals from the garden.

My father rose to make a toast. I held my breath, willing myself not to cry. Everyone hushed as he held up his glass and began to speak.

"To say that I'm proud of you, Josephine, is somewhat of an understatement." His voice broke. He took a moment to gather himself. "I had a grand speech in mind, but it appears I'm overwrought. I'll say simply this. Since the moment you were born, you've been a joy and a delight to your old papa. Phillip, take good care of my Jo, and welcome to the family."

We all raised our glasses. I clinked mine with Phillip and allowed myself a moment to stare deeply into his eyes. The future was there. My past was all around me. I'd thought of myself as daughter, sister, friend, even a librarian. Now I would also be a wife and, God willing, a mother.

More cheering as Cymbeline rose to her feet. "Papa said it was all right if I make a speech." Her voice shook. "Jo, you're the best person in the whole world and I'm sorry for all the times I've tried your patience. You make me want to be a better girl. Honestly, I didn't think there was a man good enough for you. Phillip, I've come to my final conclusion and it's that you're fine enough for my Jo, and I'm glad you're my new brother. You won't ever have to feel lonesome again because now we're your family. That's all."

"Thank you, Cymbeline." Phillip wrapped his arm around my shoulders. "I'm happy to have found my family at last."

"You've won over Cymbeline," I whispered to my groom. "Well done."

"She's all soft under that sass," Phillip whispered back.

After we ate, Fiona and Li began to play so that the dancing could begin. Instead of the classical style Li had learned at school, they played the music of the frontier. Lively, foot-stamping music that hinted at the wild country we held so dear.

Soon, our makeshift dance floor filled. A breeze brought the scent of grass and lilacs.

As the gloaming softened the light in our little part of the world, the music ceased. "I don't have a speech to say but I have a song," Fiona said. "This is for Jo and Phillip and for all the best wishes for a happy life together."

Couples drew close as Fiona sang the first notes of "Ave Maria."

Phillip held me close as we danced. My chest ached at the sheer beauty of my sister's voice and the poignant swells of sounds from Li's violin. Mama and Papa danced in the middle of the floor. Addie and Delphia sat on the grass holding hands and watching Fiona with adoring eyes. Cymbeline, to my shock, had accepted a dance from Viktor. Given her smile, she seemed to have forgotten her pledge of eternal hatred at least for tonight. Flynn and Shannon took up one corner of the dance floor, seeming to be lost in each other's gaze. Their eyes closed, listening intently to the music, Pastor Lind and Pamela sat together at a table holding hands. Theo and Poppy were dancing compatibly together like two friends who had known each other all their lives, as were Louisa and Isak. The Johnson sisters were dancing with their handsome husbands. Harley and Merry had their little boys between them as they danced. Even Lizzie had stopped fussing with the food long enough to fall into her Jasper's arms. The others from those long-ago school days huddled together in groups on the grass, enjoying cake and punch, while the youngest of the children chased one another on the lawn.

My husband's sure, strong arms wrapped around me. I nestled against him, giving him my full weight and resting my cheek upon his chest. His heart thumped against my cheek as if it were part of the music.

Fiona held the last note, and for a moment, time stood still. Yes, just a fleeting moment in time, but one that held all the beauty of the world. Like a droplet of dew on a summer rose or the scent of the first rain or the last perfect vibrato note of "Ave Maria," it was too precious to last forever. Yet it was etched into our hearts just the same. What was to come, we couldn't know. For now, however, we were all together, safe and joyful, basking in the glow of the setting sun and the love that flowed among us.

More Emerson Pass!

The first of the Emerson Pass Contemporaries , The Sugar Queen, featuring the descendants of the Barnes family is available at your favorite retailer. Grab it here: The Sugar Queen.

Sign up for Tess's newsletter and never miss a release or sale! www.tesswrites.com

The Sugar Queen

The first in the contemporary Emerson Pass Series , The Sugar Queen features the descendants from the Barnes family.
Get ready for some sweet second chances! Download a copy here: The Sugar Queen.

True love requires commitment, and many times unending sacrifice...
At the tender age of eighteen, Brandi Vargas watched the love of her life drive out of Emerson Pass, presumably for good. Though she and Trapper Barnes dreamed of attending college and starting their lives together, she was sure she would only get in the way of Trapper's future as a hockey star. Breaking his heart,

and her own in the process, was the only way to ensure he pursued his destiny. Her fate was the small town life she'd always known, her own bakery, and an endless stream of regret.

After a decade of playing hockey, a single injury ended Trapper Barnes' career. And while the past he left behind always haunted him, he still returns to Emerson Pass to start the next chapter of his life in the place his ancestors built more than a century before. But when he discovers that the woman who owns the local bakery is the girl who once shattered his dreams, the painful secret she's been harboring all these years threatens to turn Trapper's idyllic small town future into a disaster.

Will it take a forest fire threatening the mountain village to force Trapper and Brandi to confront their history? And in the wake of such a significant loss, will the process of rebuilding their beloved town help them find each other, and true happiness, once again?
Fast forward to the present day and enjoy this contemporary second chance romance set in the small town of Emerson Pass, featuring the descendants of the characters you loved from *USA Today* bestselling author Tess Thompson's The School Mistress.

Acknowledgments

Thank you to Elizabeth Mackey for the outstanding cover.

Thank you to my assistant, MaryAnn Schaefer for her tireless effort to make me look good.

Also, as always, thank you to Best Husband Ever, Cliff, for making all my dreams come true.

Thanks to my girls for putting up with their unconventional and absentminded mother. I couldn't do this without your independence and encouragement.

Both my maternal and paternal grandmother and grandfather, respectively, were born in the year 1919. I hope they're smiling down on me from heaven and forgive me for whatever errors I've made in accounting the period.

Also by Tess Thompson

CLIFFSIDE BAY

Traded: Brody and Kara

Deleted: Jackson and Maggie

Jaded: Zane and Honor

Marred: Kyle and Violet

Tainted: Lance and Mary

Cliffside Bay Christmas, The Season of Cats and Babies (Cliffside Bay Novella to be read after Tainted)

Missed: Rafael and Lisa

Cliffside Bay Christmas Wedding (Cliffside Bay Novella to be read after Missed)

Healed: Stone and Pepper

Chateau Wedding (Cliffside Bay Novella to be read after Healed)

Scarred: Trey and Autumn

Jilted: Nico and Sophie

Kissed (Cliffside Bay Novella to be read after Jilted)

Departed: David and Sara

Cliffside Bay Bundle, Books 1,2,3

BLUE MOUNTAIN SERIES

Blue Midnight

Blue Moon

Blue Ink

Blue String

Blue Mountain Bundle, Books 1,2,3

EMERSON PASS

The School Mistress, Book One of Emerson Pass Historical Series

The Sugar Queen, Book One of Emerson Pass Contemporaries Series

The Spinster, Book Two of Emerson Pass Historical Series

RIVER VALLEY

Riversong

Riverbend

Riverstar

Riversnow

Riverstorm

Tommy's Wish

River Valley Bundle, Books 1-4

CASTAWAY CHRISTMAS

Come Tomorrow, Castaway Christmas, Book 1

LEGLEY BAY

Caramel and Magnolias

Tea and Primroses

STANDALONES

The Santa Trial

Duet for Three Hands

Miller's Secret

About the Author

Tess Thompson
HOMETOWNS
and HEARTSTRINGS

USA Today Bestselling author Tess Thompson writes small-town romances and historical romance. She started her writing career in fourth grade when she wrote a story about an orphan who opened a pizza restaurant. Oddly enough, her first novel, "Riversong" is about an adult orphan who opens a restaurant. Clearly, she's been obsessed with food and words for a long time now.

With a degree from the University of Southern California in theatre, she's spent her adult life studying story, word craft, and character. Since 2011, she's published over 20 novels and a five novellas. Most days she spends at her desk chasing her daily word count or rewriting a terrible first draft.

She currently lives in a suburb of Seattle, Washington with her husband, the hero of her own love story, and their Brady Bunch clan of two sons, two daughters and five cats. Yes, that's four kids and five cats.

Tess loves to hear from you. Drop her a line at tess@tthompsonwrites.com or visit her website at https://tesswrites.com/ or visit her on social media.

CPSIA information can be obtained
at www.ICGtesting.com
Printed in the USA
BVHW042105150222
629168BV00021B/609